BREAKING THE DEVIL'S BREAD:
DARK WORDS & SHADOW TALES

Satyros Phil Brucato

Nightmare Press

Shepherdsville, KY

Praise for Breaking the Devil's Bread

Breaking the Devil's Bread offers up an array of bite-sized treats for those readers who like their stories... darker.

- Nancy A. Collins, author of *Swamp Thing* and the Sonja Blue series

In his collection *Breaking the Devil's Bread,* Satyros Phil Brucato melds lyrical beauty with stunning brutality and occasionally a touch of 90's nostalgia. Brucato not only excels at delving into the darkness of "ordinary" horrors, as in "The Lingering Fist," where a couple is forced by poverty to endure violent neighbors, but he's equally adept at conjuring the weird and fantastic, such as the carnal sorceress in "Shakarah and the Red Wheel" or the young couple in "The Green Tunnel," who encounter unimaginable evil while crossing a monstrous wilderness. All in all, *Breaking the Devil's Bread* is a brilliant collection both masterfully written and keep-the-lights-on-all-night terrifying!

- Lucy Taylor, author of *The Flesh Artist*, *Spree*, and *The Silence Between the Screams*

Brucato is a visionary storyteller whose work transcends conventional genre, weaving horror and the supernatural with a deeply insightful vision of the human experience.

- Evelyn Kriete, editor of Weird Tales, Sherlock Holmes Mystery Magazine, *Hearts of the Abyss* and *SCP: Redacted*

Breaking the Devil's Bread is a masterpiece of visceral horror, chilling suspense, and deeply human narratives. Every story is unique in voice and vision, united by magnificent prose and carrying seamlessly from one thrilling tale to the next.

- G.D. Falksen, award-winning author of *The Ouroboros Cycle*, *The Hellfire Chronicles*, and the Cities of Ether series

Written in language that careens between lush and brutal, *Breaking the Devil's Bread* is a chocolate box full of intricate explosives. Each story delights in its own unique way, while also leaving an indelible mark on the reader. It's a wild ride to dark and beautiful places, and well worth the journey.

- Richard Dansky, author of *Firefly Rain*, *Ghost of a Marriage*, and *A Meeting in the Devil's House*

Breaking Devil's Bread takes readers on a darkly imaginative journey through the deep shadows of our reality and fantasy alike. These thirteen tales drip with their own brand of nightmare fuel, from the blood-dimmed tides of "Shakarah and The Red Wheel" to the lurid wickedness of the titular "Breaking Devil's Bread" and the subtle all-too-real horrors of "Spookies Shouldn't Play with Sharp Things" and "The Lingering Fist." A feast of the lurid, the unsettling, and the unflinchingly honest, these stories serve up unsavory truths and decadent nightmares with every bloody bite.

- Coyote Wallace, author of *American Mystic* and *Sarah Corben's Bloody Revenge*

Brucato's stories weave dark, sinister webs beneath an engaging, accessible voice. Familiar phobias and unusual twists create an intriguing set of stories which flow smoothly down bloody roads to satisfying conclusions.

- Jaym Gates, co-editor of *War Stories*, *Strange California*, and *Strategy Strikes Back*

ALSO FROM Satyros Phil brucato

Red Shoes

Valhalla with a Twist of Lethe

Deliria: Faerie Tales for a New Millennium

Powerchords: Music, Magic & Urban Fantasy

Creatures of the Dark

Mage: The Ascension (series)

Mage: The Sorcerers Crusade (series)

Mage 20th Anniversary Edition (series)

Truth Beyond Paradox (editor)

Ravens in the Library (editor)

6

dedications

This book and its stories are dedicated to
Mike and Michael, Inky, Cathi, Heidi, Kelly, Wendy, Raven,
Echo, Chesh, Francesca, Katie, Chris, the Stone Mountain
White Wolf Crew, and a certain pair of beloved Coyotes.
With extra-special thanks, love & appreciation
to my dear friend Andi Pants, and to my Ever-Belovedest
Sandra Damiana Swan.

CONTENT WARNING

Stories within this book feature suggestions or depictions of injury, torture, drowning, cannibalism, addiction, self-harm, domestic violence, mental illness, child abuse, racism, bigotry of all kinds, dubious consent, sexual violation, sex magic, devil worship, and other potentially upsetting or offensive things.

Off-screen, there's also a long-dead dog, and some asshole who brags about killing a cat.

As should be obvious, the author does not endorse any of this shit. Readers are advised to heed their own boundaries and proceed with caution.

BREAKING THE DEVIL'S BREAD:

DARK WORDS & SHADOW TALES

Satyros Phil Brucato

CONTENTS

SPOOKIES SHOULDN'T PLAY WITH SHARP THINGS

If it's true that one must bleed on Halloween, then I guess I've done my part. Okay, it wasn't exactly Halloween Day when I made my sacrifice, but... well, it's complicated.

Let me explain.

I *love* Halloween. As a kid, I would sooner stay home and dress the house up with gory dummies and spooky sound effects than go out trick-or-treating with my friends. It's not surprising, then, that when my friend Thomas — a former college classmate who'd dropped out of our theatre program not long after playing the lead in an ambitious yet doomed production of *Jesus Christ Superstar* — invited me to talk to a friend of his who was setting up a haunted house, my response was *Oh hell yes*.

This would be late September in the mid-1980s. My then-wife Corrianne had moved in with me a few months earlier, and we'd been sorting out what happens when two late-teenage types suddenly find themselves stuck together and trying to be adults. The opportunity to go be a kid again — and for *money*, no less! — appealed to me. And so, by the end of September, I'd joined the team for *Gorehome 2: The Nightmare Continues*, a Halloween attraction set in an abandoned restaurant that had been scheduled for demolition.

That last part should have been a clue about what life had in store for us that month.

Our director for the project was a short, intense guy who came across like Harlan Ellison's younger brother. I don't recall his name, so let's just call him "Harlan" here. The producer, if I recall correctly, was named something like "Mike," and our cast and crew numbered about fifteen people when I joined the troupe. By that time, they'd already begun gutting the building and painting its interior black, blue, and red. Because the city had condemned it, we had permission to do whatever the hell we wanted to that building; we took full advantage of that license, and we'd trashed the place thoroughly before the attraction even opened. Walls were kicked in. Holes were cut and hacked away. Red "blood" spattered every surface, and black sheets divided the dining areas into "rooms" where different scenes were staged. In later days, folks would call this sort of thing a *haunt*. Back in the 80s, we just called 'em *haunted houses*, and the precautions used by any respectable haunt were notoriously absent. We used real knives and real sledgehammers and a real chainsaw with the chain removed. It was crazy, and dangerous, and I loved the hell out of it.

Guests to our haunt were met by a tall Grim Reaper greeted those guests and escorted them through in groups of two to six people. After encountering a vampire girl in her coffin, they'd be led into Cynthia's Room: a blood-caked "honeymoon suite" where a mad bride was murdering her husband. Ushered quickly through that room, they'd encounter a long hallway with a mad steelworker swinging a sledgehammer through the walls; a "dentist's office" where a shrieking mad dentist tortured a shrieking patient; a large room featuring a Goth chick tormenting a mutilated guy strapped to a cross; a hallway where a masked killer ambushed people with a chainsaw; and a Freddy Kruger who'd jump out at the last second and chase the guests out the exit. Along the way, various screamers and spooks would keep the party hopping. Gender-wise, we were split roughly 50/50 between women and men. (This was before *nonbinary* was a word people used as a gender identity.) We didn't have any guys who could fit into the coffin, and we preferred to make most of the tormentors women, and most of their victims men, in order to avoid the usual misogynist abuse dynamic. Most of us traded roles throughout the month, if only because the screaming and shrieking did a number on our vocal cords. I found that out in my first two nights as a performer, when a stint as the dentist and a stint as the patient rendered me unable to speak for a day or two and so I wound up on the cross for a few days until my throat recovered. I played Freddie and the chainsaw maniac, too, before alternating to Cynthia's Room.

That's when the real horrors began.

When people entered Cynthia's room, they'd see a blood-drenched bed occupied by a guy in torn and gory clothes. His belly was ripped open, with one leg hacked off at the knee. As this dying groom urged people to "Run before she gets you too," the wild-haired bride in a crimson-soaked dress leapt out from behind a screen, waving a sickle and threatening to chop them all to bits. The Grim Reaper would hustle the guests out into the long hallway, and the two "married" castmates would catch a breather until the next group came in.

That, anyway, is the way things were *supposed* to work.

In order to stage the illusion of a disemboweled dude with a dismembered leg, the groom would stick his leg through a hole in the mattress. After he arranged his torn clothes accordingly, someone else placed a plastic sheet over his bare chest and belly, then covered that sheet with fake innards and dumped a cubic fuckton of Karo syrup blood all over him. For the next few hours, that performer endured cramps, lost circulation in his leg, and froze half-naked under foam and plastic intestines, covered partially in plastic, and drenched in cold, sticky fake blood.

October's a cold month in the city where we used to live, with strong winds blowing the summer heat away. *Gorehome 2* occupied the middle of a parking lot, and so those winds blew across the empty space and cut right through the building's unheated and destroyed interior. Few of us wore more than a shredded gown, shirt, or pants; most of us were barefoot, every bit of us drenched in red sticky goo. Young idiots like us seem to generate our own heat, thankfully, but we kept from freezing to death mostly through adrenalized activity. The guys on the bed and the cross, however, and the person in the dentist's chair, were confined to one place; inevitably, we wound up being the coldest ghouls in the room. Therefore, Harlan switched those roles out every night or two, so that no one person spent each Friday and Saturday night of the month strapped into place and shivering until after midnight.

If this sounds like disaster waiting to happen, that's because it was.

Why, then, did we do it?

Mostly because it was *fun*. It really was.

We got paid each night, too, which was more than most starving-artist kids got in Reagan's America. Harlan would divvy up the proceeds from the door, take the biggest cut for expenses and profits, then deal out $20.00 or so to each cast member. It's not much, granted. Again, though, this was "the Capital of the South" in the 1980s. My job at Pizza Hut paid $3.25 an hour, plus tips (if we got any), minus taxes, and so having fun for an evening, covered in gore and scaring the shit out of people, and then pocketing $20.00 tax-free at the end of the night seemed like a pretty decent deal.

Beyond that, almost all of us were actors or artists of one kind or another. I doubt any of us, other than Mike and Harlan, were over twenty-five, and at least half of us were teenagers. I'm not certain the building had been rented legally, and I know damned well there was no insurance involved. The number of legal and ethical issues surrounding such an enterprise should be obvious, but for hungry young creative misfits such things rarely matter... until, of course, they *do*.

Me, I was a seasoned veteran of guerilla filmmaking, art modeling, and improv theatre. I'd spent college falling down hills, getting thrown into swimming pools, gagging on rotting animal guts, getting cast nude in plaster, shivering naked on a model stand, pounding myself senseless in dive-bar mosh pits, and having my chest hair burnt off with an improvised explosive device. Gory makeup and cold Karo syrup blood were my natural plumage in those days, so this was just one more adventure to add to my long list of crazy shit. Corri, bless her heart, wasn't nearly as much of a ham as I was. She'd stay home and read, safe in a warm bed full of cats, and then help me out of my Karo-stiffened clothing and into a hot shower whenever I'd get home.

Until I roped *her* into that madness too.

We'll get back to that shortly.

We were maybe halfway through October when Harlan asked me if I would be willing to be Cynthia's dying groom. Of course, I would. Hell, one of my roles in a roommate's college film involved me wearing prosthetics covered in fake blood and rotting animal guts *for over twelve hours straight*, so sticking my leg through a mattress under a coating of fake intestines seemed easy by comparison. Besides, I'd spent the previous weekend standing in place for hours while tied to the cross, wearing nothing but Karo blood and shredded jeans, so a night or two of laying on a bed sounded like a huge improvement to me. I got on well with the woman playing Cynthia, too (let's call her Julia, which was not her name), and we had fun with our respective roles. We'd improvise vitriolic banter as she'd shake her blooded, rusted sickle and scream, *"THAT'S WHY I KILLED YOU!"* In hindsight, we were probably acting out the kinds of domestic conflicts we didn't dare have with our real-life partners. We'd vicariously abuse each other, laugh, and enact neo-spousal murder over and over and over again.

That was the first night.

On the second night, we were getting close to Halloween. Only a handful of performances remained. The lines outside got longer, and the people in them got more restless from standing outside in the cold. We kicked out every stop and pushed ourselves to new extremities in order to give those people a good time. And so, when a group of guests stopped at the foot of my bed to marvel at the gory mess of my belly and leg, Julia and I took our marital discord to new intensity. "Get *out*," I bellowed, "before this crazy bitch kills you too!"

"Come along," said the Grim Reaper, trying to escort the group out of our room without touching anyone. (That's one line, reckless as we were, that we did *not* cross.) "This room is dangerous."

"Wow, cool," said one guy in the group, leaning in toward my "severed" leg and mangled viscera. "How'd they do that?"

Another guy in the group was like, "Are those *real* animal guts?"

"We must leave," intoned the Reaper.

"*Get out!*" I screamed at them. "*GO!*"

Normally, Julia stayed at one end of the room and I stayed at the other. Our contact was all verbal. As the dudes refused to move, however, she ran across the room, leapt up on the bed, screamed "*I'LL KILL HIM AGAIN!*"

And swung the sickle down toward my face.

The real sickle.

With blunted edges and a rusty point.

"*NO!*"

I threw my hands up to block her, and the sickle slammed into the back of my right hand.

THUNK.

Ow.

"We must leave this place of death," the Reaper insisted, breaking that inviolate rule and practically shoving the guests through the black curtain. His voice held a note of panic, and the chastened dudes seemed to realize that we had just entered the realm of That Wasn't Part of the Act.

"*Ohmygod,*" Julia whispered, "I'm sorry, I'm *sorry!*"

"Get Harlan." I'd smashed my left hand over the wound, pressing it closed. Both hands were, of course, covered in fake blood and real grime.

"I'm *sorry,*" she repeated. "I'm so *sorry.*"

"*Get. Harlan.*" I snarled it out, not wanting to think too much about what the pain pulsating through my hands meant in terms of damage.

The sickle hit me right where a major vein runs up the back of your hand, branching out slightly above the wound. The first blast of pain had been dull; it sharpened, though, by the time the vampire girl had hauled herself out of the too-small coffin, stuck her head in, and whispered, "Oh, shit — are you okay?" Julia had busted through the curtain between our room and the entryway, frantically asking where Harlan was. Although the guests outside hadn't yet heard the news, word quickly spread that the guy in Cynthia's room had just been stabbed for real.

By the time Julia pulled Harlan into the room, Vampire Girl and several of our castmates had gathered around and were trying to help extract me from the bed. With my left hand pressed against my right, afraid to let go and see just how *much* that vein would bleed, I needed two guys to climb onto the rickety bed, grab my arms, and pull me up. Vampire Girl peeled away the gut-laden belly sheet while Julia kept apologizing. "It's okay," I told her. "It was an accident. You didn't do anything wrong." With help from my castmates, I drew my half-asleep left leg out of the hole we'd cut in the mattress. One guy whose name and role I never learned hustled me to the one functioning bathroom, Harlan close behind us. "Oh, God," Harlan whispered. "Please don't sue us."

"It was an accident," I kept repeating. "As long as I don't get stuck with the doctor bill, that's all it was as far as I'm concerned."

Man, was I stupid. Young and stupid and heading into shock.

The bathroom was a unisex ruin. Makeup of all kinds smeared across every available surface. Ratty clothes and towels, stiff with Karo blood, draped over the toilet and the edges of the sink. That sink looked like Jackson Pollock had thrown up in it after a particularly hard night. Smudges blurred the mirror as my castmate turned the light on. After hours in near-darkness, our pupils squinched in that blast of light.

I'm gonna have to look at it, aren't I?

That was not a pleasant thought.

For some reason, that one functioning bathroom was tiny and cramped. I guess someone had gutted the public restrooms before we got hold of the place. Nameless Castmate had gotten a bottle of alcohol, and both of us were like, "Yeah, we need to clean this out before we get you to the hospital." Harlan told us that an ambulance was on its way. "Is that *your* blood?" the guys asked me, noting my gory presence. "I don't think so," I told them. "I've been keeping pressure on it since she stabbed me."

Since she stabbed me.

How surreal.

In the glaring light, I saw the spectre I'd become: Torn-up white T-shirt. Bare feet. Old jeans cut off at the left knee. Flannel shirt open to expose my chest and belly. Every bit of me caked in sticky cold red stuff. Makeup smeared around my eyes to give me a dying sort of look. Messy short hair and the beardless face I'd had back in those days. Barely out of my teens, recently married, with a hole in my hand I didn't want to look at but knew I needed to see.

Oh, well — let's do this.

It wasn't as bad as we'd expected, probably because I'd been pressing my left hand across my right so hard that the throbbing from the wound now pulsed between them both.

What we saw, in that bright harsh light, was essentially a *dent* in the back of my hand, its edges pale blue and starting to bruise. The vein had been squeezed closed on both sides, and a slash of red welled at the center of the dent.

My castmate turned on the water. I stuck my hand under it.

Well, at least I didn't *scream*.

In hindsight, I suppose I'd turned off most of my usual functions in order to deal with the realities of my situation. Shock's useful for that sort of thing, I hear. And so, as I held my hand under cold water, sluicing off as much of the grime and gore as possible without touching *that fucking blue dent in my hand*, Nameless Castmate opened the bottle of alcohol and said, "This is probably gonna hurt a lot."

I agreed. "Just do it."

He was right. It hurt a lot.

Like, a *lot* a lot.

In my various misadventures, I've dislocated my knee twice, broken several bones, had the bottom of a shattered bottle punch through an inch of rubber on my sneaker sole and then slash my hand open when I reflex-grabbed at it. I've been burnt by fires and explosions, splashed with hot oil, beaten bloody, knocked across a room by a blow in the face from a Scuba mask, hit on several occasions with baseball bats, and wound up hunched and wailing on a bathroom floor while my guts contracted from a nasty stomach flu. I've had hangovers and suicidal depressions. I've been in car accidents and motorbike spills. I tore a chunk out of my arm when skidding across gravel-strewn concrete. I've had a knife at my throat, fists in my face, splinters in my skin, and two divorces carving bits out of my heart.

The stomach flu is the only thing I recall hurting worse than the moment he poured alcohol on that pale dent in the back of my hand.

Folks talk about things being "breathtaking"? That pain was breathtaking. The only sound I remember making was a low hiss through clenched teeth. I looked away because I didn't want to see that damn dent in my hand again. It's funny how you can be surrounded by carnage and torture so long as it's not real, then feel your chest hollow out the moment you realize that you've *actually* been stabbed and now the blood welling up in the wound isn't made of colorful liquid corn.

Someone produced a clean towel. Harlan checked in to make sure I wasn't gushing blood and threatening to sue him. Nameless Castmate, Harlan, and Vampire Girl ushered me through the darkened *Gorehome 2*. Guests had begun to file in again, now with more stringent control from our stalwart Grim Reaper. The show must go on, as the saying goes, and we'd had a line of people freezing their asses off to get the thrills they paid for. By then, I'd asked someone to call Corri, and Julia — who, for obvious reasons, took the rest of the night off — went to go fetch my wife from our apartment. As I neared the entrance and saw the flashing ambulance lights beneath the curtain, I realized something funny:

The crowd outside had been standing next to a real ambulance that had pulled up outside a haunted house attraction. As my escorts led me to the paramedics, I saw people in the crowd draw back from my ragged blood-soaked form.

I probably would have laughed if I wasn't so worried about my hand.

Someone had briefed paramedics. Given the absurd recklessness of that coke-drenched era, I'm sure this wasn't the first time a Halloween haunt resulted in real injuries. They asked me how much of the blood on me was mine. "None of it," I assured them. "I've kept pressure on the wound."

You'd think I would recall my one and only ambulance ride, but my head felt fuzzy by then. The ensuing few hours blurred into a montage of *Look how brave I'm being* banter, appalled faces in the ER waiting room when I walked in under my own power while covered in apparent gore, Corri carefully hugging me at the hospital (with an affectionate, "You *idiot*"), and the ER personnel plopping me in a cold treatment room for what seemed like hours — still barefoot in torn and Karo-bloodied clothes — when they realized I hadn't actually fallen into a threshing machine. I got a few shots of morphine or something in my hand, so when the doctor came and stitched it closed, I felt disconnected enough to watch him do it.

It didn't look so bad, really. Just some pale bruised skin, the big vein pinched shut and probably coagulated by that point, and a bloodless gap about an inch long being stitched shut with black thread by a guy who'd done that job a million times before.

X-rays showed the bones to be undamaged. My ligaments remained miraculously unharmed. The sickle had punched straight to the bone, but the dull impact and my left hand had kept me from bleeding out. Eventually, after some sharp words from Corri, the ER staff got me a blanket to wrap around my shoulders. She'd brought me a change of clothes and helped me into them. By the time Julia, Harlan, and Julia's husband arrived to invite Corri and me to dinner, I was so high on painkillers and receding adrenaline that I said *Sure*. The hospital gave me a soft demi-cast cloth split to keep my wrist straight and my hand immobile, provided more painkillers and instructions on how not to fuck my hand up, and sent us on our way. Once I'd cleaned up, we shared a late, delicious dinner while I assured Julia and Harlan I wasn't suing anyone as long as I didn't get stuck paying for the ambulance and hospital visit. Hell, I said, it didn't even *hurt* that much!

Not until the painkillers wore off, anyway. Around 4:00 a.m., I was whimpering with pain as my hand pulsed lightning through my arm. I struggled in the dark with the child-proof cap on the meds until Corri, whom I'd been trying to *avoid* waking, got up and opened them for me.

The next weekend, though, I was back at *Gorehome 2: The Nightmare Continues*. I kept my right hand wrapped in plastic to avoid soiling the bandages or reopening the wound, and I cycled between the groom's spot on the bed and the victim's spot on the cross. Somehow, I'd convinced Corri to join the cast as a new Cynthia, a role she and Julia alternated in until the day after Halloween. Having been fired from Pizza Hut (from which I subsequently quit in protest) Corri had a blast, and we went home with forty bucks a night instead of twenty.

That year, Halloween fell on a Saturday. We'd planned to spend Sunday cleaning the place out and saying our last goodbyes to each other; when people began lining up outside before sundown, however, we decided to give it one more night. Dressing in our tattered, smelly, sweat-and-Karo-rigid gear, we put everything we had into that performance. The final group of guests to come through the door got the entrance locked behind them. At each room, the performers rose up from, or out of, our positions — our coffins, beds, dentist's chairs, and darkened alcoves — and began following them, chanting "*Gonna get you! Gonna get you! Gonna get you!*" This spontaneous chase began as stalking and whispering. By the time they reached the exit, with Freddie Kruger and the chainsaw maniac and the whole demented cast and crew behind them, the guests were laughing and screaming and running for that door. Running after them, we circled them, joined hands, and began dancing around them in the parking lot, chanting the *Nightmare on Elm Street* rhyme, our voices rising on each verse. As we reached the final shrieking *NEVER SLEEP AGAIN*, we burst out in laughter, cried "*Happy Halloween!*" released each other's hands, and bowed. We thanked our final guests, they thanked us, everyone was laughing and crying and hugging (we didn't hug the guests, though), and as the guests walked back to their cars, all of us waving to each other, the cast and crew filed back inside to begin our final transition back to normalcy. The phone rang one last time, and instead of the customary, "Gorehome 2: The Nightmare Continues," Vampire Girl answered with, "Gorehome 2: The nightmare is *over.*"

Most of it was, anyway.

As one might expect, I couldn't work with a stitched-up right hand. By mid-November, though, I was able to score a Christmas gig at Kay Bee Toys in the local mall, where Corri found work at... cue the Irony Bell... a cutlery store.

A week or so after *Gorehome 2* closed, we got a furious call from Harlan. Mike, the producer, had ditched out with the money and disappeared. Harlan wasn't paid, and his name was on all the paperwork, so he got hung out to dry financially. A bunch of people, it turns out, received little or nothing out of the considerable sum *Gorehome 2* had amassed. Corri and I wound up being two of the only cast members who'd been paid consistently, probably because Mike hadn't wanted me thinking about a lawsuit and so told Harlan to cash us out each night. It was a good thing we *had* been, too, because although Mike told Harlan that he'd paid off my ER visit, the first bills from that night arrived a few weeks later.

At least the motherfucker paid the ambulance fee.

When I got those bills, I panicked and lost my shit. Trying to reach Harlan, I got his answering machine. Enraged when he did not return my calls, I called Julia and got her machine as well. In a moment I regret over thirty years later, I puked lava into the phone — not blaming her or demanding money but unleashing weeks of pain and betrayal and money stress on the party who deserved it least. Her husband called me later and chewed me out for upsetting her. I apologized to them both and never heard from them again. Harlan never called me back either. Thomas and I were no longer on speaking terms, so I couldn't ask about the friend who'd gotten me involved with the production. I hadn't learned the last names of anybody involved except for Julia, so I couldn't sue anyone even if I'd wanted to... and by that time, trust me, I *wanted* to. Eventually, Corri and I were able to talk the hospital's bills down to a manageable level. I paid them off shortly before we split up a few years later.

Spookies shouldn't play with sharp things. Especially if they don't know who to sue afterward.

My hand healed fine. I still have an interesting scar on the back of it. You can't see that scar easily, however, because I'm such a furry cuss.

No haunt worth that name behaves nearly as recklessly as we did back then, though I'm told there are still plenty of spooky kids with more spirit than sense as far as that's concerned.

I still love Halloween, but never worked another haunted house.

Life is weird. Especially mine.

At least I can honestly say I haven't been bored since high school, and I've paid my dues to the Halloween spirit.

So Happy Halloween, y'all, and don't let anyone swing a rusty sickle at your face.

THE FINAL LEGACY OF BOBBO THE FUNMASTER

The bidding for the fingertips of Bobbo the Funmaster was about to begin. They floated in formaldehyde, each pickled in a separate jar, three in all. Candlelight shimmered on the glass while other mementos, shrouded beneath black velvet, awaited eager purchasers.

In the tiny dim room, four buyers held their offers, eying each other warily. The entrance fees — $500 in Bitcoin, transferred to a dark address — had secured their place at the auction. Each participant waited in a luxuriously anonymous chair at the foot of a rent-per-hour corporate podium, behind which sat a table topped with the coveted remains. The auctioneer, fifteen-year-old Harry Parks, scanned his audience. The payments they brought were better than money... but then again, Harry offered very special wares.

"My brother-in-law Kip says they used the bone saw while Bobbo was still alive." Harry scowled at the sound of his voice, still pinched with the bite of puberty, then continued: "They started at his fingertips and moved down, joint by joint, burning each stump with a wood-burning knife. Bobbo would have approved —" Harry's voice cracked. He coughed. "If, y'know, *he'd* been the one with the bone saw and the knife instead."

The four bidders — three men and one woman — eyed the three jars with approval. Bobbo had been a man of refined, if brutal, tastes. They shared his enthusiasm for the finer things in life and appreciated the irony of his demise.

"They fed the pieces into the soup vats," Harry said after a solid pitchman's pause, "boiled them off the bones, ground those up, and fed the whole mess into the production line." He held up a can of well-known chicken soup; he couldn't resist: "Mmm-mmm, good!"

Harry knew his audience by inclination if not intimacy. Each person in that room shared the late entertainer's predilections. All five were acquainted with Bobbo's parties and collections, and each one held a stake in the Funmaster's grisly end.

"Kip cleaned the place after they were done, but he saved these three fingertips. He knew you'd all want something to remember Bobbo by. These three fingertips are the only pieces left." The angelic-looking boy paused again, then held up an old-school VHS tape. "Three fingertips... and *this*."

The bidders' eyes grew wide. "Is that," asked Adrianna Carter, "what I think it is?"

Bad Juju grunted, nodding. The others sat up straighter in their comfortless chairs. This was an added prize, a worthy addition to anyone's collection.

Harry grinned. "Yep." Pulling aside a drapery on the auction table, he revealed an equally antiquated large-screen TV and VCR. His clients, after all, were traditionalists, and presentation is *everything* when you've got goods to sell. Popping in the tape, Harry thumbed a remote control and the TV burst to life.

Bobbo's shrieks began as Kip hefted the bone saw. They echoed through the massive kitchen. The sound quality was superb. This was no grainy cellphone video or *Blair Witch*ian "found footage" mess. The clarity of both sound and image spoke of cool professionalism and top-notch gear. The Funmaster's chained and naked body thrashed spread-eagled on the stainless-steel slab. The unseen cameraman tracked slowly across the killer's panicked form as the whirring saw approached, then settled on a long close-up of Bobbo's face before traveling down his arm in time to meet the saw.

In a nice touch, Kip had painted that face with Bobbo's hallmark design: The Weeping Clown with Bloody Eyes. In Bobbo's more familiar videos — familiar, that is, among certain clientele — the Funmaster grinned wide through greasepaint tears. He wasn't grinning this time, though, and the blood and tears were his own.

Harry stopped the tape. "There's more where that came from. Lots more. *Hours* more."

Bad Juju's disappointed grunt held an unsettling carnal note.

Adrianna's eyes narrowed in silent anger.

Brian Franz, the youngest collector, sneered. "*Seriously?*"

Joe Myers, the broker, smiled. Deals were his element. The tape was as good as his.

"Joint by joint," Harry repeated, scanning his bidders. "For hours."

Juju shook his white-boy dreads. "How *many* hours?"

"Two tapes," Harry answered, "shot at high resolution. Just shy of four hours of material. And those two tapes come as a set. One bid, both tapes. No exceptions." He could afford to be smug. There are benefits, after all, to having an especially sadistic serial killer in the family.

Joe's grin crooked one corner of his face. The kid had potentially useful talent.

"So, my friends..." Harry clacked the remote control to the table. "What'll it be? How much will you offer for this fine presentation of Bobbo the Funmaster's final show?" He scanned his audience again. "Three of you get the fingertips, plus whichever items from Bobbo's personal stash you might also want to purchase. The highest bidder takes home the tapes."

"I wanna see it *now*," Brian whined. The others mumbled assent.

"Sorry," Harry said. "You know how I work. This tape is one of a kind. Prime goods. Unique. If you *all* saw it, it wouldn't be *special* now, would it?"

That, of course, was the kicker. Harry knew his clientele. Sharing wasn't their strong suit. *Ownership* was.

The collectors glanced at each other like crows eyeing small but tasty roadkill. Who would get the best part of the feast? Bad Juju growled for effect. The sound got lost in a sudden, silent pulse of sex.

Adrianna's mouth twitched in disgust with her fellow collectors as she pulled at a strand of Cover Girl Auburn hair. Eyes riveted to the dazzle-dots playing across the dark TV screen, she clutched her plaid skirt and licked her lips. She needed that tape. She had to see it all.

Brian shifted with tumescent discomfort. His offerings sat bunched in the paper bag at his feet. His thatchy rust-colored hair cast red highlights in the candle glow. Acne stood out in sharp relief across pale skin. Skinny fingers wrestled on black denim. Though sure he couldn't afford the tape, Brian hoped like hell to see it.

Joe Meyers let his Brioni suit testify to his success. The contrast between his bespoke elegance and blue-collar face and name provided an effective negotiating tool. Joe's reputation, in its way, was comparable to Kip's. The broker's collection was the talk of the circuit. No pissant gorehound would, or *could*, match his offers. He'd seen to it personally.

Each bidder knew the rules: Artifacts, not cash. Each one had brought bits from their own collections as currency for new additions to that stash. Harry would be the arbiter of value, and cold Kip would ensure that everyone played fair. Even in his absence, people feared Harry's relation. These crows were mere collectors. Kip was for real.

Harry banged a gavel on his podium. The fingertips shuddered in formaldehyde. "The bidding," he declared, "begins *now*."

Bad Juju made the first offer. His black-dyed dreads contrasted with pasty skin. Juju's studded biker jacked clacked with buttons: "*Dahmer for President*," "*Help Your Planet — Kill Yourself*," and so forth. Ketchup stained his "*Charlie Don't Surf*" T-shirt, but Juju liked to imply it was something else. He pulled a jar from inside his jacket. In it, three strips of reddish flesh bobbed. Juju coughed, a wet and ugly sound. "These," he said with a practiced low pitch, "are... uh, *lips* from Jeb Markowitz' last kill. I stole 'em from the morgue when I worked at Westland." He met each buyer's eye. "Jeb skinned the soft parts from his kills. He missed these, though. I didn't."

Harry frowned, looking the contents over. "So they're lips. Big deal."

"Not just 'lips,' lips," Juju replied. He let the implication set in.

If Arianna felt disturbed, it didn't show.

"Ah," Harry said at last. "Well, I guess I have my first bid." His voice cracked again. He grimaced. "Do I have another bid for the first fingertip of Bobbo the Funmaster?"

No one answered. They all stared at the dark TV.

"Only three of their kind." Annoyance tinged Harry's voice. "One of you might get the whole set."

"What about the soup cans?" Adrianna asked, her mind damp with writhing red visions. To see the sweet schoolteacher's face, you'd never know the company she kept.

Harry shrugged, his salesman face slipping. "Kip and his buddies just dumped Bobbo in the vats. No one knows which batches of what he ended up in."

Adrianna's mouth twitched with disappointment.

"Come *on*, guys," the auctioneer continued. "This first bid is *lame*."

Juju growled. "Man, *fuck* you."

Harry ignored him. "Just think: This is *Bobbo* we're talking about here. His last will and testament, screamed out and written in blood."

Silence.

Things were not going as planned.

"Bobbo, the *Funmaster*," he rallied. "King of the cut-ups. Host of those full moon carnivals we all knew and loved!"

"Speak for yourself," Joe muttered, "you little pervert." Joe's tastes were too refined for crude torture parties where guests both present and virtual helped Bobbo turn homeless folks into howling pinatas.

"Is one lousy bid —" Harry's voice cracked again. Dammit. "All I'm gonna get for this first fingertip?"

Brian raised his hand like the classroom misfit he was. "I've got..." Harry smiled. "...one of Linwood Briley's home movies." Brian stood, quivering, and pulled a Super 8 spool from his bag. "It's not... y'know, anything *special*, but it *is* from Linwood Briley and... y'know, he's a *lot* bigger than Jed Markowitz."

"Yeah, *eat* me you little fuck." Juju glared. "At least Jed Markowitz never got *caught*."

Brian blanched. Joe and Adrianna exchanged looks and shook their heads.

"I have two bids," Harry cut in. "Do I hear three?"

Nothing.

"Going... going..."

No response.

"Sold to my friend Juju for..." He cocked his head for affirmation. "Ellie Sanderson's, I think it was...?" Juju nodded. "Um... '*lips*. Courtesy of Jed Markowitz and our man Bad Juju.'"

The dreadlocked connoisseur stepped up and exchanged his first offering for the fingertip.

After a long pause, the bidding continued.

# # #

The table beside the podium stood littered with ghastly artifacts by the time Harry got to the videotape set. The candles had melted to guttering nubs. Sweating a bit in the stuffy room, the auctioneer eyed his new additions. Soon, he'd have one of the best collections in the circuit, especially if something happened to Joe Meyers. Harry made a mental note to prime Kip in the businessman's direction. It was a breach of etiquette, of course — but then, collecting *was* collecting.

The others sweated too. After getting past his initial setback, Harry had played them with the skill that made him famous among the collectors' breed. A jiggered thermostat and a few brief previews from the prize had worked their magic on that small yet eager crowd. Each bidder coveted the video set with a lust that thickened the heat of the room. Juju had shucked his leather jacket, but Joe Meyers sat resolute in his suit and tie. He had more class than his competitors and would be damned if he'd let down a single edge. Harry had to admire the bastard.

Adrianna's blouse lay open to the fourth button. No bra. Sweat sheened her cleavage and she made no effort to wipe it away. From the auctioneer's perch, the moisture caught the light and Adrianna knew it. Teenage boys are open books, after all, and Adrianna specialized in all kinds of media.

Harry sipped the last of his ice water, scanned the buyers, and lifted his gavel. "The last item of our sale is the videotape set, that last will, testament, and dying graces of our friend Bobbo the Funmaster. You've seen the goods. It just gets better from there. What will you bid for this one-of-a-kind spectacle?"

The claim was more-or-less true. Though he'd kept a copy for himself, Harry's word was good in the collector circuit. Kip had given his brother-in-law the proverbial leg up, and so despite his youth Harry Parks had credibility. Going back on that word was bad for business and everyone in that room knew it. Just as they knew that making copies and splitting the cost was not an option here. Each collector *had* to own an item that no one else could claim.

Bad Juju, as usual, began the bidding war. "This jacket," he said, reverently hefting a ratty buckskin coat, "belonged to Squeaky Fromme during her Family days. I verified it with her online. She says she wore it during Helter Skelter but a friend borrowed it before she got busted." Juju displayed faint stains on the suede sleeves. "That's the blood of *history*."

"You're fulla *shit!*" Brian's anger burned through his usual whine. "You can't prove that!"

"I've got Squeaky's email." Juju's pale face squinched. "Right here."

"That could be *anybody's* email," Brian grated. "It doesn't prove *shit*. You probably just picked that up at some fucking thrift store."

"You callin' me a *liar*, queerboy?"

"Gentlemen." Joe's voice dripped sarcasm. "I'm sure Mr. Parks will want the final say about the authenticity of that jacket." His eyes met Harry's with a challenge: *Let's see how good you are, boy.*

Harry faltered briefly under Meyers' gaze. Then rallied, more determined than ever to set Joe up with Kip's bone saw, pronto. *Chill out*, he cautioned himself. *Deflate this fucker later*. The slow way. The fun way. *That* tape, he'd wager, would fetch decent market value too. Without a word, he took the coat from Juju and appraised it with a seasoned eye. Juju handed him a folded printout. Harry appraised that too.

"It looks old enough," he finally said. "The stains *do* look like blood, and the email exchange seems genuine. I'll accept this offer." He passed his gaze over all four bidders. "You all *know* better than to rip me off." No one contested his decision. "I have one Helter Skelter jacket, worn by Squeaky Fromme. Do I have a counteroffer?"

Meyers raised one discreet finger. "I have," he said, taking out an envelope of photos, "vintage crime-scene photos from Jeffrey Dahmer's apartment."

"Man," sneered Juju, "*everybody's* got photos from Dahmer's apartment. That shit's old *and* weak."

Harry nodded his agreement. *Not good enough*.

"And," Meyers added, "autopsy photos of Charles Manson himself. *Real* ones, not Dark Web forgeries." He fanned through the photos, showing just enough to display their contents.

Juju growled. "The fuck'd you get *that?*"

"We all have our sources, young man." Joe didn't bother hiding his contempt. "Not all of us have to work in mortuaries."

"*Jeeze*, Joe." Adrianna favored him with her favorite glare. "Juju's right. You *are* old and weak."

"Not all of us," Joe countered, "employ *your* methods, either."

She gave Joe a slow blink of contempt. "I teach *teenaged girls*, Mr. Meyers. No insult you could possibly imagine would scratch the surface of what I hear every day at work."

Joe had no reply to that.

"This is a *trophy* auction," she went on. "Not a slideshow for dead celebrities who never got their hands dirty. Put up or get out."

"Lady, gentlemen," Harry soothed. "Let's please stay civil here. There's no sense in getting all riled up..."

"Show us the tape," said Juju.

Brian nodded, vigorously.

Harry shook his head. "Can't do that. I've already shown you enough." He took another sip of water and failed at *not* staring down Adrianna's cleavage. The room was too hot. The bidding had gone on too long. Harry's tactics had backfired on him. The last bits of his control slid off like rivulets of sweat. "That's what we're here for," he declared, his voice cracking once again.

"That's what *you're* here for." Joe aimed for a target he could hit. "We got what was promised. Your decision to spice things up was not something any one of us agreed to."

"He's not wrong." Adrianna aimed at Harry too. "We're done playing games, kid. Quit fucking around and show us the goddamned tapes."

That wet and carnal pulse shuddered in the air.

Harry wiped a trickle from his hairline. Styling gel stick to his fingertips. Once more, he scanned his audience. Their words fuzzed. Their faces blurred. He reached for his ice water. The pitcher was empty.

"Show," Juju growled, "the. God. Damned. *Tape.*"

"I can't do that."

Brian giggled.

"*Won't,*" Adrianna replied. "You *won't* do that."

Joe shuffled through the photos, then returned them to the envelope.

Adrianna crossed her arms and leaned back, sweaty, in her chair.

Brian's eyes were wide. Unblinking. Sweat ran into them. He didn't care.

Juju's jeans bulged ominously. Brian's, too. The latter had stopped trying to conceal it. Adrianna noticed. So did Harry.

Juju rose. "Harry..." his voice dropped, subsonic. Fearfully gentle. "Show us all the tape of Bobbo."

"No."

"Harry." Adrianna's sigh was every rejection Harry'd ever heard. "Quit wasting our time."

"*No.*" Hurt sent steel into the word. "Now *back off.*" Harry steadied himself. His voice, for once, did not crack. "You all know my rep," he continued. "And you all know Kip. What he did to Bobbo will be *nothing* compared to what he'll do to you, and Bobbo took a *very* long time to die."

Juju clenched his fists but sat back down.

Joe Meyers frowned. "May we all *finally* get back down to business, please?"

Brian giggled again. Girlish, high, and brittle.

"What the *fuck*," Juju snapped, "are *you* laughing at, queerbait?"

Brian reached into his paper sack.

"Do you have an offer, Brian?" Harry stepped back into the familiar auctioneer role.

The thin boy nodded. He drew out a zippered baggie. The severed organ inside had been drained, stuffed, and treated with the care of practiced taxidermy. "I..." He giggled again. "I bid Kip Morrison's severed penis. I've got the rest of him at home."

Harry gaped.

His gavel dropped.

Adrianna leapt from her chair. Juju moved just as fast.

They trapped Harry between them. He jumped back. Hit the wall. Fell. Adrianna grabbed his wrists. Juju flipped the table full of bids. Stained clothes, murder weapons and pickled body parts crashed to the floor.

Tools spilled — knives, screwdrivers, a claw hammer, and a dull-toothed hacksaw.

Formaldehyde sprang from shattered jars.

Joe Meyers flicked a bit of wet dead meat from the cuff of his tailored, dry clean-only pants.

Brian rose, setting aside his baggie. He wasn't giggling anymore.

Adrianna yanked Harry to his feet. Juju kicked his legs out from under him. The teacher flipped the boy around and raked his face through the glass. Juju slammed his knee into the auctioneer's back, twisting Harry's arms behind him.

Adrianna released Harry's wrists and grabbed his sticky, blood-moist hair. Ran his face through broken glass again and again and again. Vented wet, hungry animal sounds.

Joe Meyers *tsk*ed as he picked up the remote control and returned to his chair. This spectacle, as usual, was beneath him. He did, however, like to watch.

Brian shuffled through the tools, rejected them, then returned to his bag and withdrew a Piranta Tracer skinning knife. He popped the blade and smiled at Harry's reaction.

Harry opened his mouth to scream. Juju stuffed it with glass shards, then clamped Harry's jaws shut. Juju turned to Adrianna, Harry's face held tight between his hands: "Ladies first."

"*Thank you*, kind sir." She dipped her head in a half-bow, locked eyes with Harry, and slapped him hard until the glass ripped through his cheeks.

"Careful," Juju warned her. "Don't cut your hands. I've done that. It hurts."

"He might try to swallow it," said Joe.

"Good point," said Juju. "Thanks." He wrenched Harry's mouth open and held the auctioneer at arm's length as Adrianna reached past him, grabbed Harry's throat, squeezed, and shook the boy. "Spit it all out, you little shit," she ordered. "You're not getting away from us *that* easily."

Gouts of blood and bits of tongue, cheek, and teeth spattered to the floor as they wrangled Harry to a seat, pinned his arms, and let Brian cut his clothes away.

Joe pressed Rewind. "It's been ages," he said, "since I used one of these things."

"At least *one* of us," Adrianna said, "is old enough to know how."

Meyers chuckled. "At least," he agreed. "Now let's all enjoy this from the beginning..."

# # #

As promised, the tape lasted almost four hours. Harry lasted almost as long.

When the four collectors parted, each had fond new memories, fresh treasures for their collections, and their own little touch of Harry in the night.

BUT THEY CALL ME JO

I was twelve when the darkness claimed me.

Mike had this great idea. Mike, my closest friend. The guy who thought playing in construction sites and drainage tunnels was the Best Thing Ever. Mike, whose parents were never home and whose house smelled like incense and old books, and whose folks had an old-school stereo that played vinyl records in their living room. Who had a whole wall devoted to faded sleeves and bright new collector's editions and box sets of CDs and record albums you could hold in your hands and drop a diamond needle on when you wanted to hear the voices of the dead.

Mike with curly black hair and a mouth full of lies so bold that even *I* knew he was full of shit because whenever Mike spoke, he was lying and that's just how he was back then.

My best friend was good to me. And so, he *was* my best friend. I never had many of those. These days, I have even less of them. I haven't spoken to Mike since the day he pointed a gun in my face, but I'm getting ahead of myself and that doesn't have much to do with the darkness and the day it took me in and left itself inside my head.

I lived a different life in the days and years before then. I was shy, sure, and quiet in ways parents appreciate and other kids mock. I had a head full of spaceships and monsters of the fun kind. Life-and-death dramas played out on pages and screens, not in flesh and words that hurt to recall. Life back then was special effects and homework and parents trying to hang on to the little kid I didn't want to be anymore.

I still thought I was a boy at the time. My body told me otherwise. And my parents. And the kids at school. And the pervos passing on the street who couldn't just let a kid be a kid and figure that shit out when we got around to it. Especially them.

I was lucky. No one forced the issue on me. Came close a few times, yeah, but not the way I know it got forced on other people. Mike accepted me. My parents accepted me.

No one forced me to decide who or what I was back then.

Until the darkness.

On the day it swallowed me.

It was Saturday afternoon and a thunderstorm hung on the edges of the too-hot, too-bright sky. A construction company was building a new housing development by Mike's place back then. "Hey, Joie," he'd said when we'd gotten bored with listening to old Yes albums and had drunk enough Cokes to make us feel like we could vibrate through the floor, "I found something cool the other day."

"I'm surprised you could find it without a microscope."

It took him a minute. Then he got it. We laughed. Everything's funny when you're twelve. "Not *that*," he said when we caught our breaths. "I'm *serious*. I found this really cool place near the construction site. Let's go check it out!"

It says a lot about my friendship with Mike that even at twelve I didn't question a boy wanting to "take me somewhere" and "show me something." It says a lot about him that he didn't betray that trust.

Not intentionally. Not until later.

We felt the hot breath of the storm ride in on the humid afternoon.

Back then, Reedsworth Farms still looked like the farmland it once had been. The prefab developments hadn't yet sprouted industrial acne all over Westland County, or left the pockmarked craters of abandoned industrial parks, tree-stripped soil, and houses built too fast and cheap to last. You could still see the horizon from Mike's front yard. That day, the horizon was turning black as Mordor on the march. We liked playing in the rain, though, so the idea of a thunderstorm adventure on a hot afternoon appealed to us. We pounded off across the asphalt toward the new construction site nearby.

To imaginative misfits like us, buildings under construction loom like dinosaur skeletons from strange dimensions. With the roaring machinery shut down for the weekend, those structures breathed an eerie silence. Sudden cracks from across the fields tolled the advance of Mordor's dark horde. Wet-blanket heat pressed damp T-shirts and shorts to our skins, filling our lungs with heavy cotton. Careful of debris, we scooched under the portable fences intended to keep kids like us away. In that heat, its silence broken by incoming thunder, we could envision ourselves survivors of an alien apocalypse, stalked by titans who spoke their name in storms.

We stealthed our way through bellies of alien war machines, forgotten ruins, and the remnants of vast battles fought before our time. Occasionally, we'd whisper to each other, caught up in the fantasy of invasion and the potential for discovery. That second risk wasn't entirely unfounded. Security guards made their rounds as we hid in shadows. Their voices and the electric snap of radio replies sent our hearts jumping inside our chests. With a secret language born of such adventures, Mike and I gestured each other through the maze. Above us, light dimmed from the approaching clouds.

That's when we found the hole.

In hindsight, I can't imagine what it was for. My adult mind discards possibilities: A drainage tunnel? A cable pipe? An escape hatch from an unbuilt panic room? I have no idea. In the years since then, I've compared my memories of that concrete void against everything I know about construction sites. None of it makes sense.

But it was there.

I know it was there.

Because, of course, we crawled into it.

And that's where darkness crawled into me.

# # #

Why are we built to self-destruct? What draws kids on a hot afternoon to squeeze into a narrow black tunnel burrowed beneath a construction site? I have no idea why we did what we did that day. Only that Mike nodded to the tunnel, I nodded back, and we went in.

Scrawny kids that we were, Mike and I still had to get down on hands and knees to enter that tunnel. Gritty concrete dust bit into our palms and scraped our kneecaps raw. The humid darkness of that pipe drew us forward, Mike in front of me, me watching his faded-denim butt. The light behind us reached a few yards into the void. Far in the distance, a speck of light encouraged us to keep going. As we advanced, the scuffle of our skins against the concrete muffled and the echo of our breaths bounced back to us off the narrow round surface. Behind us, the light darkened. Thunder rumbled down the pipe.

"Is it getting *smaller?*" My whisper hissed down the endless concrete pipe. My heart thumped hard against my ribs. Bits of rock lodged in my palms and knees, scraped raw and probably bleeding.

"No." Mike's reply barked back at me, ghosted with echoes and sanded rough by the drainage tube. The strain of crawling through that circular tightness cramped my shoulders and my back. Mike's legs, butt, and feet began disappearing as the dim light faded.

"We should go back."

"We *can't* go back."

He was right. There wasn't space enough to turn around. Going back meant…

My heart beat harder when I thought about trying to crawl all that distance *backwards*.

"What if…?"

"Shut *up*." Though we still whispered, our voices bit back at us like snakes coiled in the confining dark.

Snakes. Spiders. Whatever kinds of bugs might live this far underground. Rats, maybe. Rabid cats or dogs or moles or…

My mind scrabbled on sharp and ugly thoughts.

"Mike…"

"I *got* it," he insisted. "There's light ahead. I'm almost there."

I didn't see any light ahead. Not much reflected off Mike's backside, either.

"Dude…"

"*Shut UP.*"

Our breath rasped against those walls.

The tunnel rumbled as the storm broke overhead.

Rumbled and hissed.

"Is that…?" Mike's voice held a panicked whine.

Water.

I felt it splash against my palms and kneecaps.

The tunnel went from dry to wet in seconds.

The light faded.

The darkness roared.

From dryness to a trickle to a stream to a splash, the water rushed to fill the pipe.

Our sudden screams crashed back at us from the concrete walls, the weight of their humid stinking darkness pressing in on us from all sides. Whatever words we yelled got lost in the frenzy that kicked in when my brain shut off.

Mike slammed back into me as he tried to back up, and I tried to back up, and we both got stuck in a screaming tangle of panicked limbs.

We wrestled and shoved as the water splashed against us. I bashed my skull on the concrete walls, saw flashes of light and pain and the glow of sunshine far away.

Mike scrambled over top of me and crawled a beeline back the way we'd come. The faint shine of sunlight still beckoned from the entrance.

I thrashed around, repeatedly banging my head, tearing my skin on the rough concrete. Both of us kept shouting. Our words blared together in a nightmare roar. My throat ripped itself raw. My ribcage squeezed against my frantic heart and lungs. "*I'M STUCK*," I kept screaming. I remember that part, anyway. "*I'M STUCK I'M STUCK I'M STUCK I'M STUCK!*"

Mike yelled back at me, his voice drowned out by the thunder in my ears.

My head wedged against my shoulder, my legs locked under me, I felt water rise and pour against my face. Bolts of pain shot through every joint. My lungs clenched. My heart hammered.

I felt the darkness tighten.

Squeeze.

Crushing me.

Swallowing me.

Then the words, cutting through the chaos in my head.

Now, it whispered, *you belong to me.*

# # #

Mike's ribs cracked under my fist.

I don't remember throwing that punch at all.

All I recall is Mike saying, "I'm *sorry*, I'm *sorry*," over and over again in my doorway. Then something crunched and my hand was in a fist and Mike was on the ground, and his parents stared at me like I'd grown three heads and an extra set of hands.

Mike tried to breathe. And couldn't. He laid there like a busted doll, eyes wide, mouth open, blinking hard and panting and holding one hand over his chest as if he might jump-start his lungs with some sudden electric-fingers burst.

"Mike?" His Mom looked down, knelt down next to him. Mike kept gasping. "Mike? *Michael?* Baby, are you okay?"

I still held my fingers in a fist.

The search party found me in the fields two days after things went black. I'd been soaking wet, covered in scrapes and scabs and grime. Nonverbal, they told me later. As one said,

"You looked like you'd seen Hell." It took three days before I could talk again, and the last thing I remembered was being stuck in the pipe as water and darkness rushed in.

I never told anyone about the voice in my head.

Everyone said my survival was a miracle.

It *had* been. Just not the kind they thought it was.

Mike came to my house with his parents after I'd been cleaned up and checked out and released from the hospital to go home.

As I'd heard later, Mike escaped, waited in the rain for me to follow him, and finally ran off to fetch security guards. They'd sent in guys with flashlights and rope once the water level dropped. I was gone. Wherever I came out, it wasn't where we went in. Mike got in a world of trouble. Got arrested, from what I heard. My survival got him mostly off the hook. Obviously, he felt bad about the whole thing.

I wanted to feel bad about punching him in the chest. Standing there, over him, I couldn't feel anything but a faint sting in my knuckles and a deep cold everywhere else.

Mike's dad looked like he might hit me himself.

Then Mike finally took a deep breath, wheezed, and coughed a few times. "Ow," he said. "Ow, that really fucking *hurts.*"

No one scolded him for using the F-word.

My mouth kept trying to apologize. Nothing came out. It took several months and lots of therapy before I began using complete sentences again. My mind worked fine, but words got lost in translation somewhere between where I *thought* about saying them and where my voice actually began.

"Now *look*, young lady..." Mike's father finally found his voice.

"Not lady," I replied. My own voice grated on the words.

"It's..." Mike coughed again, wincing. "It's cool, Dad. I deserved that." His eyes glared like a wounded animal at me. His parents helped him up as Mike stumbled over contrition. It was his fault, he said. "I'm just glad..." Mike looked for signs of his best friend in my face. I don't think he found me there. "...you're not dead," he finished.

We didn't speak again for months.

Our parents, of course, forbade us from seeing each other again. We listened about as well as anyone listens to their parents at that age. After many weeks of moving through the school halls like a ghost, an object of intense yet distant fascination, I found myself at Mike's locker between classes. "You okay?" I asked when he arrived.

"A few cracked ribs."

"I'm sorry."

"So am I."

If this had been a movie, we might have hugged while a pop song tugged on the audience's heartstrings. As it was, we walked off toward class together, not talking, whispers from other kids trailing in our wake. Because I had more leeway to be late to class, thanks to my "incident" and its effects on me, I guided Mike to Geometry and just said, "Later?" at the door.

He looked me over again. Nodded. "Yeah. Yeah, that'd be cool."

It *wasn't* cool, in hindsight. But we tried. That darkness hung between us both, swallowing everything we'd been before that day.

We kept up the old rituals. Backed each other up when the rest of the world gave one or both of us shit. Listened to old records in Mike's parents' house. The distance we kept from everybody else, though, was nothing compared to the distance ripped between us by that day.

Our best friends drowned in that pipe, in the darkness.

Someone else survived.

And neither Mike nor I knew how to reach across that gulf to find our friend again.

#

The blood didn't care how I felt about myself.

When I grew up, there weren't nice words for the kind of person I am. "Tomboy" was the most polite term. That, or "androgynous." Short hair and skinned knees were my childhood trademarks, so when puberty kicked in I'd added ace bandages, not makeup, to my daily morning rituals. By that time, my knuckles got skinned more often than my knees. I fought like a boy, took no one's shit, and earned the nickname *Psycho Jo*.

The darkness left its mark on me. In strange ways, that was a blessing. People gave me space, for the most part, and understanding when I decked some asshole for getting too close. My grades stayed high, thanks to my parents accepting that "class participation" would never be my strong suit. Most folks assumed Mike and I were a thing. We never so much as kissed. Despite the gulf where our old friendship used to be, he had my back and I had his. When he dated Amy, I approved. When she dumped him, I beat the shit out of her.

That last part broke whatever bond we'd had left.

"What the *fuck*, Joie?" I'd never seen him so mad. I caught a two-week suspension over that beating. Mom and Dad had to talk them out of expelling me. Mike's face flared red as he clenched his fists. "What the fuck is even *wrong* with you?"

"She hurt you."

"That doesn't mean you get to *break her face*." I'd only just broken her *nose*, actually. To be fair, her face was pretty much a mess.

"Sorry."

"That was *not cool*." His voice bunched up with quiet tension. Mike's eyes narrowed.

Darkness began seeping in around the edges of mine.

That's how I learned to sense it coming. The edges of my vision would start dimming and I'd hear water tricking when no water was there.

I whipped my head around and squeezed my eyes shut. My hands had already snapped into fists.

"Sorry," I repeated. My words got lost in the sound of water.

"You *FUCKING SHOULD BE*." I felt Mike's spit on the side of my face.

I smashed my skull against the wall so hard the world lit up behind my eyes.

"Get *away*," I growled.

"*Fuck* you."

"*GET. AWAY.*" His face was inches from mine when I opened my eyes.

Whatever he saw in those eyes made him run.

I slammed my head in the wall again, arms wrapped so tight around themselves that I dug scars in my biceps with my nails. Rushing water roared in my ears. I kept straining to open my eyes. All I saw was black. Darkness flashed with stars forged from my pain.

I threw myself down and rolled myself raw. There was blood on the pavement when I finally stopped.

There'd be no apologies this time. No more quiet reconnections.

Whatever friendship survived the tunnel died that day.

# # #

Darkness ripples. Its touch is cold.

As the waters reach my lips, shapes unfurl, black upon black.

From the absence of light comes the essence of Not-Light. A petal-vortex of overwhelming void. Alive in an awareness crucible, it writhes. Scuttles. Licks my skin. Past my skin. To my bones. To beyond.

Trapped, immobile, I breathe it in.

Void ripples up my nostrils, down my throat.

Fills me. Gestates. And expands.

I become Void.

And Void is ice.

Light seeps in, unwelcome, blinding. Faint light, but too much to bear.

Shivering, I uncoil on the stone.

Void-chill runs in rivers down my face, trickles from my ears, pours from my nose. Cough. Buckle. Vomit darkness into darkness.

Get up.

Void-voice scraping like iron nails.

Wipe the darkness from my mouth. Above me, light. Dim. Fading. Flickering. Through bars.

Too high to reach. Too faint to see by.

My hands are bone-shapes chipped from ice. Sheened with pulsing luminescence.

Cramped limbs untangle, too many limbs, a spider's limbs bent to impossible degrees.

Get up.

Slip and skate in frozen black. Hell-pins prickle bones and skin.

Shuddering, shaking, try to stand.

Four legs now. Two legs. Two arms. Vertigo reeling in my skull.

Not-Light flows on the edges of my sight. Up angles. Up walls.

Walls within a darkened cell.

A cell paved and shaped with ice, lit from distant glow above.

Wake up.

I can't.

Wake up.

I won't.

You will. We will you to wake.

Rocks underfoot. Sifting brush of rough weeds on scabby skin. A light. Two lights. One brightens. Turns toward me.

"Hello? *Hello?*" A man's voice. His shape. "Holy shit — *I found her.*"

It's not me they found, though.

I'm not her.

I never was.

My name is Void.

But they call me Jo.

# # #

No one calls me "girl" at Lexa's. Or *kid*. Or *she*. Just *Jo*. I'm Jo.

They know what happens otherwise.

High school passed with a few bloody noses and a lot of stony silence. People stopped trying to define me. I stopped caring what they thought. I never dated. People asked. I never said yes. Desire, for me, felt like an arm I'd laid on the wrong way for too long. I could still feel the weight of it, attached yet cut off from complete sensation. When I'd try to move it, it hurt and threatened to break. Eventually, I just got used to that dead weight. Sure, I knew I was missing vital bits of life. The void inside me, though, snapped back with cold teeth each time I reached for something more. Finally, I stopped trying. Numbness took over where feeling used to be.

Even my parents avoided looking me in the eye. They were grateful, I think, when I moved out.

Clocks tick. Time moves on.

College slid off me like butter in a hot Teflon pan. After three semesters, I gave up and went to work. By then, I'd attracted the right kinds of attention from the wrong sorts of people. After those people made some assault-and-battery charges disappear, I went to work for them. Lexa's needed security. I needed a paycheck and the chance to beat folks into cooperative states of mind without going to jail for doing it.

We all have our place in this world, I guess. My life fell between the cracks of it, so that's where I found a home.

Lexa's only *looks* like a dive bar. The club squatting in a concrete box is just there for show-and-tell. The heart of the place beats three levels down, beneath locked doors and storage rooms. Building inspectors never see it. Club patrons don't see it either. Most employees don't even know it's there.

There's where Lexa's *real* business takes place.

I learned the truth bit by bit. Not through rumors, which is how you tend to learn such things. Through hard-won trust. No one in the know said a goddamned thing. No one talking knew the truth. I won my place near the inner circle by doing things no sane person would want to do. I knew where certain bodies were buried because I helped put them there. By the sixth or seventh corpse, I could put them *literally* on ice. With a mental shrug and a brief flash of darkness, I froze bodies almost solid with my hands. That, it turns out, is a *very* useful talent when your employers run a club like Lexa's.

"So, Jo," Mr. Lake said to me one night. "What do you believe in?"

"Not much." I still spoke in small words and tiny sentences. Words are a liability. Too many words can pile up, fall down, and bury you. I knew that from experience. I let eyes and fists speak for me instead. They tend to be safer and more honest than words.

Mr. Lake wasn't someone you'd expect to be running a place like Lexa's. Shorter than me, stocky but well dressed, streetwise as a Disney princess at first glance, he seemed more like an accountant than a gangster. Those tend to be the most dangerous people, though. Not the ones who can break you in half. The ones who get folks like me to do it for them.

"Are you a *god-fearing* man, Jo?" The words rode a razor between sarcasm and sincerity.

I could ride that edge too. "Depends on the god, I guess."

"Follow me," he said. "I have something to show you."

We went down more stairs than I'd seen there before.

Neither of us spoke, so we descended in silence.

I had lots of time to think of things as we made our way down.

I'd seen all kinds of debauchery by then. All kinds involving *adults*, anyway. If some deep secret lay beneath what I already knew, I wondered, then what was I *about* to see? What would my limits be if I *did* see something terrible? What would I do about it if I witnessed something I couldn't turn blind eyes to? And, most worryingly, what would Mr. Lake and the unseen muscle I knew was following us down those stairs do about it if whatever was in that basement was more than even *I* could excuse?

Then there was that odd spin he'd put on "god-fearing." Sarcastic, but reverent too. I doubted Mr. Lake was about to introduce me to their bible-study group, so that mystery haunted me as well.

Knowing what happened to people who really fucked up bad at Lexa's, what was about to happen to me? Was there some mistake I'd made without knowing it? Was I about to become one of the screaming playthings whose cooperation in Lexa's games was not, as they say, safe, sane, or consensual? What could I do if I *was*?

Such thoughts chased each other through my mind as we went down.

And down.

And down some more.

"No questions, Jo?" he asked as we reached a thick steel door at the bottom of that final set of stairs. "I can hear them buzzing inside your head."

I shrugged. "I'm good."

"Oh, we know," he said. "You're very discreet. We're noticed that. And we appreciate it. That's why you get to see what you're about to get to see."

I steeled myself.

"Don't worry," Mr. Lake continued. "You're not about to be punished. You're about to be rewarded."

He ran a key card through the slot. Heavy locks clicked open. A hiss of air escaped. He reached for the thick steel lever that opened up that door.

Light bled into the dim stairway as he pulled the big door open.

I'd expected some hidden dungeon.

I was wrong.

# # #

I heard water trickling before the door had fully opened.

Inside, it was beautiful.

The room beyond that door glowed a pristine white, lit by tastefully concealed illumination. This wasn't the clinical harsh light of exposure. It was the soft warmth of luxury.

A spotless gallery awaited us. A handful of couches and chairs, upholstered in white leather, sat expectantly on white-tiled floors. Two small fountains, bubbling happily, poured water into a complex array of channels. Through those channels, water flowed.

My amazement must have shown on my face. Mr. Lake chuckled. "Not what you expected, is it, Jo?"

I shook my head, not trusting my words.

"Come on," he said, holding the door open for me. "I'll show you around."

We slipped off our shoes on a mat by the door. Tracking club grime on those white tiles seemed like blasphemy. Through my socks, the floor felt warm. "It's…" I let my voice trail off.

"Not many people see this room," he said. "Only the special ones. And yes, you're one of us now."

As we stepped inside, I sensed an odd chime echo off my bones. Silent resonance, like a song in a frequency I could *feel* but couldn't *hear*. Welcoming, yet alien.

"So, you *do* hear it." Mr. Lake smiled. "Even after that awful din upstairs, you're still open to the finer things in life." He nodded further into the room. "That's what I like about you, Jo." Again, he repeated, "You're one of us."

One of *who*, though? What did he mean?

The water channels, I noticed, formed designs in the tile floor. At their edges, that warm floor chilled. I hesitated at the edge of one. Mr. Lake stepped past it, though, so I followed him. We wove our way through that design. "Our patrons," he explained as we went, "have special needs. Not the trite desires of the flesh. Something different. Something more." I began feeling slightly dizzy. The chime in my bones intensified.

I noticed odd sigils cut faintly in the walls.

"This is a nexus," Mr. Lake went on. "The absurdities upstairs feed essence into this room. *Energy*, if you will. It sustains us. It sustains... our patrons."

My unease returned like fire.

"What...?" I began.

Then I saw it.

We rounded a set of folding screens, the kind you see in Japanese films. White paper stretched over white lacquered wood frames. Behind them, another design in the floor. This one had been etched with shining gold and black complexity. Though cut into the tiles, interwoven with the water channels, these designs seemed to float in the air above the floor. Hovering and pulsing, they shimmered with cold light I *felt* more than I *saw*.

And in the center of that design...

I shook my head to clear it.

What I sensed there remained.

If reality was a fancy candle you'd left too long in a hot car, it might look something like what I saw in that design.

Except that it was moving. And breathing. And alive.

Someone slammed me in the face with a mirror made of ice. It shattered and I felt myself falling into every flying piece of it. All I *knew* and all I *was* exploded into that cold and endless moment. I was everywhere but nowhere. I cascaded through forever as a blast infinite shards.

Behind them all was nothing.

The essence of Not-Light.

The Void inside, outside, everywhere.
A trillion fragments of a broken whole.
My last illusions, gone.
My memories of that childhood dark returned.
From everywhere, I heard his voice. Resonant. Eternal.
"I knew you'd recognize it, Jo," he said. "Welcome home."

# # #

"Give him back," Mike said. "Give me back my friend."

The gun in his hand wasn't pointed at me.

It pointed *past* me, into the void behind my eyes.

I don't know how he found me. I hadn't spoken to Mike in years. I found out later that he'd been asking questions around Lexa's and trying to track me down. Why, I couldn't say. Maybe he remembered the friend I'd been to him. Or he still felt guilty about leaving me behind in the tunnel that day.

As Mike faced me with that Glock, his hands shaking, his voice frantic, his reasons for being there didn't matter. Just the gun, and how he knew I wasn't Joie anymore.

I'd gotten careless, I guess. After the room, and the secrets in that room, and the secrets I found *beyond* that room, my awareness had expanded outside human comprehension. Time, space, the weight, and force of earthly physics, all showed themselves as lies to me. Like one of the superheroes I'd watched and read about as a kid, I'd become so much *more* than just another guy. Moving through a crowd on the street or in the club, I sensed heatbeats and essence and the things they *might do* or *had done* in the moments before or after those people did those things. I moved before they could think of moving. I froze bodies without touching them with my hands.

So I froze Mike in place before he said another word.

Then I hauled his cold but living form downstairs.

Mr. Lake eyed me as I carried my old friend towards the door that led to the stairs which led to our secret space beneath the club. Ronnie, Lexa's main muscle guy, moved to stop me. Mr. Lake shook his head. Ronnie stopped. I did too.

Mr. Lake met my eyes. Looked at Mike, whose frost-filmed eyes were the only part of him that moved. Looked back at me.

The Void in Lake met the Void in me.

He nodded.

I carried Mike's stiff body down the stairs.

Strong as I am, it was a rough climb. Mike's brittle body cracked. Bits of him broke off. He tried to speak, or scream, or appeal to that kid I used to be when we would listen to Yes in his parents' living room. Against my skin, the cold seeped in. It didn't bother me, though. That cold, I was used to. It was, after all, part of me.

I said nothing.

My key card slid like ice through the reader. The locks opened. We went inside.

I left my sneakers at the door, hefted Mike in my arms, and carried him over water, toward the screens.

His eyes rolled and begged and wept.

Sounds wheezed from his throat as Mike saw what waited for us there.

By that point, I knew the song between the stars. That melting-wax reality had become my comfort zone.

Our patrons have needs.

They meet ours. We meet theirs.

I set Mike on his feet. The gun, by then, had chipped and frozen past uselessness. I searched Mike's eyes with mine.

The deep breath I took then reverberated across worlds.

With the same nod we'd used as kids, I motioned toward the grand design. Toward the living smear of realities inside.

"This is where the tunnel goes," I said. My words buzzed with the chiming in my bones.

"They're waiting for you there."

No screams. No last words. No drama as I pushed him in.

Just the look in his eyes as he'd seen what waited for him behind my own.

#

Ronnie was next. Then Shelly. Then Grace. And Rollo. Now, finally, Mr. Lake.

Not all at once, of course. I was careful. They had their talents. I had mine. I'd learned plenty in my years between the cracks. Like how to make folks disappear before anyone noticed they were gone.

The white room sings to me as I shuck my sneakers and carry Mr. Lake past sigils and over water, toward the screens.

Unlike the others, he doesn't try to fight. His eyes focus on what waits beyond for us both.

"Thank you," I say as we stand beside the grand design. Inside, that cosmic hunger waits. "I appreciate all you've given me. This isn't anger. This is fate."

I heft Mr. Lake in my arms: "You're not being punished. You're about to be rewarded."

Before I toss him, I see him fall.

The endless instant flickers, the moments *of* release, *before* release, and *after* release stacked and playing on top of each other, rolling like puppies on a bright summer day.

He disappears. Like Mike did. Like the others.

He was wrong, that day, Mr. Lake was.

He thought I was one of *his* people.

I'm not, though. My patron claimed me long ago.

A different darkness, from a different universe. Similar, but realms apart.

I should feel something.

All I feel is ice.

That shattering ice-mirror that broke *the Jo I was* into *the Jo I've now become* shimmers before me. Calling me in.

Beyond that space, my patron calls.

It's time.

I must return. Then go beyond.

The cramps in the shoulders of the child I was flow away like water down a pipe. The chiming in my bones rises to a pitch I can finally, delightfully, *hear*. Tightness in my chest, held in all these years, melts. Expands. Rises in my ears. Then drifts away.

In my throat, a wordless song. A hymn past darkness. To something More.

It's time.

Deep breath.

I close my eyes and fall forward. Fall *inside*.

Clocks tick. Time disappears.

# # #

No impact. Only peace.
　　No fear. No pain. No memories.
　　There are no words beyond the darkness.
　　My name was Jo.
　　Now I'm only Void.

BUY A BEER FOR HANK

I dare you.

No words in the English language, especially when spoken by an attractive woman, are more likely to get a young guy to do something gloriously stupid.

And, so, one night around 1996, I found myself striding toward the DJ booth of my favorite Goth club, prepared to make an ass of myself. My then-girlfriend Wendy had spoken the magic words, and so I, of course, had donned the mantle of a most magnificent fool.

Back then, for reasons that are obvious to anyone who knows me, I was throat-deep in the Goth scene. How could I not be? Great music and wild bass-heavy dancing wound like ivy through a wrought iron fence? Check. Tongue-in-cheek fascination with spooky stuff? Check. Beautiful people spinning through clouds of smoke-machine fog, decked out in everything from black leather buckles and boots to bare feet and gauzy white dresses? Sure, sign me up for *that!* Though I'd seen *The Hunger* almost ten years earlier, and wished that I could find a club like the one where Bauhaus serenaded vampire lovers, I finally discovered the joys of Goth-Industrial clubbing in 1993. From there, they became my regular haunts, so to speak, for the decade to come. That night in 1996, the club was called No Exit and the manager was hosting a Gothic lip-synch contest.

No Exit was neither fancy nor low-rent. Like most such clubs, it was a concrete box fancied up by bright lights, black walls, lots of shadows, and a smattering of props. In No Exit's case, those props included a handful of tall wrought-iron candelabras, stocked — in clear violation of fire codes — with real burning candles. I think the space spent its days as an arty internet café of the sort that was popular when few Americans had the resources for home-computer internet access. On Wednesday and Friday nights, however, the tables got scooted into backroom storage and the Goths came out to play.

Back then, in Atlanta, darkwave types had many playgrounds to choose from. The most popular was the Masquerade, a three-floored monstrosity converted from a mill into one of the city's most vibrant (if dilapidated) nightspots. The Chamber was next in line — a decadent temple of fetish culture whose vast dance floor and potent sound system made it a go-to destination despite its distance from Downtown proper. The Vault — reputedly converted from an actual bank — proved short-lived but memorable, with two tiny dance floors but unusually strong drinks. And for the hardcore, there was 688 Spring Street: a cramped subculture bunker redolent of tobacco and cloves, with concrete floors, cinderblock walls, exposed iron beams, and an eerie neighborhood whose denizens were scared off by those weird-ass freaks in black. No Exit, then, had competition. Despite a booming economy and a nightlife rep, 90s Atlanta was full of places to go. Thus, the club's founder (let's call him Daniel) got creative with No Exit. He won my heart on opening night by spinning some Loreena McKennitt and Faith and the Muse. He hung work by local artists, and on the night of the dare in question he announced that Gothic lip-synch contest. First prize was $50, and contestants were to leave their shame at the door.

As I recall it, the club's main room featured a sunken dance floor surrounded by a common area raised by four or five steps of ascending layers running around the edges of the dance floor. A black, painted railing surrounded the sunken area, broken up here and there with passages to let people move between levels. A small stage projected out from the upper level into the dance floor area, marked not by rails but by two standing candelabras. The DJ booth rose opposite the main entrance, at the back of the club's main room. On No Exit nights, Daniel let the smoke machine go wild. Although not as dense as the fog in more upscale clubs like the Chamber or the Masquerade, No Exit's fog gave the light-rig plenty of smoke to play with, wreathing the dancers with enough haze to keep us all from feeling too self-conscious to dance like the morbid aesthetes we were.

Around midnight, Daniel stopped the music and declared the beginning of the contest. Aspiring luminaries were to go to the DJ booth, tell Daniel which song they wanted to use, and then — assuming he had it in his collection — get up on the stage and go for the glory.

The first few people played things pretty straight. We all applauded them for having the guts to up on stage before the rest of us broke down and did the same. The first performance I remember, though, involved my friends Paul Mercer and Regeana Morris from the Goth band The Changelings, plus two other friends of theirs whose names I don't recall, doing an *a capella* rendition of the guitar riff from the INXS song "Devil Inside." As the three women sang, Paul stepped back from them and began fashioning an invisible noose. The song faltered as the three singers looked back at him. Paul mimed hanging himself as they changed the chorus into a dirge, slowed to a mordant chant, and then — with a final mournful "Doo-doo doodle-oo doo-doo-doo" — they bowed their heads and shuffled offstage.

Welcome to humor, Gothic style.

Wendy and I, leaning on the railing, applauded. "I think we just saw who won," I said.

"You should do it," she replied.

I laughed. "Nah, I'm not in a mood to make a fool of myself tonight."

"Go ahead." Wendy had a magnificent grin. "Go up there. I *dare* you."

So, I did.

To be honest, I had already been contemplating a foray onto that stage. An inveterate ham, I'd pictured myself up there giving vent to a particular song. I even had that song picked out in my head. And so, when Wendy offered up that most efficacious dare, I knew what I would tell Daniel to play, and I knew he had it in his collection.

"Play 'Ghostrider,' by Rollins Band."

Any child of the 90s is familiar with *The Crow*. To those of darkwave temperament, that film's soundtrack was our *Hair*, our *Grease*, our *Saturday Night Fever*. A hallmark of that sonic bible is the six-minute edit of Rollins Band's ten-minute cover of the comic-book homage by the techno-anarchist duo Suicide. Where the original is a skittish bunny-hop of jagged keyboard stabs overlaid with wispy echoing vocals, that cover bludgeons you with piledriver slabs of guitar fuzz, bronco-busted by Hank in all his gravel-throated glory. It's not "Goth" per se, but no Goth worth that name at that time lacked a copy of the *Crow* soundtrack. As Daniel mispronounced my name over the PA, I slouched to the stage and assumed the hallmark Henry Rollins stance.

I'd first discovered Rollins in 1984 by way of another film's legendary soundtrack: the movie *Repo Man*, featuring Black Flag's "TV Party." Shortly afterward, my friend Big Bob hipped me to the band's debut album *Damaged*, which remains among my favorite punk rock albums. Black Flag had several frontmen, but Rollins remains the most memorable. His feral mix of muscular hypermasculinity and hip-swiveling gender-bending gave him a hallmark stage presence — one I adopted as I wrapped the microphone cord around my fist and assumed the wide-legged stance of Hank Rollins at bay.

The ominous fuzzy opening notes lumbered through the club's speakers. I glared up at my fellow club-goers from the patented Rollins underlook — chin tucked down, eyes rolled up to gaze through the eyebrows. I squared my shoulders, shook my hips, clenched my throat tight.

"Ghost. *Rider*. Motor. *Cycle*. *Heee*-roh..."

The mic was live, so I locked the words down in my throat as I hurled myself into Rollins Mode.

Anyone who's seen Hank perform knows that Rollins slammed every ounce of energy in his muscular form behind every move he made onstage and every word he belted up his gravel-strewn larynx. Wendy once described Rollins Band as sounding "like an angry man throwing heavy machinery at the floor," and that's as accurate an assessment as I've ever heard. "Ghostrider" distills the essence of Rollins' intensity into a cascade of punishing beats and distortions that's heavy even by early 1990s standards. In that spirit, I squeezed my eyes shut and gave my performance everything I had to give.

For the first few minutes, I played the game straight. Silently mouthing the familiar words, I bent myself into

Rollinsonian contortions. Unlike Hank, I wore my hair long; in place of his bike shorts and bare chest and feet, I had my trusty motorcycle jacket, jeans, heavy boots, and the inevitable black band T-shirt. Aside from those differences, I gave as faithful an impression as I could.

Partly from intensity, partially for courage, I kept my eyes shut tight.

During the instrumental bridge, however, I opened my eyes and beheld the dance floor.

Previously empty, it now boiled with a handful of my friends doing a slow-motion mosh pit.

So I did what any self-respecting punk rock veteran would do: I threw myself into the crowd.

For endless moments, we rolled and tumbled in sludgy grace, ramming into one another with slow but potent impact. Paul, my buddy Michael-Also-Named-Rollins, and a few other folks whose names I can't recall three decades later, all played Black Clad Bumper Cars off one another's shoulders and backs. Then, as the break transitioned into the next verse, I hauled myself back up on stage and went full-blown apeshit.

Peeling off my jacket, I drew it back, threw it on the stage, and started hopping up and down on top of it. Grabbing a lit candelabrum, I held it up and shook it, punctuating Hank's cries of *"FIRE-FIRE-FIRE-FIRE-with-FIIIIII-AHHHHHH!!!"* Hot wax splattered all over me — my jacket, my face, my arms, my T-shirt and hair. Still moving as slowly as it was physically possible to move, I slammed the candelabra down, dropped to my knees, beat my head against the stage, wrapped the mic cord around my neck, and mock-strangled myself to death with it.

The song faded. I opened my eyes.

Cheers and applause from everywhere. I think even Daniel was clapping in the DJ booth. Wendy wore that huge, wicked grin of hers. She had — of course — been right.

No one tried to follow that performance.

I won.

As befitting a prize won in such a ridiculous manner, I spent my $50.00 on CDs, one of which replaced my worn-out tape copy of Rollins' classic *The End of Silence*.

One of these days, I hope to tell Hank this tale in person, presenting that absurd tableau in all its glorious physicality. I know Henry doesn't drink anymore, but I still feel like I owe him a beer or something. I'm not sure if he'd laugh, glare, or beat the shit out of me. Judging by what little bit I know about the guy from interviews and his spoken-word performances, though, I think he'd get a kick out of it.

If nothing else, that night scored me fifty bucks, an amusing story, and the assurance that when I choose to make a fool out myself in the name of a pretty girl's dare, I probably won't be alone.

ECHO CHAMBER

"I know it's not much," Brian said, "but it's the best we can do for now."

Dennis nodded as he took the envelope from Brian; inside, three weathered $50 bills folded around a gift card. "The card's got an additional hundred-fifty on it," Brian added. "That's a food allowance for you. Anything that's left when we get back, you can keep."

"Cool. Thanks." Dennis nodded again, tucking the envelope into his pocket. "Half now...?"

"...and half when we get back." Brian nodded. "Plus, if you do a good job, you can pick out a few goodies from the warehouse next week." His voice held a note of apology, and he reached behind his neck in the age-old gesture of silent discomfort. "Sorry we can't do more."

Dennis shook his head. "It's all good, dude. I know how things are these days." He did, too. He'd gotten this gig by way of his buddy Rig Chen, graphic designer and de facto art director for Storm Dragon Game Studio. The company was hurting, and Dennis knew it. He was hurting too. Even at three hundred bucks for a week's work, he needed this gig more than he wanted to admit.

Brian Beckett, Storm Dragon's co-founder and acting CEO, continued rubbing the back of his neck. The past five years had aged him at least ten. Brian still looked fitter than you'd expect the head of a gaming company to look, but the stress was starting to show. His rangy good looks had begun to grow hollow and a bald spot crested his once-boyish hair. "I think this'll be a good con for us," Brian said, his words straining toward optimism. "There's a lot of anticipation about the new line, and I think it'll go over well this year."

Dennis Kitcher nodded, grinning. "I heard. Rig says it's badass."

Brian grinned back. "It is. Wanna see?"

"Of course!"

Around them, the offices of Storm Dragon Game Studios bustled with activity... or at least did the best approximation of "bustling" a company can do when it consists of nine people and a cat. Editor Kathleen Crowley hauled a case of bottled water toward the door, while the company's sales manager Travis reset the reception office's phone messages. Outside, incongruous against the background of a neighboring cemetery, an Enterprise rental van purred near the main entrance, packed to the brim with luggage, pillows, and boxes of stock. Marjorie Stoner, the warehouse manager, sat behind the wheel, battered combat boots kicked up on the dashboard and a bored look creasing her face. Her sweaty assistant Scott shoved another cardboard box into the van's crowded interior. Meanwhile, the company's CFO, A.J., checked the offices for burning candles, smoldering incense, or drugs left in conspicuous places. "Geeze, guys," he told Cheshire Martin and Echo Stern, the company's two remaining rock-star designers, "I hope y'all are getting that out of your system before the drive."

In the kitchen, the two women held court with a belching contest. True to her name, Echo seemed to be winning. "C'mon, Chesh," Rig urged, "you can beat her!" He waved to Dennis as his friend passed the kitchen with Brian. "Dude! You made it. Thanks!"

"Thanks for getting me the gig, man," Dennis replied.

"Hey, Rig," Brian added. "Wanna come help me show off your masterpiece?"

"Cool!" Rig exclaimed as Chesh ripped forth with a devastating burp. "I call this duel in favor of the pretty redhead from Atlanta!"

"Jesus, Rig." Echo sneered in mock disgust. "You're such a fucking suck-up."

"Um..." Dennis held the new book at arm's length with fascinated disbelief. "It's... wow."

Chesh prodded Rig in the belly as his friend scanned the pages. "Hey, Mikey," she said, "I think he likes it."

"God," Rig whispered back, "that shit's *archaic*, yo."

Brian stood behind them, his hand again clasping the back of his neck. "So," he asked Dennis, "thoughts?"

Dennis pored over the pages of the lush hardcover, his eyes darting across the red-and-black images within. "It's gorgeous," he allowed. "They're gonna let you sell this at *GenCon*?"

"Nope," Rig said, grinning. "They already said no."

"Then why—"

"...are we piling into the van?" Echo added, leaning one elbow on Chesh's shoulder and the other on Rig's. "Because we're going black market with this bad girl."

Brian winced and Dennis turned his head to her in confusion. "I don't follow you."

The brawny designer flashed a grin that had floored fanboys and fangirls alike for almost a decade. Her biceps flexed as she leaned her weight against Rig and Chesh. "They told us in advance that we couldn't sell *Crimson Key* on the exhibition floor," she said. Dennis felt his heart catch as Echo's mischievous brown eyes locked on his own. "So, we won't. We'll be selling it outside the hall, out of the van and our backpacks..."

"...and making sure everyone else knows about it," Chesh finished, offering the cock-eyed smile that had inspired her nickname. "TikTok is our new best friend."

"That way," Echo finished, running her fingers through Chesh's red-dyed bangs with knee-buckling effect, "we keep everything we make from the *Crimson Key* sales, generate scads of free publicity, *and* hold exclusive distribution of the hottest-ticket item at GenCon!"

Brian's expression showed what he thought of the arrangement. Still, desperate times called for desperate measures, and Storm Dragon was pretty damned desperate. If *Crimson Key* didn't pan out, everybody'd be looking for work. And then there'd be the legal battles over ownership they'd face if the company went belly-up. Gavin McRea, Storm Dragon's co-founder, wanted the Intellectual Property rights to everything the company had produced. No one here wanted to see him get them.

Rig fished a folded flyer out of his pocket. "What'cha think, yo?" He held it out to Dennis. *Crimson Key*, read the words grouped around a scalding hot bondage babe. *Dark Erotic Roleplay — the book THEY don't want you to see!!!*

"Seriously?"

Rig frowned. "You don't like it?"

Kevin backpedaled. "It's not *that*, exactly..." He noted Echo giving him a look that might be appraising, thoughtful, hostile,

or some combination of the above. "It just seems a bit...
extreme?"

"Extremity," said Echo, "is the point. Everyone's concerned
with being so fucking *polite* that everything has just gotten so..."
She searched for the right expletive. "*Boring.*"

"And boring," Rig added, "does not save companies."

"Or," Echo finished, "*jobs.*"

And jobs were not anything anyone could afford to lose.

Two years out from the biggest economic crash since Black
Friday, everyone who still had a job was struggling to keep
it. The new guy in the White House talked a good game, so
to speak, but layoffs were still the order of the day. "Hope"
was a slogan for banners and election parties. Hope didn't pay
the rent. *Attention* did. *Extremity* did. And yeah, sex did too.
Storm Dragon had been founded on all three, and if they were
lucky this year, those traits might keep the place in business.

Fortunately, Chesh and Echo excelled in those regards.

Seven years earlier, everyone at GenCon had declared Echo
and Chesh to be the hottest booth bait in the show. They
were wrong. The two young women weren't booth bait — they
were Storm Dragon's newest game designers. Gavin's furious
departure that year had left Storm Dragon in the lurch. Enter
two college friends who'd met in their local gaming group.
Echo and Chesh had started off as interns but didn't stay that
way for long. In short order, the girls charmed Brian, teamed
up with Marjorie, kicked ass on everybody else, and led Storm
Dragon to its hottest days that decade.

Trouble was, it had still been a lousy decade. The
book-based roleplaying market had crested in the mid-1990s
and then steadily declined. Between collectable card games,

miniature games, computer games, and those thrice-damned Massive Multiplayer Online RPGs, the demand for Storm Dragon's specialty collapsed almost as soon as the company released its first product, *Angelicus: War in Heaven*, in 1995. Computer-game license attempts hadn't panned out, and two ill-fated card games and a misconceived zombie board game soon drained the company bank account to critical levels. If it hadn't been for the wildly successful *Angelicus*, Storm Dragon would not have survived the turn of the millennium. As things were, that survival had been a near thing.

And then suddenly, there'd been *Blood, Roses & Steel*, a swashbuckling success story with a heavy live-action component. In the hands of the traditional dude-male game designer, the game might have warranted a shrug. Thankfully, *Blood, Roses & Steel* had come from two smart, attractive, badassed young women instead. When McRae quit, Echo picked up *Angelicus* and ran with it, hard. The resulting books — and some tie-in jewelry — had kept the company afloat while Chesh and Echo created *Blood, Roses & Steel*. The pirate-themed RPG arrived just as Disney's own pirate films made pirates cool again. The timing had been just what Storm Dragon needed... and when the two designers hit the con circuit with gleaming corsets and cutlasses, the game exploded. Since then, Echo and Chesh had been golden. Still, book-based games no longer paid the rent. *Crimson Key* was a make-or-break gamble. It was all-hands-on-deck time at Storm Dragon Games, and the storm, as the saying goes, was upon them now.

Thankfully, it seemed, Chesh and Echo were ready to face it. Being female game designers, they were obviously used to storms.

"So — you like it?" Chesh asked Dennis. A full head shorter than her friend, the designer stood as curvy as Echo stood lean. Her short hair blazed red as a bull-baiting flag. She looked, Dennis realized, like the model for half the pictures in the book. He felt the spit dry out in his mouth. "Um, yeah," he mumbled, glancing between the pages, her face, and the floor. "I do. A lot."

"Cool," she added, her tone suggesting that she'd known as much already. *The dudes at GenCon*, he reflected, *are doomed.*

"Check *this* out, yo," Rig added. He took the book from Dennis' hands and flipped to a section printed in graceful red ink. The sumptuous line art recalled Alphonse Mucha by way of de Sade. "We adopted the LARP system from *Blood, Roses & Steel*, then added some real kink and sex magic!"

"*Dude!*" Dennis grabbed the book back as the designers laughed. The pages swirled with arcane designs. "Are those real, like, real occult thingies?"

"Kinda," Rig confessed. "I messed with 'em a bit."

"We didn't want to put real magic in a game book," Chesh said, her cropped bangs twitching as she shook her head.

"Not cool," added Echo. "Seriously not cool."

"You never *know* what people will do with it," Chesh added, smirking. *Are they messing with me?* Dennis wondered, and decided that they were.

"Echo did some kick-ass research," Rig said. "She got all these wild books back in her office, and..."

"Guys," Brian interjected in his *Boss said so* voice, "we really need to go."

"Yeah, I guess we gotta," said Rig, disappointed. "Still, check that shit *out*, yo!" He pointed to some ominous squiggles. "My head hurt for *days* after I drew that shit!"

Dennis scanned the diagrams, which looked like tantric spaghetti on crack. "I see why, man," he said, nodding. "That's seriously complex!"

Echo squeezed Rig's shoulder affectionately. "Rig came through, big-time," she said. "The book wouldn't be nearly as good without his art."

Dennis eyed Chesh, connected the dots between her looks and his friend's illustrations, and glanced down at the floor again. *Lucky bastard*, he thought. *I wish I could draw like that!*

"So, Dennis," Echo added. "Have you been to the office before?"

"Nope."

"Lemmie show you around then," she said, taking his arm. "If you're gonna be stuck here for a week, you really should know what *not* to touch."

# # #

"See the books up there?" she asked, pointing to a series of battered spines crammed into the top layer of Echo's bookshelf.

"Yep," Dennis answered.

"*Don't. Touch. Those*. If and when you want something to read, you're welcome to browse through anything else in here. But not those. Seriously." She looked eye-to-eye with him. "This is so *not* a Bluebeard's keyhole thing. I mean it. Those books are old and rare and valuable, so pretty please, with sugar on top, don't fuck with 'em."

"No problem." Dennis decided he could get used to looking eye-to-eye with Echo. She was tall enough... or he was short enough... or something. *Damn*, he thought, *do I have stuff in my teeth? Did I brush before I got here? Is my breath doomish?* She didn't seem to mind his proximity, but closeness to a woman like Echo made a dude self-conscious.

Dennis himself wasn't that bad, really. Just kinda... y'know, *geeky.* He spent too much time playing *World of Warcraft* and not enough out in the sun. Dennis hadn't worked up a sweat since that warehouse job two years ago, and his hair stayed stuck in that awkward range between "delightfully scruffy" and "Dude, see a barber." As Echo leaned against the bookshelf, her six-pack abs teasing the edge between her Venture Brothers T-shirt (with the sleeves ripped off) and a low-rise set of urban camo cargo pants, Dennis found himself poking between his teeth with his tongue. Her office smelled like coffee and girl-sweat. Its walls glared with sullen prints by Royo and Brom. She'd painted those walls a dark forest green and the light oak of her bookshelves made them pop in the dim light. He recalled the pictures in the books she'd just written, and his mind wandered. *She just invited me into her office*, he thought, *and told me I could borrow her books.* Did that foretell further intimacy? Or was she just being polite, pitying or both?

"So, yeah," she continued, "feel free to come in here while you're here if you need something to read or anything. Just put stuff back where you found it when you're done. I have a system here, and I'll be hacked off if it's ruined."

Dennis put his hands up, open-palmed. "No problem," he said again. "I'll make sure that I keep track of anything I move."

"All good," she said, flashing that killer grin. She leaned in closer to him. "Hey, we really appreciate you coming in on short notice like this. Thanks."

"No prob—" He threw himself into verbal reverse. "I'm glad to do it." He glanced around, noting the pagan-god statues and vintage McFarlane action figures. Three swords hung by brackets on the wall — one, a wooden practice sword, the crossed ones, actual steel. "Cool office," he said at last. "I like it."

"It works."

He indicated the swords. "You really use those?"

"Ten years of kenjutsu, plus some fencing and a stint in the SCA."

"Bad*ass!*" he breathed.

Echo brushed his arm with her hand. "Thanks," she said, and he could almost spot a shy girl underneath her grin. It was easy, he thought, to see why Echo made such a hit at conventions. She had a gift for seeming aloof and intimate at the same time. The combination made him flush. "I spend way too much time in here," she went on, "so I have to make sure it's comfortable."

Against one wall, a Papa-San chair rested against the wall, its contours draped with blankets and pillows. "You sleep in here, too?" he asked before he'd thought better of doing so.

"Yep." She grimaced. "More often than I'd prefer to."

Dennis flushed at the mental image of her curled up in that chair. "Bum..." he started to say, but his voice caught. He coughed. "Bummer."

She giggled. "People still say that with a straight face?"

Face burning, he shrugged. "I guess."

She slapped him lightly on the shoulder. "Well, you can look through the books, except for the ones I told you not to touch." She grinned with just a hint of edge. "But you should probably do your sleeping elsewhere."

"Oh, no question." *I might be a perv*, he thought, *but at least I'm not a creep*.

#

"So, you canned the interns?" Dennis whispered when Echo and Chesh had gone to finish loading the truck. Out back, a small Ryder rental idled, its cargo bay stacked with product.

"Dude!" Rig shook his head. "They were totally skeezing hard on Kat."

"And they *lived*?"

Rig chuckled like dry leaves crunching. "More or less. Echo, Chesh and Marjorie took turns tearing strips off 'em before Brian finally gave 'em the big ass-boot."

"No doubt!"

"You do *not* fuck with those ladies, my friend," Rig said. "They've had every kind of shit this industry can throw at 'em — an' when you think about who most of the people in the gaming business are...dude, that's a *LOT* of shit!"

Dennis nodded. He knew some gamer-girls, himself. Until today, though, he'd thought all game designers were dudes. "So, you're driving the truck up with Chesh?"

"Me an' Cheshire, all the way to Indie!"

"Dude..." Dennis glanced in the direction of the departed designers. "Are you and she like...?"

Rig laughed. "Me and she are like *friends*, yo. Friends and brothers-in-arms. Yeah, sure, we spend some nekkid time, but it's not like that. That's like business. She's an artist, man. So am I. We make art and war, not love."

"Sounds all right, man," he said, jostling his buddy's arm. "Not prying, just frying."

Rig looked at him. "'Frying'?"

"Forget I said that."

"Done."

"Yeah. Well, hey — I'm glad for the caretaker gig. Thanks."

"All is good, grasshopper," Rig said, checking his desk drawer for a flash drive. He found one, nodded to himself, then stashed it in his black Tripp jacket. "All is good. ' sides," he added, "I'd rather have you here minding the shop for a week than leave *those* two geeks gone wild in charge while we're away." Rig scritched absently at his spiky black hair. "They were on my last nerve in a *week*, yo, and I was glad to see 'em gone."

"Their loss..."

"Your gain."

"No doubt."

"Hey," Rig added, dropping his voice to conspiracy level. "The intern slot's still open. You want I should drop a bug in the boss's ear while we're conning?"

Dennis nodded. "Yeah. A fucking centipede, dude."

Rig laughed. "Right to his *brain*, man. Right to Brian's brain."

"Thanks, dude."

Rig shared the infamous fist-jab with his friend. "You got it, yo. Just don't fuck shit up, you got it."

#

The key ring rattled as Dennis locked the door. Up Boulder Avenue, the Ryder truck's taillights flashed red for a moment at the intersection, then disappeared around the curve. Above the tree line, dimming skies hinted at dusk. Six days until the Storm Dragon crew returned. Six days, and the office was all his.

Cool.

"Keep visitors," Brian had told him, "...to an absolute minimum. We don't expect you to be a hermit, but for God's sake don't host any parties here. Honestly," he'd said, rubbing the back of his neck again, "I'd rather you didn't have anyone out here except the pizza delivery guy."

"Understood," Dennis had replied in his most professional voice.

"Good." Brian fished out — with some hesitation, Dennis noted — a bright new key. "We had to change the locks last week," he said as he handed the key to Dennis. "I think you probably heard why."

"The interns."

"Yeah." A cloud of anger drifted across Brian's face. "They probably won't come back, but they know we'll be gone, so..."

"Travis gave me the security company code," said Dennis. "And I know how to call 911."

"Good man."

"And if all else fails," Dennis added, "I can always grab a sword from Echo's room."

Brian laughed, and all was good with the world.

There was beer in the fridge (good stuff, too, he noted — Canadian microbrews and some Sapporo), a ton of books, and no end of games to play. *Of course*, he thought, *I'd need someone to play them with*... and since Brian had discouraged visitors... Oh, well. There was still online gaming, and this time out he'd get *paid* to sit on his ass and veg on *WOW*.

The office sat in a crappy run-down industrial space on the curve of Boulder Road. All by its lonesome self, it nestled between two empty office fronts, a bunch of trees, and that nearby cemetery. Train tracks passed by the intersection of Boulder and Stone Ridge. Not long before the van pulled off, a freight train had rumbled past, shaking the floor like thunder. "Is that a storm?" Dennis had asked, and Chesh had laughed at him. "That's what I thought, too," she said, her red bangs fringed across her eyes. "When I first got here," she continued," I kept looking for thunder clouds and wondering where they were."

"That's why," Marjorie added as they checked the warehouse one last time, "Brian and Marcus called their company 'Storm Dragon.' It used to be 'Rabid Hamster' or something like that, but when they moved into this office space, they always thought it was getting ready to rain."

"So yeah." Dennis nodded. "Storm Dragon. I get it."

"Sounds better than Rabid Hamster, anyway." Chesh stretched herself into interesting shapes. "God, I hate long drives!"

"Now these," Marjorie continued, indicating rows upon rows of stock, "have been taped shut while we're gone. If you open them," she said, her jaw tight with menace, "I *will* know, and I'll feed your spine to my iguana."

"I'll keep 'em shut," Dennis assured her.

"You'd better," she said. Watching Marjorie move with the grace of a wrestler and the single-minded focus of a Shaolin monk, Dennis wondered why anyone in right mind would even dare to risk her wrath.

Marjorie showed him how to take deliveries, pointed out the pallets that needed to go out, and handed him inventory instructions. "Everything I know about has gone out already," she'd said, "and most of our customers will be at GenCon, too. Still, I want to keep track of anything that comes in. So, if and when a truck arrives," she asked, her face mild yet significant, "what do you do?"

"Follow the instructions, keep out of the way, and open nothing."

"Right." Her grin revealed some missing teeth, and her nose lumped like it'd been broken once or twice. The shoulders beneath her hoodie stretched with muscle. Her tattooed forearms would make Popeye doubt his chances in an arm-wrestling match. *Those interns*, Dennis thought, *had been the dumbest motherfuckers on earth.*

As a fresh train rumbled past, Dennis checked the sky. It *did* look like it might rain tonight. He felt sorry for Rig and Marjorie, driving through the storm. *Yeah, right*, he reflected. *They're going to GenCon, and you're holding down the fort.*

All things considered, though, this wasn't a bad place to be.

# # #

Batshit the Dementicat — named for her tendency to tear through the offices at lunatic speed — arched with tortoise-shell abandon. Dennis scritched her under the chin as he wandered his temporary home. In his arms, Batshit stretched out her paws and tilted her head back for more effective spoilage. Outside, the sunlight faltered and a train rumbled past on its tracks. The pizza guy would arrive at any moment; in the meantime, Dennis paced the Storm Dragon halls, cat in hand, and contemplated his evening's activities.

His ramblings took Dennis through a dim-lit office space. Posters from previous Storm Dragon releases (*"Angelicus: Thy Name is Wrath!" "Blood, Roses & Steel — a Girl's Best Friends!"*), scatterings of art prints, and the doleful "wall of shame" where awful submissions were posted for mockery at large... Dennis scanned them all. As Batshit pawed Dennis's chest, Dennis eyed the empty offices. More than half, he noticed, were *empty* empty — or at least abandoned by regular staff. The layoffs that had bled the company dry had turned those forlorn offices into dusty storage space. Old computers, battered toys, stacks of expired promo material... *Damn, dude*, thought Dennis, *this shit's kinda depressing*. Even game companies, he reflected, could be grim places to work.

Most of the doors were closed. Some sported shiny new doorknobs, with keyholes that the other doors lacked. *I guess that was to keep the interns out*, he guessed. *Or maybe me?* The thought troubled Dennis, though he couldn't say why. Echo, however, had left her door open — had, he reminded himself, explicitly invited him to go in and borrow anything he wanted or needed. *Except those*, he recalled, glancing up with inevitable curiosity at the volumes on her top shelf. *I'm supposed to stay away from those.*

What better way is there to invite someone to do something he's *not* supposed to do?

Echo's oak bookshelves reached almost to the ceiling. Unlike the OfficeMax specials that filled the offices, these looked expensive and serious. The forbidden volumes ranged across the bookshelf nearest to her desk, an obvious reference library within easy grabbing range of both the computer seat and the Papa-San chair. A grungy pair of Reebox nestled beneath her desk, their weather-beaten look at odds with their meticulous arrangement. On the wall nearby, a new poster for *Crimson Key* ("*Sin & Sorcery at the Devil's Knee!*") gleamed within a glass frame. Rig's work, Dennis noted... and damned if the model didn't look like Chesh. She knelt in an alluring pose, her parted lips and half-shut eyes reflecting strength, submission, and sarcasm all at once. That kind of image would seduce boys and girls alike. *Those posters*, he thought, *will be very popular this weekend.*

And then, there were the books...

What *is* it that makes us do the things we're not supposed to do? Dennis scanned the shelf, eyeing the titles with a scuttling thrill of curiosity, arousal, and distaste. *Screw the Roses, Send Me the Thorns. The Encyclopedia of Erotic Wisdom. Dark Eros. The Sadian Woman.* There were art books with titles like *Bondage Obsession* and *Cry for Pain*. There were other titles, too — ominous tomes of old leather and gold-etched spines: *Hymns of Matangi. Daughters of Joy. Codex Licentia. The Feast of Flutes.* A roleplaying supplement, *The Book of Erotic Fantasy*, perched incongruously in the midst of these disconcerting volumes. *Oh, well*, thought Dennis, *I guess Echo's system makes sense to* her, *anyway.*

As he thought so, his hand reached toward the top shelf. Batshit mewed her displeasure as those fingers ceased their tribute to her majesty. *Dude*, Dennis reflected, *don't go there. She said not to...*

So just take out one at a time, he replied to himself, *and put 'em back in the right place when you're done. She won't know.*

His tingling fingers slipped across the spines. Rested on *Cry for Pain*. Began easing it from its place on the shelf.

DEENG-DONG! Dennis jerked his hand back at the sound. Batshit spilled from his arms with loud complaint, hitting the floor and racing off before the source of that sound kicked in. *Oh yeah — the door.* The electric bell rang again as his heart hammered against the ribs that restrained it. Slipping like a sinner through Echo's open door, he hustled off to get the pizza.

Minutes later, he returned, his fingers smelling slightly of garlic and cheese. The pizza cooled on the break room table, filling the office with the welcome scent of chow. Still, the bookshelf drew him back. When he walked into the office, he saw way. The copy of *Cry for Pain* tilted out from its position on the shelf, held there by the press of other books. *Oh, crap!* Dennis thought. Not a half-hour into his week and he was already breaking the few rules they'd given him! Reaching up, he pushed the slender volume back into its proper position...

...then slipped his fingertips across the heavy-bound spine of *Feast of Flutes*. The other books shifted slightly, as if inviting him to ease the volume from its place among them. Shaking with guilt and curiosity, Dennis slid the book out... and then caught himself and stopped. *Nope*, he thought, and pushed *The Feast of Flutes* back where it belonged.

Someone's watching me.

He turned slowly toward the door, expecting either some wild-eyed demon or — worse yet — Echo.

Batshit the Dementicat *rowww*ed at him, her eyes shining in the dim light.

"Yeah," Dennis said aloud. "I need to get my ass of here and go eat some pizza before I do something really dumb." With those words of wisdom, he followed Batshit the Dementicat toward the kitchen, pulling Echo's door closed till it clicked shut behind him.

# # #

"Dude," he whispered aloud, "this fuckin' *rocks!*"

Dennis stretched out in the break room, his high-topped Keds propped on a neighboring chair, his belly plumped by half a Meat Lover's pizza. Batshit nestled on the table next to him, gnawing on a crusty peace offering he'd left on her very own paper plate. A deep purr signaled her acceptance of the new cat-slave.

His hunger sated, his fingers wiped thoroughly on a half-dozen paper napkins, Dennis now turned his attention to the copy of *Crimson Key* that Brian had given him before they left. "All yours, Dennis," Echo had said as she blew her wet-inked signature dry. "You're the first one outside the company to see it." She handed it to him with a grin. That flash of teeth alone had been worth a week of baby-sitting real estate. Every member of the staff signed the book for him — even Scott, whose contribution to *Crimson Key* consisted of hauling it around the warehouse. It was a collector's item of immeasurable value now. Better still, it was actually *good*. Really good.

"*Life*," it began, "*is lust. Lust for pleasure. For power. For immortality. In this lust beats the heart of our existence. And from it, those of us without fear or scruple bring lust to its grandest heights.*" Written in Echo's lilting prose, the book went on to describe a world where ultimate pain and pleasure were the keystones of enlightenment. Players in this world were invited to become *Talashi*, masters of sensual bliss. The game drew bits of *Vampire*, *Witchcraft*, the Kushiel and Gor novels and God-knew-what else and then wrapped it up in the romantic dedication of two young women who clearly believed in what they were doing... or who at least did really good imitations of people who did.

He had to wonder how much they truly practiced what they wrote.

The art was every bit as good as the writing, if not better. Rig had outdone himself here. Each illustration looked like a page from the *Kama Sutra* by way of Luis Royo channeling Gustav Doré on an absinthe-cocaine bender. The book was smaller than usual, more like a novel than a game textbook. Its hard red cover gleamed with red-foil embossing. *No wonder Brian's nervous*, thought Dennis. *The printing alone must have cost a fortune.*

Years back, Chesh had won awards for her world-building work on *Blood, Roses & Steel*. If anything, she'd surpassed herself on this book. *I wonder if they run a* Crimson Key *game here*, he thought, and then wondered what he'd have to do to receive an invitation if they did.

#

A crash jolted Dennis from his reading reverie. Another crash dimmed the light. Something rattled the ceiling overhead — a metallic wash of sound. Dennis looked up, puzzled, as the light came back on. "Jeeze," he said after a moment, "is that... *rain?*"

Apparently, it had decided to storm after all.

Rain roared thick against the corrugated roof. Putting his signed copy of *Crimson Key* on one of the few clean countertops, he rushed out to see if everything was safe. Light flickered from outside as he headed toward the plate glass door.

Across the parking lot, sheets of rain steamed against the asphalt. Branches caught in the sudden tide surfed out from the edge of the grass. A sudden southern storm boomed down from the pink-gray sky. Dennis winced as yet another bolt of lightning knocked the power out.

This time, it stayed dark.

Great.

Candles, he thought. *I know I saw some somewhere.* Thankfully, it wasn't quite dark enough to render the office impassible. The maze of doors and corridors glowed with what was left of daylight. He grabbed his book and fumbled his way in the direction of Chesh's and Kathleen's offices. They had candles, he recalled. Lots of them. Now if only they had matches, too...

Again, he flashed sympathy for the drivers caught in the blast. *It can't be easy*, he thought, *driving a truck or van through this shit!* He hoped that Rig and Marjorie had cleared the path of the storm before it hit. Kathleen's doorknob rattled but refused to open. Locked.

Okay, fine — Cheshire's office, then.

It was locked, too.

Don't they trust me? he wondered as the building shook again. But then, given those asshole interns, why should they take chances? *Hmmmmm... there must be flashlights around here somewhere. Why didn't they cover that stuff in the tour?*

Batshit the Dementicat raced past Dennis, yowling distress. She darted into an office down the hall. He heard dull thumps, a meow, and a muffled crash. "Um, Batshit?" he called out, and was answered by a boom of thunder.

A dull red glow infused the front offices. Dennis glanced up to see the sky bloom into a disconcerting crimson shade. "Uhhh," he said, shaking his head. "That can't be good." Tornado? Forest fire? Incursion of demonic forces? From where he was standing, nothing seemed unreasonable.

You did this, he thought. *You were fucking with the books.*

"Oh, *please!*" he spat, aloud. "I put the damn thing back — I didn't even *open* it!" Still, the idea nagged at him. What if — in breaking Echo's rule — he *had* brought on some kind of...

That was too stupid to consider.

He went back to searching the drawers. Finally, he found a small Maglite with half-dead batteries at the bottom of the reception desk. Lightning flickered through the red skies, throwing the rain into silver shards.

Dennis popped his cellphone. No signal. He blinked. No bars. The display glowed with bright blue promise, but the reception field was blank. He tried the phone anyway. Dead.

"You're kidding, right?" he said, but got no answer.

Outside, a green Prius — headlights glaring — sheared down Boulder Avenue, fishtailed across the rain-slicked pavement, and disappeared beyond the trees. Dennis waited for the sound of a crash, but nothing followed.

Caught between the dark labyrinth of offices behind him (populated by Batshit and God-knew-what-else) and the red-tinged storm on the other side of that fragile-seeming door, Dennis stood thoughtfully for a moment, hefted the tiny Maglite, and sighed. "This," he said, again aloud, "is gonna be a *long* few days."

# # #

As the shock of the storm wore off, Dennis headed toward Echo's office. There'd been candles in there, too, and the room hadn't been locked... or had it? *She left it open for me*, he recalled, *and I closed the door*... He hustled toward the room through dark hallways, lit only by the faint beam of the Maglite and a wash of distant red from the sky.

In that disconcerting twilight, the posters seemed to shift and dance, their faces following as he passed. Dark fantasy was Storm Dragon's stock-in-trade, and the hungry figures on the walls capered with sinister allure. A half-naked witch girl howled from her stake. A grim knight, bristling with spiky plate armor, hefted an ax large enough to chop Buicks in half. A blaze-eyed beast-thing hefted a young chick in artfully tattered clothes. In the red-washed shadows, these cheesy archetypes reached something dark and primal within Dennis' skull, pulled it out, and had a snack.

Around him, the walls rattled with the fury of the rain. Rolls of thunder shook the floor beneath his sneakers. Batshit yowled from her hiding place, commanding the new cat-slave to find the source of this disorder and make it stop at once. Echo's office lay at the far end of a narrow corridor, flanked on each side by closed doors on the facing walls. The first bore a picture of a scar-faced man pointing a huge pistol at the viewer. "*I'M BUSY*," the sign declared. "*GO. AWAY. OR. DIE.*" The second door held a poster of the Devil grinning with mustachioed aplomb. A short-haired brunette lashed a two-fisted dude with her riding crop. A blonde in torn lingerie cringed behind him as the poster proclaimed that "*SATAN WAS A LESBIAN!*"

Echo's door was blank. And slightly open.

I could have sworn, thought Dennis, *that I closed it when I left.*

The Meat Lover's pizza waved *Hello!* to him from within his guts. *Remember what we shared?* it cried. *Set me freeeee!* He clamped down on the churning below his belt line and gently pushed open Echo's door.

Behind him, storm-sounds rumbled down the corridor like Lucifer belching through a megaphone. *Six more days of this?* he wondered as he stepped gingerly inside. The dark green walls felt oppressive now. The bookshelves bore their burdens with stoic resolve. Dennis spotted three fat red candles clustered on the paper-strewn desk.

DEENG-DONG! Dennis shrieked, springing back from the desk. Again, the doorbell rang. His heart threw a hissy fit inside. *Someone's at the door*, he thought through a hopping maze of panic. *Someone's out there in the storm. I should let them in.*

No, his wiser self replied. *You really shouldn't do that.* Still, he set down his book, grabbed the candles, and hustled toward the door.

Batshit hissed from her hidden niche. Dull thumping sounds echoed down the hall. Dennis passed the posters again, grimacing at their lurid splendor. *Dude*, he pondered, *why the creeps?* There was nothing in these hallways worse than the stuff on his walls at home. *Those* posters didn't freak him out, he puzzled, so why should these?

Red light still glowed on the reception area walls. Weird shadows danced off boxes and furniture. That annoying doorbell pitched its electronic insistence through the halls. "*Christ!*" yelled Dennis, "Knock it *off*, already! I'm *coming!* Jeeze!" The muffled thumping grew louder as he reached the doorway, entered the reception area, and stopped.

Outside the plate glass office front, clustered by the door and bumping together beneath the overhang, a crowd of people packed themselves against the glass. One leaned his shoulder against the doorbell, sending that affronted *DEENG-DONG!* bouncing through Dennis's skull. The red skies threw the crowd into silhouette, casting thick black shadows across the sullen carpet. The people outside were soaking wet. Silver drizzles spilled across their limbs. Instinctually, Dennis flicked the light switch near his hand. Nothing. He raised the Maglite. Its illumination shimmered off the glass. It caught the faces of the crowd. Or what was left of them.

"You," said Dennis, "are *shitting* me."

Back behind him, Batshit hushed. Far off, deep in the warehouse, something boomed against the loading dock door.

The impact echoed through the office building, blunted but not silenced by the doors and walls.

Again, he sent the timid light brushing across the features of the crowd. Their gaunt faces. Their sunken eyes. Their bared teeth and tattered clothes. The occasional missing limb.

"Seriously?" Dennis shouted. "*Zombies?*"

Lots of zombies.

"But I didn't *DO* anything!" he wailed. "I put that stupid book back on the shelf! I didn't even *open* the damn thing!" The loading dock door thundered again behind him. Batshit had nothing to add to its eloquence.

"This is *bullshit!*" He crossed his arms defiantly. "I did not do *anything* to deserve a fucking zombie horde! And zombies are. *So. Played. Out.* Fuck. *OFF!*"

In answer, the shambling things beyond the glass door moaned, their rotting mouths swelled with preternatural hunger.

"Uh-uh!" Dennis insisted. "Take it elsewhere, dudes!" The zombie by the doorbell pushed the button again. "*AND CUT THAT SHIT OUT!*" Dennis banged the wall beside him, and the zombie lurched away from the buzzer. "That's better," Dennis said.

Now what?

Okay, zombie hordes. He'd seen this movie already. You beat their brains in and ran away until either the Army showed up, the zombies ate your guts out, or someone bigger and meaner than you arrived to kick some ass... yours included. The plate glass, he noticed, was reinforced with thin wires. It would hold, but probably not for long. There were zombies at the back door, too. This wasn't good. No phone, no lights, no way out. *George Romero*, he reflected, *you suck*.

Mental inventory time. The Maglite was useless. The kitchen held a microwave and some junk in the fridge. The knives and forks were probably all plastic. There'd be box cutters back in the warehouse. And yeah — Echo's swords. *Well, that's a 'duh,'* thought Dennis, turning back toward Echo's chamber. Swords it was, then. He'd never used one in real life, but it couldn't be *that* hard. Sharp, pointy, made of metal. Swing at things until they die. It's not like zombies used swords, too.

I don't want *them eating my guts out*, he thought.

And so, he went to fetch the swords.

# # #

...which would have worked better had they been sharp.

"Practice swords," he cried. "*Dammit!*"

Still, a set of aerodynamic baseball bats was better than no weapons at all. So as the zombies battered themselves pulpy against the front door (and the unseen yet ominous-sounding trespassers at the loading dock added their efforts to the overall din), Dennis tucked one dull metal blade into his belt, did the same with the wooden sword, took a practice swing with the best of the lot, and accidentally demolished a plaster bust of Cthulhu on Echo's desk. "Oops," he said, wincing as pieces bounced off the dark green wall. "Sorry, Echo."

He wondered if he'd get the chance to apologize in person, or if his intestinal spaghetti (*possibly*, he thought with a grimace, *polished off by the cat*) would be the closest thing to contrition she would see. *Talk about spilling your guts*, his inner voice added. The image of a Tom Savini special effect with his face on it reintroduced Dennis to the Meat Lover's pizza in his aforementioned guts. *Hiya*, it said. *Miss me?* A sharp, sour taste rose up the back of Dennis's throat. *With my imagination*, he reflected, *who needs zombies?*

As Dennis picked up the biggest chunks of Cthulhu's shattered skull, he noted a loud cracking sound from the vicinity of the front door. The warehouse still rang with the sound of zombie fists on corrugated steel. The cat had probably disappeared to whatever dimension cats head off to when things get bad. *Alas, poor 'Thulhu*, Dennis mused as he placed the busted head on Echo's desk. *Dude, we hardly knew ye.*

Anger surged again. He looked back up at Echo's books. "It's not *fair!*" he spat. "I put you back without reading you! Dude, why are you fucking with me now?"

Dennis, said the calm inner voice, *Why are you talking to a bookshelf?*

He slammed his free hand against the bookshelf in frustration. "'Cause I don't *want* zombies to eat my guts out! 'Cause all I wanted was to score an easy gig and a few bucks for rent! 'Cause I was tempted to read those stupid books up there and I didn't and *IT'S NOT FAIR!*" The zombies out front took up the cry, moaning loud enough to be heard down the hallway. Dennis felt chills racing underneath his skin. It was one thing to play *All Flesh Must Be Eaten*, and another to be the main course for real.

I'm a gamer, he thought. *In a gaming company's office. That's got to give me some kind of advantage here.* In a way, after all, he'd been training for this his whole life. *Problem is*, he thought, *zombie-survival horror games don't teach you how to fix the problem. They just stall your messy and inevitable death.*

As if to provide an express stop for that train of thought, he heard the front door shatter and bodies spill through. The warehouse shuddered beneath the blows at the loading dock door. *There's a side door, too*, he thought. *They're probably at that one, also... or already through it.* He heard thumping in the hallways, clumsy bodies butting into walls and doors as they plodded through Storm Dragon's office space.

Dennis glanced around. At the green walls. The heavy bookshelves. The desk and Papa-San chair. Echo's computer and the seat beneath that desk. Cued by the hollow sounds from the warehouse door, he looked up at the flimsy drop-tile ceiling. And then at the door and the hallway leading to it. He swung the sword again, this time in a more careful arc. Dennis smiled. *It's a defensible position!* To get him, the zombies would need to cram themselves down the hallway, pile up against the door, and expose themselves to attack if and when they smashed it open. The ceiling wasn't worth a damn, but since when could zombies climb? Although, backed into a corner, he might just survive this mess! *As long as they don't hang around until I starve*, he thought, *I may be able to wait them out.* And if they *did* come for him here, down that long and narrow hall, he could hold them off like those dudes in *300* until someone came to help him out... or at least till he died like some barbarian badass on a Frazettian heap of corpses. *That*, he decided, would be *cool*.

It sounded like a plan.

But a *cowardly* plan.

Dennis scowled. He kinda *had* been training for something like this his whole life. Even though that "training" took place in his imagination or on a computer screen, the adrenaline rush had been real... and so had the feeling of victory when he'd won, or at least gone down fighting. He glanced around Echo's office again, this time feeling ashamed. The swords he'd taken, the action figures on her desk, the games she'd designed, the posters she'd framed... this was the domain of a woman who worked out hard, practiced with swords, and collected and created fantasies of heroism.

Heroes didn't hide and wait for monsters to come kill them. Heroes went looking for adventure. And if it killed them, well at least they died with style.

Would Echo want him to make a last stand cowering in her office? Would she respect that? Dennis shook his head. *He* wouldn't respect it, either. It might have been *smart* to stay there, but it wasn't *heroic*. And if he'd learned anything from a lifetime of fantasy, it was that it was better to be a cool corpse than a live coward.

And then the crashing began.

First, it seemed as though someone had overturned a table full of silverware. Then the unmistakable *BOOM!* of something heavy dashed against an office wall. Another "something" — this one glass — shattered against the kitchen tiles. An object both mechanical and fragile (*the microwave? A computer?*) whoooshed through the air and slammed against carpeted concrete floor. *Holy shit*, he thought, *they're trashing the place!* This wasn't incidental damage — it took effort to make that kind of mess. Vandalism, not hunger, appeared to drive the zombie horde.

"Like *hell*," he said aloud. "I'm gonna kick some zombie ass!"

He strode forward manfully and tripped over the swords in his belt.

# # #

One of the benefits of a sedentary lifestyle is a built-in cushion when you fall on your face. Dennis felt the impact mostly in his front-loaded gut and the wrists he'd put out to slow his descent. By the time he was eye level with the floor (which needed *serious* vacuuming), Dennis was more angry than stunned. With a grunt, he pushed himself upright, yanked the swords out of the way, and watched a computer monitor bounce itself to pieces at the far end of the corridor. The red light from the sky illuminated just enough office space to reveal moving shadows and shimmering ruins. From the floor, the Maglite cast a dim yellow sun against the doorway's edge. Dennis felt the vibration of some other item being smashed. Snarling with territorial offense, he hauled himself upright, rearranged the swords, and started down the hall.

Glass glittered across the carpeting as Dennis crept out and raised Echo's blade.

Not ten feet away, three zombies stomped the remains of his pizza into the rug. None appeared to sense him.

Heart pounding, Dennis tiptoed into position, drew back the sword, and swung it powerfully into the nearest wall.

Dude, he thought as his palms stung with impact and the zombies turned, as one, to face him, *how the fuck did you miss hitting a zombie from behind?*

"*RUGGGHHH!!!*" cried the nearest zombie, jaw slack with decayed disbelief. He pointed at Dennis, his skull bobbing like a bobble-toy as he glanced between the other walking corpses as if to say, "What a *dork.*"

"Eat me," Dennis snarled, immediately regretting his choice of words.

The first zombie had been a beanpole. The second one looked grannyish, while the third had probably gone by "Bubba" in his past life. All three zombies had endured some fairly extensive rot, and they seemed to have died or been buried in formal clothes. Now, however, those clothes hung in muddy ruin. The zombies gaped at Dennis for a moment, flexing their devastated hands.

Then they attacked.

This time, Dennis was ready. He yanked the blade from the drywall and took the zombie's bobble-head off at the neck. That neck crunched like a handful of crepe paper wrapped around some Kentucky Fried chicken bones. That skull hurtled through the air and bounced off the second zombie's face, knocking the Granny corpse askew. Dennis brought the sword around in a backswing, mulching through Bubba's ribcage and spilling rank intestines across the floor. "Holy hopscotch *Christ!*" he cried at the wave of rot-formaldehyde stench. Who knew death could smell so *bad?*

Dennis recoiled as the first and third zombies collapsed in stinking heaps. *Huh,* he thought in the part of his mind that wasn't gagging, *they're pretty fragile.* The second zombie steadied herself drunkenly against the wall. Dennis let loose a barbaric yawp and brought the sword down through Granny's skull. *BWANG!* The metal blade shuddered against the bone.

Both combatants staggered, knocked away from one another by raw kinetic force. Dennis swore with geeky eloquence, his palms stinging from the impact, as half the zombie's face slid down her sundered skull. Granny shuddered for a moment and then joined her fellows on the floor.

"That was easy," Dennis marveled.

Then a laptop hit him in the head.

# # #

Something rank and squishy pinned him to the floor. Behind the dark wall of pain, he sensed a pile of soggy weights on his back. A cold, wet tile floor pressed against his cheek. Nasty fluids bathed his face. The smell made him cough. "Hey!" cried a female voice, "he's *alive!*"

"Good," replied another voice. Echo? A muddy Doc Martin boot came down beside his eyes. Dennis tried to speak but the effort sent sparks of bright pain across his head. Someone started lifting the weights off his body. *Dude!* he thought. *Zombies. I'm buried underneath dead zombies!* The redundancy behind the sentiment did nothing to alleviate its Ick factor. Dennis tasted his Meat Lover's pizza heading for a swift return trip.

A crunchy burden lifted off his head. Dim light greeted his half-open eyes. Groaning, Dennis squeezed them shut again, clamping his lips shut tight and swallowing the pizza down. Rolling over slowly, he opened his eyes again and looked up.

Echo towered over him, the crotch of her cargo pants posed right over his face. "I thought I told you..." she said as she tossed the last zombie aside, "...to leave my goddamn books *alone.*"

"I *did* leave your goddamn books alone," he rasped. "I had nothing to do with this."

She wiped her hands on her pants. "You swear?"

"I swear." Despite the view, he closed his eyes again. His head felt like aliens were kegging it up in the back of his skull.

The lights had come back on. All around him, the office was trashed. Broken bits of zombie flecked the walls, floor, and drop-tile ceiling. Not far off, yells and thumps and crashy sounds suggested that the battle was not yet won. Echo reached a slime-coated hand toward Dennis. Groaning, he took it. "Okay, then," she said. "Sorry if I was wrong."

Together, they shoved the other zombie corpses off him. "They didn't eat me?" he marveled.

"No," she said. "I think they just came to fuck shit up."

"Good," he replied. "Not good that they came to fuck shit up, but..."

"...good they didn't eat you," she said with a grim smile. "Yeah, I count that as a win too, I guess."

"Man," cried Rig, rushing over with a brain-clotted baseball bat. "What the *hell*, dude?" He helped pull Dennis to his feet. Dennis clenched his jaw against the pain. Still, he held the sword he'd taken from Echo's room, its blunt and battered edge smeared with zombie gore. "Check *you* out, yo!" Rig exclaimed, slapping Dennis on the shoulder. "You went *Conan* on those muthafuckas!"

"Not bad," Echo observed. "Though you probably would have done better without two swords in your pants."

Dennis shrugged. "I wanted backup in case I lost the one in my hands." He regarded the spray of bodies, fluids, and destruction. As near as he could figure it, he must have gone berserk when the zombie clubbed him with the laptop. There was indeed a Frazettian strew of carnage from the break room to Brian's office. "Did *I* do that?" he marveled.

"Looks that way," Echo said. "I'd guess you buzzsawed your way through the bulk of 'em, then tripped over the bodies and got dogpiled in the corner."

"And that's around when we showed up," Rig added with a cocky grin, "and played piñata with their undead butts." He shook a splatter of gunk off the bat. "We figured they already ate your ass. But hey..." he added when Dennis grimaced, "I'm glad they *didn't*, yo!"

"Yeah, me too." Dennis added. "So, what's up with that — you coming back so soon, I mean?"

Echo laughed, a nervous sound punctuating the smack of a crowbar against a distant zombie's head. The door toward the warehouse was open, Dennis noticed, and Marjorie was making all zombies on her turf rue the day they had returned from death. Around them, the office was a shambles. "God," Echo said as she surveyed the damage, "I really hope *Crimson Key* does well at GenCon."

"Yeah," Dennis agreed. "Like I said: What's up with that? Where are the others, and what brought you back so soon? Not that I'm not grateful and all."

"Well," Rig said, "we're about half-hour out when Echo sees the sky go all red 'n' shit." He prodded a zombie with one pointy-toed boot, but the sack of bones and bloated skin remained stubbornly deceased.

"So, I tried to call you," Echo said, heading back toward her office, "and got nothing. We called the office, called your cell..."

"Yeah," said Dennis, following her lead. "I tried calling out, too. Everything was dead... well, y'know, the phones and power and stuff. The zombies showed up later."

"I still want to know," she said, grim, "where they came from, and why they all came here."

"It didn't happen everywhere?" Dennis asked as they passed through the hallway and returned to her room.

"Nope," she said, brows creased with irritation. "Just here."

"Which means..."

"It was personal," she agreed.

"There was some *serious* arguing, when Echo told Brian we needed to stop!" Rig followed them down the hallway, checking the locked office doors.

"I'll bet," said Dennis, flushing with embarrassment when Echo spotted Cthulhu's head on her desk. "Sorry," he added. "Bad practice swing."

Echo frowned. "Dammit. That was an old Sideshow Collectable, too." Her attention, though, focused on the top shelf of her reference library. Spotting something, her eyes narrowed. "You said you left these alone, right?"

Damn, thought Dennis. "Um, pretty much, yeah."

Her mouth curved dangerously. "'Pretty much,'" she mimicked. Echo reached up toward the volumes. "Then what," she snarled, "is *this*?" Dennis gaped as she slid *The Book of Erotic Fantasy* down from the shelf. "Well?"

"I had nothing to do with that," he replied. "It was there when I got here."

Rig stood in the doorway, blocking escape. Echo brandished the book as if to hit Dennis with it. "So how," she demanded, "do you *know* that?"

Dennis spread his gore-slimed hands. "Okay," he said, "I looked at them, yeah. I read the titles. I was curious. I did *not*," he insisted, looking her dead-on, "pull them down, or move them, or read anything from off that shelf... or any *other* shelf, either." He pointed to the copy of *Crimson Key* they'd given him, perched on her desk where he'd left it. "All I read tonight was *that*..." He looked at Rig. "...and it was awesome, and you did a great job with it and I hope it sells a million copies so *GET THE FUCK OFF MY BACK!*"

In the warehouse, a zombie went *squish* beneath Marjorie's bootheels.

Echo glanced at Rig. "You believe him?" she said.

Rig shrugged, looking at his friend. "Fuck yeah."

Echo nodded. "Me too."

Dennis sighed with relief. "Cool." Then he added, "But who *did*?"

# # #

"Those idiots," Echo said, careful not to step in the bloody shreds that had once been their ex-interns. The cemetery mud was churned red with their messy and inevitable demise. She fished a tattered page of *The Black Seals of Ganzir* from the mud. "I knew," she said as they surveyed the ruined graves, clawed open from the inside out, "that I should have kept that book at home."

The red skies had faded to their rightful black by the time Echo, Rig, Marjorie and Dennis sorted out the mess. They'd decided it would be best if no member of Storm Dragon Games — not even a hired hand like Dennis — was anywhere near the offices when the delivery truck came by the next day. "That way," said Marjorie, "we have what the politicians call 'plausible deniability' when the cops show up."

"What's that mean?" asked Dennis.

"It *means*," she said, her own voice full of meaning, "that we don't know *shit* about what happened." Dennis got the feeling she'd had experience covering up crimes.

"The place is enough of a wreck," Marjorie had continued, "that they won't be able to pin anything on anyone here." They'd already wiped the hilts of Echo's swords clean. The evidence of Dennis's presence in the offices would be explained by his new intern status.

And his alibi?

"Well..." said Echo, shrugging, "...wanna come to GenCon?" Naturally, he'd said yes.

Now they stood in the middle of the last loose end: A churned-up graveyard with two fresh bodies and some old pages of a book. Empty cans of cheap-ass beer littered the site for yards around. The dead boys had embarked one hell of a bender before hauling out the book and calling up the bodies.

"So, what do we do with *them*?" Dennis asked. By now, he was feeling kinda detached. *Still*, his inner voice insisted, *I think we'll have a few rides on the Nightmare Express soon, don't you think?*

"I don't think we do *anything*, yo," said Rig. "I think we let Five-O figure out what lies to tell, not us."

Echo nodded. "Stupid bastards," she said, each word crusted with sorrow and disgust.

"Dude," said Dennis, shaking his head in agreement. He felt bad and all... *But hey*, said the inner voice, *they called up what they couldn't put down.* You *didn't do this.* They *did.* And with that, his conscience could agree.

Echo ground the remaining pages under her Doc Martins, blotting out their weird designs. The rain still fell hard enough to wash away all signs that they'd been there. By morning, they'd all be in Indiana, facing a new kind of zombie horde. "Let's get outta here," she said, glancing at the sky. "We've got *Crimson Keys* to sell."

"We do?" said Dennis, liking the sound of *we*.

Echo smiled as she took his arm. "Yeah," she said, "I guess we do."

A SCORPION'S PRAYER

Ms. Simmons had it coming. The dog's head made sure she got it. Trouble is, those things never go the way you think they'll go. Now that dog's head waits at the threshold of my dreams. If it barks again, this time I'll answer. I left the shadows of those trees long ago. If that night taught me anything, though, it's that human eyes are too rational to see what's truly going on.

My friends and I were the last generation to run wild through our woods. In those years before Stranger Danger and faces frozen on waxed paper and bound for the dump, we enjoyed freedoms bought with blood offerings to gravel and concrete. Snapping, crackling, and popping all the way, we'd haul ourselves to school in packed and stinking buses, or else hike the proverbial "six-miles-each-way-to-school-uphill-both-ways-barefoot-in-the-snow." We stayed out past sunset and got yelled at for missing dinner. We had G.I. Joes (the real ones, with fuzzy hair and Kung Fu Grip™), snuck into R-rated movies, and watched memorably terrible cartoons. No cellphones. No internet. No parental guidance, as they say. At night, we'd sprawl around on shag carpets stretched between cheap-paneled walls, our cable-less TVs delivering inane sermons before signing off with Star-Spangled salutes to pledged allegiance. On warm or chilly nights, after our parents stopped whispering or shouting behind closed doors, some of us would creak our windows open and slide off into the dark.

That's what my friends and I did, anyway. The night belonged to us until everything went wrong.

Young Bear's name was Tom. That's not the name we called him, though. We had our own names for ourselves. Tom was Young Bear. Kristeen was Fox. I was Scorpion. Tom called me that because, as he put it, stinging folks was just my nature. I didn't mean to hurt anyone. He was right. I didn't. That doesn't absolve me of the blame for what happened.

I hadn't meant to open that door.

But I did.

"You're just a bunch of wild animals." That's what Mrs. Libby called us. She almost said, "wild banshee Indians," which is what she called her own kids all the time. She slammed her lips shut on that expression, though, when Young Bear gave her The Eye. He was good at that. It usually worked, too, especially on adults who wanted to think of themselves as good people. Young Bear had glossy black hair he wore in two long braids down either side of his face. His mother started braiding it when their neighbors referred to him as "that little hippie," which was *not* an endearing expression when we were kids. Hippies back then were The Enemy. Drug-crazed cultists shooting up in the pages of Reader's Digest or freaking out on TV. Kids with long hair were crimes in progress. Indians, though? They cried on TV, or celebrated Thanksgiving when they weren't getting gunned down by John Wayne. Indians could have long hair without being hippies, and Young Bear said he was part-Indian, and so even though his mother told him, "No, dear, you're Italian," she taught him how to braid his hair so people like Mrs. Libby would shut her mouth on expressions like "wild banshee Indians" when he was around.

(Folks didn't say "Indigenous" back then. "Native American" was rare. Most folks just said "Indian" when they weren't using rougher words. The past speaks a harsh language. Those who were there can never forget it.)

That's where he got our animal names, too. "Tom's a stupid name," he said. Not Indian *or* Italian, it fell out of your mouth and lay on the carpet like a lump. Young Bear hated "Tom," so he took Mrs. Libby's insult and ran with it. I became Scorpion because sharp things came out of my mouth, stinging worst the ones I loved. Kristeen became Fox because she was thin and raw and didn't talk much but liked to howl and bark and jump off the embankments of Shooter's Creek like a cartoon in the hands of gravity. Fox was more boy than girl and more animal than either one. These days, they'd probably call all three of us "autistic." Back then, we had harder words: *Weirdo. Spastic. Retarded.* All those words meant the same thing: No friends except each other and the woods and the stack of comics in Young Bear's closet.

Words change. Feelings linger.

The name he gave me came from a Russian fairytale. In it, a scorpion asks a frog to carry him across a river. "I can't do that," the frog says. "You'll sting me." "If I sting you," the scorpion says, "I'd drown." So the frog agrees, and the scorpion climbs on and the frog swims across the river, and the scorpion stings him, and they drown. "But *why*," says the dying frog. "I'm sorry," the scorpion replies. "I didn't mean it. It's just my nature."

Nice story, huh?

Young Bear's mom worked at Able Drugs. She worked so late that Fox and I went home long before she'd return. Young Bear's dad was the subject of rumors and speculation. He'd been in Vietnam. He'd lived on a reservation. He was in the Mafia... or *had* been until he ratted out the Godfather and went into hiding or ended up wearing concrete shoes. Young Bear was a toddler when his dad disappeared. Even so, he claimed he felt his father's blood in his veins. Who that father was or had been was a funhouse mirror of how Young Bear felt about himself. His mom was nice, and quiet, and always tired in the way you get when your dreams become someone else's paycheck.

Young Bear cooked for himself: canned soup and TV dinners with little pinches of salt and pepper. He read the comic books his mom brought home from work, and he watched the news well enough to lecture us about what Carter was doing wrong, and so he seemed worldly compared to Fox and me. Our parents worked late, too, trusting us to not burn our houses down while they sat in gas lines or called from the office to remind us to do our homework before they got home. All three of us lived a Peanuts life, grown-ups buzzing the background until we'd cross one line too many and get grounded or suspended from school again.

I got suspended from school a lot. My mouth was a stinger, and my fists were claws, and so bullies like Leonardo Castinelli (who unquestionably *was* Italian) bounced words and punches off my carapace. A ball of quiet punctuated by taunts and brawling, I was a headache for my teachers and a consistent source of disappointment for my family. I told lies often too, like the time I'd informed my little brother that our *real* father had been killed in Vietnam (he hadn't) or regaled some kids at school with tales of seeing an airplane flip over and crash on a runway, blood spilling from its windows like ketchup out the sides of a Big Mac. Young Bear and Fox knew what a liar I was, too, which is why they both laughed when I told them about the van in the woods with the dog's head inside of it.

They laughed until I led them to it.

I'd found the van during one of my solo ventures into the woods on the far side of our school. Back then, the Greatest Generation had begun hacking down the wilderness to replace it with schools for their grandkids, housing developments for their families, and the shopping malls, which would soon become our generation's rite of passage. Young Bear, Fox, and I occupied a borderland between rural woodlands and suburban sprawl. Lakemount Middle School topped a big hill overlooking our neighborhood. And somehow, sometime before the school was built or the chain-link fence surrounding our school was erected to keep woodland animals out and human animals in, someone had driven a hippie-style VW van off one side of that hill and left it to rust among the trees. I'd climbed that fence and clambered down that hill one day, drawn by the call of something I still can't name.

The van hunkered down on four flat tires, its headlights blinded, a thick broken branch punched through its windshield like a spear. Rust furred the fading orange paint. For a moment, I could have sworn I saw arcane writing scribbled across the side of the van. Looking closer, I realized it was patterns of shadows dancing over scratches and rust.

At least, that's what I tell myself it was.

The sliding side door stood open, wrenched off its track and rusted into place.

In later years, the horror movies that populated video-rental stores would warn kids like me against what I did next.

I hadn't seen those movies yet. Even if I *had* seen them, though, I would have done it anyway. I wasn't called Scorpion for nothing.

Scaling the fence and skidding down the hill, I dug my heels into the dirt to keep myself from landing on my face. Gravity pulled me forward. Curiosity drew me down. The van's interior glowed with fading sunlight, its contents half-visible behind that rusted door. I saw warped paneling and a smashed table tilted by the force of impact. Every window I could see was shattered, bits of scattered safety glass glinting in the sun. Wary of that glass, and of the thorny underbrush, I picked my way through tangled roots and crackling branches.

That's when I saw the head.

At first, I took it for an optical illusion, like the writing I'd seen from the hilltop. This close, though, it was obvious. A German Shepherd's head, severed by a ragged cut, lay desiccated on the floor of the van. The head snarled in silent defiance. Despite its leathery skin, the dog's eyes remained vivid, eternally open, yet uneaten by flies. I looked for a body. Didn't find one. The head sat alone, propped by gravity against the underseat cabinet between the driver's area and the passenger compartment. A single dried-brown spatter of blood marked the head's passage from the center of the floor to its resting place.

Mortality prickled my skin and scalp.

Clouds passed across the sun. I thought I'd seen the dog's eyes close, but it was just another trick of the light.

Dull fur and skin stretched tight across the dog's skull. A hint of bone glowered in the dried meat of its neck. The ears, somehow, still stood erect, as if listening for a voice that might save that dog from eternity. Even so, time marked its end. That head, like the van, had rested here for years, undisturbed by the world growing up nearby. Timeless in a changing world, it hinted at truths childhood could reach for but not yet understand.

As patters of rain rustled the leaves, I'd trudged back up the hill, lost in fascinations I could not speak.

Until later, when I did.

"No *way*." Young Bear was unimpressed.

Fox was, though. "I wanna see it," she said. So we did.

It was still raining when we descended that hill again, sloshing and skidding through the muddy grass. Water spotted Fox's glasses and glistened on Young Bear's black braids. Clothes plastered to our skins. Twigs snagged our clothing and stuck to our skins. The dog's head glared back at us from the van's dark interior. Its eyes caught the gleam of floodlights illuminating the schoolyard up the hill.

We'd hit full night by that time. Young Bear's mom was still at work. Fox's mom was off somewhere doing God-knows-what. My folks thought I was doing homework with my friends... which, in a way, I was. Students of mortality, we stood outside the van in the rain.

"We should bury her," Fox said.

"We should leave her alone." Young Bear had picked up Fox's choice of gender without dispute.

"She wants to go home," Fox replied. "I can hear her."

We didn't dispute that, either. Fox had a way of being right about things no one else could see.

"I'm not going in there," I said. Despite my curiosity, the thought of climbing into that rusty sepulcher seemed like a really bad idea.

"We should get home." Young Bear's enthusiasm had waned. "Mom's gonna be home soon. She'll be pissed if I'm all wet."

"Where would we bury it, anyway," I asked. "We don't have shovels or anything."

Fox leaned into the gloom van. She sniffed it like the animal we'd named her for. "She smells like the moon."

"Gross," I said. "You can *smell* her?"

"I'll bet she smells like *ass*," Young Bear added.

"Like *your* ass," I added.

"You'd *know* about smelling my ass, paleface."

"She's singing."

Young Bear and I both shut up. Fox said weird stuff all the time. This was weird even for her.

"That's creepy," I said.

"She *is*, though," Fox insisted. She started to climb into the van. We both grabbed her. "Fox," said Young Bear, "*no*."

She snapped her teeth at him. He let go. She turned to growl at me. I did, too.

Fox often made jokes about eating people. After she'd bitten you a few times for real, though, they didn't sound so much like jokes. I wasn't the only one of our group to get suspended a lot from school. The bullies didn't bother her anymore, though. Picking on me or Young Bear was fun. Picking on Fox was dangerous.

"How is the dog's head singing," Young Bear asked. His ability to respect whatever crazy shit she said was one of the reasons Young Bear was the de facto leader of our pack.

"She's caught between worlds," Fox answered. "This body is like her reflection. Someone broke the mirror. This is just one piece of it."

This idea might not sound like much if you've been toking up and listening to *Dark Side of the Moon* in your college dorm. We were just kids back then, though. *Young* kids. I didn't so much as *smell* dope until years later, and aside from a butchered version of "Money," Pink Floyd wasn't a band you heard on the radio stations we listened to in those days. Fox thought around corners, though, in buildings I couldn't even see. Young Bear nodded like he understood. I didn't understand but I nodded anyway.

"What difference," I said, "will burying her make?" Taking their cue, I'd also begun thinking of the dog's head as a *her*. "I mean, if only part of her is here, how will it matter if that part is someplace else? And won't she be uncomfortable if her face is underground?"

"You're right." Fox squatted down beside the van. "She wouldn't want dirt in her eyes. She can't breathe if she's buried. We'll have to think of something else."

I didn't mention that a severed head wasn't breathing anyway.

"How did she get here?" Young Bear had a way of making the whole conversation sound like the most natural thing in the world.

"The dust knights hunted her down." Fox took off her glasses and tried to wipe them on her soaking tee shirt. Mud from her fingertips smeared the lenses. The floodlights turned us all an uncanny shade of green. "She ran down a moonbeam and they caught her here and cut her to pieces. They threw pieces all over the universe. This is just the piece we can see right now."

"Why?" Young Bear squatted down next to her, leaning his back against the van. Behind them both, I saw the dog's eyes gleam. I shivered. "Why did knights chop up a dog?"

"She's not really a dog," Fox said. "She just looks like one to us."

"What *is* she, then?" This from me.

Fox opened her mouth and tried to shape it around sounds I couldn't hear. What came out of her mouth didn't sound like anything I'd heard before, even from Fox.

I'd like to blame my shivers on the rain.

"Where does she want to go?" Young Bear stood up. "If we're gonna take her somewhere, then we need to do it soon. I have to get home. Mom's gonna kill me as is."

"The elf cathedral," Fox said.

Of course, she would.

In those days, tree forts were easy to find. Any bunch of kids with a few scraps of lumber, a hammer, some nails, and a pronounced lack of acrophobia could build one. Many of us did. This tree fort, though, was something else entirely.

I'm sure I remember it stranger than it was. That said, we called it "the elf cathedral" for a reason. Most tree forts use scrap lumber. Ones built for playgrounds often used railroad ties. This fort seemed to be shaped from trees — not broken branches or dead trunks but living trees woven together by titanic hands. Those trees arched and flowed like wet clay sculpted by a master artisan. They smelled like moss and wet wood and the thousand scents of forest. If I could go back there now, if it were still there to return to, I might realize that it was a cunning illusion of childhood memories. But those memories are all I have left now. Of the elf cathedral. Of everything. So that's what I recall.

Fox climbed in and gathered the dog's head in her arms. We crept through the edges of the woods as the rain poured down. Floodlights shimmered, their glow fading as we moved further from the field. It was long past nightfall. Thick clouds obscured the moon and stars.

Nights got *darker* back when we were kids. The constant glare of light-noise we take for granted now was subdued back then. Softer. Quieter. Streetlights were rarer. Porchlights often winked out when the family went to bed. People shut off the lights when we left a room, and stores didn't waste electricity by blazing away all night. If you lived near the woods, like we did, dark was *DARK*. As we trooped deeper into the woods — Fox up front, then me, then Young Bear — we moved more by feel and memory than by sight. Twigs, stones, and branches prodded our feet as we squelched through the muddy paths winding up and down the hills. This wasn't our first time traipsing through those woods at night, in the rain, or both. That night, however, our play held a different tone and a much more solemn purpose.

Fox whispered to the head, her words lost in the rustling hiss of rain.

I wished for dry clothes and warm dinner and *Happy Days* on the TV.

Young Bear said nothing. Occasionally, I had to look back to make sure he was even there at all.

Finally, we reached the elf cathedral. *Felt* more than *seen*, it loomed up out of the trees, *part of* those woods yet *apart from* them too. The place held a presence, especially that night. Crouched at the heart of the forest, too far from the surrounding neighborhoods to be some rich kid's toy, it called out to animal misfits like us. Radiating weirdness, it felt like home.

The forest breathed deep as Fox knelt in the mud by the cathedral's dark mouth.

For the first time since we'd left the van, I heard her speak: "We've brought her home to you."

I swear something hummed inside that mouth.

Young Bear stepped up beside me. "What do we do now," I whispered to him.

He shrugged. "She seems to know what she's doing. Let her do it."

Bowing her head, Fox began wailing. Softly at first, her voice rose in a wordless undulating cry. We'd howled and barked in those woods before that night, calling out to each other in the dark. That rain-drenched cry came from somewhere and something *else*. My arms rippled. Little hairs rose. Cold fingers gripped my throat and pulled my scalp tight. The cathedral's clearing stilled. Rain stopped trickling through the leaves. Fox raised her head and drew it back, her throat swelling with unearthly sounds. Hardly visible even to our acclimated eyes, she uncurled from the mud, her knees bending in ways human knees shouldn't be able to bend.

The darkness hummed again, the pitch rumbling underneath her cry.

I darted my eyes toward Young Bear. He was mumbling something I couldn't hear.

The cold hands crushed my ribs so tight I could barely breathe.

Moving with an odd flicker-step, Fox stepped towards the cathedral. She extended her arms with the dog's head in her hands. Like an offering. Like she was Salome without a plate.

I tried to call out *Don't*, but my voice wouldn't work.

She stepped into the blackness of the cathedral's mouth.

We followed, drawn in against my will.

Blackness swallowed us.

Blackness that breathed thick, cold, mossy breath.

I came to, stumbling through the rain. Mud caked on my fingers and smeared across my shirt.

Alone in the woods, and *very* late for dinner.

# # #

"What *happened?*"

Young Bear shrugged again. He'd gotten in trouble. We all had. Fox's parents grounded her. Mine grounded me. We met up at school the next day to compare notes. The mud under our fingernails assured me that we'd done *something*. I just couldn't recall *what*.

Fox held more stillness than usual. Most times, she did a lot of what folks these days call "stimming": waving her hands, twitching her fingers, chewing on her lower left lip, chewing on the ends of her hair, or humming to herself until someone told her to knock it off. That morning, though, she hardly moved. Her often-wild hair was clean and brushed. Her clothes were cleaner than usual, too. Fox's eyes, however, blazed with an intensity rare even for her. Something was going on in there. Something big. What it was, though, she wouldn't say.

"The last thing I remember..." I told them, "...was walking into the cathedral after you. And then walking in the woods by myself. What did we *do?*"

"We built an altar," Young Bear said, "and put the head on it."

"Why?"

He shrugged again. "It seemed to be the right thing to do. A cathedral needs an altar, right?"

"It's what they wanted." Fox's voice shimmered with determination.

"They," I asked.

"The dog. They are infinite. They contain multitudes."

I didn't understand the Walt Whitman reference back then. I'm not sure Fox did, either. I don't know if she absorbed it from someone else, if that line somehow transmitted itself through the dog-head's consciousness, or whether she'd actually read and remembered the poem. Knowing Fox, any of those options could have been true. It's not like I can ask her now.

"So, the dog's head asked us to build it... her... *them* an altar?"

Her face squinched up. "Kinda? It was like I just *knew* we should do it."

"She told us," Young Bear added, "and we did it. You really don't remember?"

"I really don't."

They filled me in — mostly Young Bear, with a few remarks added by Fox. As they spoke, flashes of sensation filled my head. Against a field of total darkness, I felt mud between my fingers, rocks gritting against my fingernails, washes of wet wood and loam and rot and raw wildness in my nose, chanting from Young Bear and wailing from Fox, neither speaking a language I could understand. My memory recoiled and left me dazed and silent as they spoke. Most of what they told me got lost in a haze.

Together, we entered our next class.

Ms. Simmons' class.

My least favorite class of all.

Ms. Simmons was a teacher of the old school. The school that resented not being able to beat the shit out of students anymore. In place of physical discipline, Ms. Simmons had refined the sort of social cruelty most often observed in teenage girls. She doled out that cruelty with a Joker grin and a too-sweet voice. After all, she was *only* trying to *help*. Stick-thin and beady-eyed, she moved through our class like a raptor. Plain and simple, she was a ghoul. And ever since the day she caught me doodling a cartoon of her with a long tongue and KISS makeup, breathing fire, Ms. Simmons held a special grudge against me.

I've always hated math. Thanks to Ms. Simmons, I hated it even more. Large groups of numbers seem to dance around when I look at them. Every time I see them, they read differently to me. Solving long equations is a nightmare. I had a special nightmare waiting for me that day, though. Ms. Simmons was introducing us to fractions. Guess who her first test subject was.

"Now, *class*," she said, her voice pitched toward sugar-shock sweetness, "fractions appear complicated, but they're *really* quite simple. Each fraction is divided into two parts, split by this little slash right here." She indicated the line between numbers. "The top one is called the *numerator*, and that number represents the fraction of the whole. The bottom one is called the *denominator*, and that number represents the whole. Got it? It's easy." Her Joker grin stretched to a predatory width. Her eyes scanned the classroom. I already knew where they would land. So did everybody else. I felt every gaze in the classroom settle on my back.

As Ms. Simmons sketched an equation of fractions multiplied against each other, she continued. "If you're *clever*, you can figure all of this out very easily." She turned back to us and dropped the anvil. "And since we all *know* that no one here is cleverer than *Mis*ter Hastings, I'm *sure Mis*ter Hastings will be glad to show us how this equation can be solved." Her grin sharpened further, as if to slice her face in half. She speared my eyes with her own. "*Won't* you, Mister Hastings? Of *course*, you will."

I heard Fox growl. Young Bear reached a hand toward me. Locking eyes with Ms. Simmons, I rose to meet my impending humiliation.

The hate in my heart as I walked to the blackboard changed all our lives that day.

I got suspended, naturally. Again. Between the "backtalk" I gave Ms. Simmons when she needled me for fumbling the equation, the "*Fuck you*" I snarled as my classmates laughed, and the sock in the jaw I gave Leonardo Castinelli when he ragged me about it after class, I racked up another parent-teacher conference, a new trip to the office, another chewing-out from Mr. Cunningham (the man masochistic enough to become a middle-school principal with a name like *that*), additional chewing-out from Mom and Dad (who were *So Very Disappointed In You* again), and some more days added to the grounding I'd received. By the time the whole miserable pageant ended, me in my bedroom with thoughts blacker than the nighttime sky, I was ready to call upon any power unholy enough to facilitate revenge.

In hindsight, I shouldn't be surprised that my stinger rose so high and descended so fast.

It is, after all, my nature.

# # #

My hatred kept me awake long after midnight. Waiting for my folks to fall asleep, I ran the day's events over and over in my mind until I thought I might explode. Finally, I heard the TV in their room snap off. Snores followed not long afterward. Even then, I lay in my bed, fixated on the path to the cathedral and the words I would say when I arrived.

I can't explain why I thought praying to a dead dog's head on an altar in the woods seemed like a good idea. We all do crazy shit, especially when we're young. That night, the compounding humiliations of that day and the saccharine sound of Ms. Simmons' voice and the look in her eyes as she made me a classroom laughingstock again burned away all rationality my twelve-year-old self might have contained. All I wanted, by the time I heard my parents drift off to sleep, was to hear her scream and to know I was the cause.

Why a dog's head, you might ask?

Because Ms. Simmons was terrified of them.

Ms. Simmons hated dogs. Freaked out at the sight of them. She once gave Fox detention just for barking like one in class. She called it "a disruption," but I could tell there was so much more than mere annoyance in her eyes. Kids can smell terror. Ms. Simmons radiated it. To my young and furious self that night, the idea of calling up the spirit of a dog to haunt my nemesis seemed like the best idea I'd ever had.

Obviously, it was the worst.

By the time I slid through my bedroom window, lowering it carefully behind me and wedging a stick between the sill and the window's bottom edge, I was ready. Swiss pocketknife nestled in the pocket of my shorts, I crept barefoot through the yard and melted into the shadows of the trees in our back yard. Around me, the neighborhood slept, windows glowing here or there but mostly dark and shut. Air conditioners hummed. Clouds eased across the sky. A light drizzle soaked my tee shirt to my skin. The mud beneath me muffled my steps. It was a familiar ritual, this nighttime venture. This time, though, I had more purpose than insomnia.

"*Pssst.*"

I jerked my head.

Young Bear gestured to me from the trees. "I thought you might be going out," he whispered as I approached. "You okay? We were worried about you."

"Is Fox here?" I whispered too.

"I haven't seen her tonight. I think she's still at home."

"Let's see if she's at the cathedral."

"Man, let's stay *away* from the cathedral." His voice held more gravity than usual.

"Why?"

"You *know* it's not safe."

Irritation surged. "What do you *mean* it's not safe?"

"Keep it *down*." He pointed to my parents' window.

"I'm *tired* of being 'safe.' Did today in class look like I was safe?"

"Are you *trying* to wake up your parents?"

"*Fuck* my parents."

"Not with *Castinelli's* dick." Yeah, we were twelve years old. "Man, you got him good."

"My knuckles still hurt."

"His jaw still hurts too, I'll bet."

Still whispering, we headed toward the woods.

For a while, it seemed like old times. We made jokes about the neighbors, warned each other about the yards where dogs were liable to be out, and watched for cars and other late-night walkers. Rain dripped off us in the humid night. Still, the hate burned deep and red in me. I snapped at my old friend too often. My teasing stung him more than usual. By the time we reached the woods' edge, our playful tone had worn thin. Even by Scorpion's usual standards, I was an asshole to him that night.

I wish I could undo what I did next.

"Man, I mean it," he said as I moved toward the path that led to the cathedral, "don't go down there again. *Please.*"

"Why?" Venom dripped off that single word.

"I'm just... man, just *don't.*"

"What's so special about it?"

"Don't you remember?"

"Remember what?"

His eyes scanned my face. Looking for a sign, I guess, that I was joking. He didn't see one. "Really, you don't?"

"Really Nope. I don't."

"How come you can't remember?"

"Remember *what?*" The second time, my voice rose near shouting.

"Mike..." I glared. We didn't use the names our parents gave us. Not with each other. "*Scorpion,*" he corrected, "doesn't that freak you out a little bit?"

"Doesn't *what* freak me out?"

"That you don't *remember* anything."

"I remember *some* things," I said. "I recall you and Fox chanting some stuff, and that I guess we did some sort of ritual but..."

His reply got lost in a welling black surge of rage. I could see his lips moving but I couldn't hear the words. Instead, I heard Ms. Simmons' voice telling everyone how clever *Mis*ter Hastings was.

Underneath that voice, I heard dogs barking. *One* dog, really. The dead one who wasn't dead.

Young Bear's mouth moved. The dog's bark came out.

He was barking at me.

The furious night closed in, darker.

"Why are you barking at me, man?"

"*What?*" he said.

"You're *barking* at me," I snarled at him. A surge of jealousy shot through me then. In hindsight, maybe I was jealous that he and Fox shared something I didn't have. Something I didn't get and wouldn't understand. I think maybe I had a crush on her, that there was some stupid hormonal shit going on, and

I felt like maybe they had a thing going on that I wasn't part of. It pissed me off. "Are you like *Fox* now?" I added. "Always barking?" I did a cruel mimic of her autistic animal sounds.

"Hey, man." Young Bear's eyes narrowed. "Not cool."

"What?" I waved my hands in an exaggerated mockery of Fox, stimming. "Aren't we *animals*, Young Bear?" An ugly new thought bubbled up. "Or is that just for you and Fox? *You* get to be animals. I get to be the *insect*."

"Scorpions aren't insects. They're arachnids."

"*I don't care.*" I'd stopped whispering and started yelling.

"Man, keep it *down*."

Beneath our voices, the dog barked louder.

"What is *wrong* with you?" Young Bear was looking scared.

"There's *always* something wrong with me. *Always*. Haven't you noticed? I mean, *you're* the one who named me after a fucking *insect* or *arachnid* or whatever it is, with the poison and the stinger and the stabbing in the back and I'm just supposed to be *okay* with that, 'Young Bear'?"

He held out hands, palms out, placating. "I'm sorry. I'm *sorry*. I didn't mean..."

"Didn't mean *what?*" The rage rose me hard. "That's I'm *different?* That you can't *trust* me? That I'm not really part of your cute little Indian club and you just keep me around for —"

"Mike, *STOP.*"

He said something then that got lost. I mean, it just went *blank*. I remember him talking and the expression on his face. I didn't remember the words he said until many years later, though. Even now I'm not sure I remember them right.

The rage in me burned so hot and deep and black that the woods closed in.

It was stupid. We were kids. I can justify all the reasons I was an asshole that night. None of them make the next things I said right.

"*Fuck* you, Tonto," I sneered. "You and that crazy dog bitch deserve each other."

If I could reach back in time and slap those words out of my mouth, I would.

Young Bear slapped them out for me.

Punched them out, actually.

I found myself on the ground.

"Fuck *you*, Scorpion," he snarled. "We've been trying to *help* you. Maybe you're not *worth* helping."

"I don't *need* your help."

"You don't need *friends* either," he shot back. "Now you don't have any more."

Young Bear stalked off as I lay there in the mud.

I wish I'd apologized. I wish I'd swallowed my pride and gotten my muddy ass in gear and said whatever it took to take back what I'd just done.

Instead, I curled up in the mud and let the hate burn deeper while the dog barked in my head and the rain came down on us all.

# # #

I walked to school the next morning. The last time I'd taken my bike to school, it wound up with thumbtacks in both tires. My bookbag dragged at my shoulder, heavier and bulkier than usual. Though I'd bathed the mud off when I got home, and had stuck my wet and dirty clothes in a plastic bag at the bottom of my closet, an ugly, earthy smell surrounded me. There was no way I was getting on the bus smelling like that.

Besides, I had things to think about, and a prayer to guide me to my destination.

Dog of the Woods, make her scream.
Dog of the Woods, make her beg.
Dog of the Woods, make her suffer.
Dog of the Woods, be my revenge.

It's not poetic. Most spells aren't. All that Latin stuff you see in movies and say in church sounds impressive and mysterious. They're all really simple, though, when you know what the words mean. You need something. You ask God. Throw in a bit of flattery and a lot of repetition and maybe God will hear you.

Or *something* will, anyway.

The words in my head matched the rhythm of my sneakers on wet pavement and the weight of the bookbag digging into my left shoulder. Rain drizzled down and soaked my hair. I was a million miles inside my head.

Lakemount Middle School hovered in the mist, each step drawing its buildings darker, closer, and more solid. Its red brick bulk suggested a colossal tomb. Its halls and rusty lockers stank of young sweat and industrial disinfectant.

Moving from the lonely mists to the rain-slicked halls, I elbowed my way through milling peers, our sneakers squeaking on tiled floors.

Dog of the Woods, keep me sheltered.
Dog of the Woods, keep me safe.
Dog of the Woods, be my vengeance.
Dog of the Woods, make her scream.

I wish I could take that whole week back.

Especially what happened next.

Young Bear hadn't said a word to me. Fox glared at me from her desk. The weight of their disdain pressed down as I took my seat. Taking out my notebook and the math text for Ms. Simmons' class, I left my bookbag's buckles open and the flap pulled back. That earthy smell rose. Faint barking echoed in my head. A few kids leaned away from me, noses wrinkling at the smell. Glancing at Fox and Young Bear, I saw their eyes go wide. Fox shook her head, her mouth dropping open, silently mouthing *no no no no no*...

"*Peeeee-yew!*" Leonardo Castinelli clutched his nose with drastic theatricality.

"*Mis*ter *Hastings*." That saccharine voice cut through the barking in my head. "Did you forget to wash behind your ears?"

Laughter from the class.

The room darkened.

"Maybe I need to write *another* note to your parents, *Mister* Hastings." Her voice cut through that darkness. "Remind them to get you to *bathe*."

I closed my eyes.

"Dog of the Woods," I whispered. "Dog of the Woods," I prayed.

Laughter pressed in.

I breathed deep.

Behind my eyelids, I watched the universe expand.

Sparkles and pinwheels of light became shapes, runes, faces, clouds. Diamonds of lightning crackled and spun. The pressing crush of laughter and rain and plastic and disinfectant ripened into a surge of dirt and mold and rotting trees and dead-dog stench. My ribs expanded. My skull. The universe inside.

I sensed the skittering of tiny legs across the tiles.

The humid pant of hound's breath thickened with decay.

My skin hummed. My bones sang. My lips whispered.

A god heard.

A howl welled up from the soul of the world.

The limbs of the elf cathedral writhed in darkness, their bark fingers lacing and winding and sliding in patterns no human math contains.

Laughter, rain, and howls chased each other through the night.

"*MISTER Hastings*." More laughter. "Have you gone to *sleep*? Are you sleeping in my *class*, Mister Hastings?"

"Dog of the Woods," I whispered. "Make her scream."

She did.

They all did.

I opened my eyes when the tearing sounds began.

I think I'd expected the ghost of a dog.

When I'd carried that severed dog head in my bookbag — having fetched it from the elf cathedral and wrapped it in my KISS Destroyer tee shirt and then whispered prayers to it all the way to school — I *want* to think I'd just meant to scare Ms. Simmons with a barking phantom that would rise from the weirdly preserved head.

I don't want to think that maybe, as I'd pulled that head from my bookbag, eyes shut tight, laughter pressing down on me and strange worlds unfolding behind my eyelids, I'd also whispered *Kill*.

It *did* kill, though.

It killed everybody in that room.

Except for Fox, Young Bear, and me.

The thing that swirled up out of my bookbag and stormed across the room was a vortex of eyes and teeth. Shimmering like the air over a blacktop on a hot day, it held the vague *suggestion* of a dog as seen through the eyes of a mosquito, all facets and layers shifting and howling but never resolving into a shape a human eye could catch. It slid, viscous, through the air but tore through Ms. Simmons and our class. "How," went a sick joke we told as kids, "do you fit a thousand dead babies into a Volkswagen Bug? *La Machine!*" La Machine was the name of a food shredder. That's what I brought to school that day.

I don't *think* I meant to.

But I'm afraid I *did*.

When the door slammed open and the hallway screamed and the shower of bits and fluids that used to be human bodies with names like Simmons and Castinelli and a roll call of kids whose faces I've forgotten but whose names still echo in my head... when our childhoods exploded in a fractured spin of time, I think I remember Young Bear screaming *What did you do? What Did You Do? MIKE, WHAT DID YOU DO?*

I think I recall Fox barking and howling those words that were never words in this world. Her hands flying and weaving patterns like the limbs of the elf cathedral, her eyes feral, spit foaming from her mouth and scattering in slow-motion as a thousand dead babies hit the blades of La Machine in the center of a classroom where no one ever taught again.

I *think* I remember those things, anyway.

My memory, though, is not what you might call "reliable."

#

I remember...

The vortex of eyes and teeth and webs of red and purple fluids looking back at me from behind Ms. Simmons' desk, the wood burnt and splintered and dripping with saccharine smear.

The men like giant black beetles, wrapped in shells and carrying guns.

The look in Young Bear's eyes as the men bundled him up in blankets and handcuffs and carried him away.

Fox screaming and flapping her hands as they bundled her up too, and took her through the door and down the hall where her barks and howls echoed back at me.

My face on the wet, warm tiled floor, spitting out blood and bits of Leonardo Castinelli's brain.

The man looming over me, dressed in a black-and-white suit now splattered with drying red, his face like something a silverfish might envision if it dreamed of becoming a man. *The dust knights*, I remember thinking. *The dust knights are here.*

Walls. Doors. Needles. Drugs.

Too many questions, no answers making sense.

In the end, they found no weapon. No dog's head. Nothing. Just a bookbag and a muddy KISS Destroyer tee shirt and a room painted with sixteen children and an aging math teacher, plus three kids of questionable sanity and what would turn out — in my case, anyway — to be a lifetime's supply of fractured mental health.

They hosed off the walls and closed down the school. Some men and women with deep voices and dark suits made everything else go away. The mess. The questions. And me. They made me go away too.

I never saw Fox or Young Bear again. I heard his mother still worked at Able Drugs until it went under about fourteen years ago. I couldn't tell you if that's true, though, because I finished school, and spent the next few years after that in a series of white rooms, and green rooms, and the kind of rooms where you have nothing to do all day except think about what you *think* you remember and how you *think* you got there and how, someday, you might *maybe* "reenter society again" to find out that your whole fucking family had forgotten you and that everything you'd known was gone.

I still dream of the elf cathedral. I hear those woods burned down.

I still dream of the dog's head, too. Of red rain in the classroom. Of Ms. Simmons, breathing fire and teaching classrooms of the damned in hell. With my luck, I'll wind up in that class someday. I'm not in any hurry to find out.

I think I finally remember, too, what Young Bear said to me that night.

"I recall you and Fox chanting some stuff," I'd said. "And that I guess we did some sort of ritual but..."

"No, man — *you* did the ritual. Not me. It was *you*."

He tugged on one of his braids. Looked away from me, toward the darkness. "You were, like, *obsessed*. It was scary. You were scaring me, man. Scaring *Fox*, too. I had to talk her into sticking around. You were talking to that dog's *head*, man. You held on to it so hard I kept waiting for it to pop. Me and Fox tried to get it away from you. We tried *everything*, man! We tried tricking you, and convincing you, and wrestling it away from you, and... and *nothing* worked." He looked for a second like he might cry. His face tightened. "I just wanted to go get dinner. I got in trouble trying to help you. So did Fox. Man, Scorpion, you sting us every time."

"Why'd Fox take it out of the van, then?" I asked him.

"*She* didn't." Young Bear gave me The Eye. "*You* did."

"I did not."

"Yes, you did, man. You carried that thing around like your favorite toy."

"You're lying."

"That's *rich*, coming from you."

"What about all that howling Fox did, and that ritual and stuff."

"That was *you*, Mike. That's what I'm saying. *It was all you.*"

"Why are you barking at me, man?"

"*What?*"

In that last exchange, the moment right before I dropped the stinger into his back and drowned the three of us forever, I think Young Bear said, "Mike, *STOP.*"

I wish I had.

Because the next thing I think he'd said in the woods, as best as I can recall it now, went something like this:

"'*Black Dog of the Woods*,' you kept saying, Mike. "'*Black Dog of the Woods, destroy it all.*' And then you just opened your mouth and all this *sound* poured out, and at first, I thought you were fucking with us, but then I saw the dog's eyes, *THAT DEAD DOG'S FUCKING EYES*, start glowing green. That's when Fox ran. 'It's waking up,' she told me. 'Get away from him. It's got him and it's waking up.' And I was like, 'He's our friend, Fox. We've gotta help him.'"

Young Bear had glared at me. "*This is the river*. That's what Fox said. 'The river has him, and this is his nature.'"

"*Fuck* you, Tonto," I'd sneered. "You and that crazy dog bitch deserve each other."

I deserved to get punched out.

I deserved those lost years afterward.

And I deserve whatever's coming next.

The Dog of the Woods waits for me. She's patient. She lives in dreams. She shimmers somewhere that human math can't measure and where human eyes can't follow. When she comes back, the carnage won't stop with one classroom and an annoying teacher. "*Destroy it all*," I prayed. And she will. This time, she'll destroy me too.

I hope she does. The alternative is worse.

I'll be damned if I know what she saw in me that night. I *am* damned ever since. When I finally answer her calls and open my mouth and let the sounds of the hate inside me pour all over whatever's left of my life and this world, those tides of black will rise and sweep us all away.

The river has me.

It always did.

I don't mean any harm, though.

Really, I don't.

It's just my nature.

FORSAKEN ANGELS

They don't speak of her, but she is there. There in the darkness carved from earth and bones and rats.

In the foggy streets above, where mist gathers on the cobblestones, they build a new cathedral each time a plague comes through. They stoke their fires and raise their voices in broguish hymns, their Latin too mangled to reach the ears of God. The day-folk light candles to their saints, and wrap knots and charms and pretty lies to ward off the touch of Death's own angel.

And when Death comes (as Death is wont to do), they call the carters to send departed loved ones on a rumble-throated tumble through cobbled streets towards oblivion.

Toward *her*, and those like her.

To the cast-off refuse of their world, where hungry angels wait.

To the gates and the vaults and the pits where they feed, those dead souls who Death's touch has refused.

The carters throw their locks and tilt their wagons and drop their wares beneath the streets. And every so often, when the Deathless grow more numerous than rats, the carters feed those vaults with oil, straw, and torches, and then raise another stone prayer to the glory of their Lord.

They don't like to think she knows this. But she does.

And this time, when the wooden carts make their rumble-throated way down the winding streets between cathedrals, their masters sweating and cursing in the mist, she'll be waiting. And she will not be alone.

Forsaken angels wait below in flame-kissed vaults never spoken of above.

But when the locks get thrown and the carts get tilted, and the bodies fall, those angels will be prepared to rise.

Not for solace or for light, but for new gospels writ in blood.

BREAKING THE DEVIL'S BREAD

I have no regrets. Nor do I make apologies for what I am or what I have done. My sins have set me free, and I anticipate the coming dawn as the first step of my eternal journey.

The pain within my shattered legs keeps me awake. This, I know, was your intention. My friends in agony, you have bent your love for a broken god to the task of breaking other bodies in his name. Your droning chants of mercy ring hollow in the ears of those whom your mercy has denied. Throats screamed too raw for prayers curse you and your god. Most of the folk you mangle in these rat-beshitted crypts are more innocent than you have ever been. And yet, following your perverse whims and maggot-drooling falsities, you crush that innocence to pulp, burn it shrieking on your pyres, and consign it to the hands of the god to whom you claim allegiance. A god whose scriptures... and, oh yes, my friends, I *have* read them without bursting into flames quite yet... proclaim an endless torture pit to all but the handful of elect he has chosen to carry from this world to his paradise. Such a just and loving god, with such gleeful, earnest servants! His truest justice sets honest souls aflame.

Just as you, within hours, aspire to inflame my own.

Long before I reached these chambers, I befriended agony. I cannot rest now, not for the blood-encrusted ruin of my legs, but rather for the joy my coming tortures will ignite. I have learned to love pain, you see, to crave it like a lover's touch. To torture me is to arouse my lusts. To condemn me to eternal torment is to grant me an eternal bliss.

Clever boys that you are, you have left my hands intact. Pen and paper, too, I see. And enough light to see them by. For such courtesy, I presume you seek confessions. New pornographies to warm your chilly cells. Lists of names, perhaps, with which to fill these vaults? New properties you can add to your treasures in this world? Whose trusts should I betray on these final parchments? The ones who sold me my forbidden books? Whose temptations led me to the lap of Lucifer? Whose feet danced beside my own as the fat of babies sputtered in the fire? Whose coins you would snatch for the coffers of your bishops, and whose land you would claim in the name of your god? Who was it, you wonder, that first whispered brimstone promises to me, whose words first spread my soul like a virgin's legs to let the Devil have his way? On that quest, I fear I must disappoint you. If you expect a testament of denunciations, then look to other men, not me. I, you see, am far too proud of my depredations to share credit with the innocent. Pride is a sin most delicious on one's tongue.

I know the reason I must burn. I know the fear that drives you like children beneath the lash. Your god is a drunken father whose rage demands submission. But I have freed myself from fear. I do not cringe from your god's polluted pages, his scriptures of lies, or his maze of terrors. I have looked into your eyes as I dangled in your chains. There, I saw men whose every waking breath is a prelude to damnation. Each day, the hell-mouth gapes wider still. And it waits for *you*. For the inevitable feast when your tired, pious souls join the mortal pageant of all flesh stumbling through those hungry jaws.

You know this. You feel its teeth descend. Each day, each night, each breath brings you one step... perhaps sometimes *many* steps!... closer to that appalling end. And to the flames that wait beyond. That wait for *you*, my friends, as much as you deny that fear. Each innocent you consign to fire or brand with the kiss of blazing iron is a sacrifice with which you hold that fear at bay. Each prayer you mumble as they scream is not for *their* souls, but for your own. If you can pacify your Lord, perhaps he'll spare you the fate He has decreed for all of us.

A fool's wager, yes, though understandable.

If I were you, perhaps I'd make it, too.

To blunt the teeth of that voracious mouth, you adorn your halls with broken trees and chant profanations to a gilded king. As if such vanities could save you from your father's wrath! In faint spectres of illumination, you enshrine false words and bend your knees to men whose tables crawl with pestilence and whores. And yes, I can assure you, those rumors trickling through your congregations regarding the corruptions of your Church are fact. I myself have shared their revels, procured their whores, broken the Devil's bread with them. I have seen the virgins raped, tortured, and discarded in the pits behind the nunneries. I have sliced the skin from inconvenient infants, watched their bones blackened and scattered and fashioned into relics to mollify the gullible. I have helped befoul the girls sold into service, stripped their innocence and whipped their skins beside the Abbess in whose service I would later bury those girls in secret graves. Unbeknownst to your superiors, I have sent succubae among their revels and then laughed to watch the seed of bishops tossed on demons' tongues. You, my friends, bow to devil-slatted patriarchs, awaiting their instructions in the litany of God.

I have seen the wormwood you adore. Beheld it with my eyes. Drunk it with my wine. The ink with which I write these words, the ropes with which you've bound me, the wood on which you broke my limbs and build the pyre to consume my mortal form are all purchased with the blood of the children of your god. When I soon reach Hell, I shall share a laugh with Lucifer and raise a cup to your damnation while he dips my soul in pitch and lights it all ablaze. As my laughter turns to screams, I will mock you even then. I, at least, am honest in my sins. They have made me a freer man than you.

Oh, but where *are* my manners? You have not provided the instruments of wordcraft — instruments I recognize from among my own possession — so that I might condemn *you*, but rather so that I might condemn a host of new fodder for your flames. What other hope, after all, could tempt you to waste such precious instruments on a dying man? To appeal so dearly to my vanity, you must have great faith in my indulgent self-regard.

In this, I cannot fault you. It is a well-known fault of mine.

I cannot fault you, either, for providing me this final testament. How seldom, truly, do you get such opportunities? To find a prisoner who can write more than perhaps his name, whose crimes are so copious in evidence that no amount of wealth or favor could free me from the stake? And what gracious irony is it that your prisoner could furnish, from his appropriated household, the instruments by which you amuse yourselves while condemning me, and others, to the flames?

Let us not forget the vanity of your god. The one, or so I hear, whose very existence is the Word. To this god, the secret and forbidden words you share are proof of his divinity. Why else would so many of you bend your backs and stain your hands inscribing tedious scribbles on books no eye but yours will read? Could it be, my pious cousins, that you strain your gaze in candlelight out of sheer boredom with this world? Or is there some illicit thrill that sends you crawling across pages to find infamies your imagination alone could not provide?

I like to think it is all of these and more.

If I am to furnish pretenses to seize your next batch of innocents, then I had best get down to the business of providing them. This candlelight and ink will not last until dawn.

By the light of this diminishing candle, I see Beelzebub's handmaids swarming on my legs. The sap oozing from my limbs draws them to the feast. Through pain's haze, I sense the tickle of their own legs, the tongues thrusting into wet ruins that cling to tiny hairs. When this form of mine is ash, I will live on in the eggs nurtured by these flies. Their buzzing prayers will sing my requiem. The maggots nurtured on my flesh will nestle in your gardens and squirm throughout your food. My brothers in anguish, *you will soon devour me*. Whether in the ash on your beards or the flies alighting on your tables, you will taste this sinner long after my corpse has fled. And someday, Satan willing, the descendants of these flies will feast in turn on your ripe corpses, nourishing my spirit with the cannibals who once consumed my skin. Each fly upon my legs is a vessel of immortality. I want them to feed well tonight, for I will have nothing more for them tomorrow.

But you? Ah, *you*, my brothers, will fat them for millennia.

In these halls, far from your savior's sight, you have made a Hell on Earth and peopled it with innocents. I can see their eyes in other cells, hear them weep and scream and pray to the same Father who delights in their extinction. Their huddled forms look away when I glance in their direction. Even bound in chains, I still inspire fear. You, though? Your gentle hands inspire dread more chilling than my wickedness. For all my well-attested crimes, I pose no threat to these companions. The machines you christen with your holy spit, the invocations you proclaim to justify their pain — *those* things are the harbingers of agony these wretched souls abhor. You kindle greater fears than I, and terror is the Devil's bread. At Mass, you crack the flesh of Christ. But here, among the keening damned, you bake the souls of men and serve them up at Lucifer's feast.

Delicious! I am bound by iron, and you by irony!

But come! Let us explore my sins! That *is*, after all, why you've permitted me this final table of indulgences. The candle has begun to gutter out, and I would not leave you empty-handed. I see you now, you know, fists clenched around your cocks as you strain to read confessions and pepper them with memories of burst flesh and cries to God. The church's walls are cold, but you warm them with your lusts. Is this, my brothers in atrocity, why so many women feel your lash and grouping hands? Why each shaved and battered girl is interrogated past excruciation? Why you conjure up absurdities with which to justify each new torture you invent? Of course! Feigned chastity has sapped your loins until only blood will free them. The blood of innocents and ashes of the just. You name me among the Adversary's brood, but your sins are a thousandfold worse than mine. I know you as brethren though you deny yourselves. Hide that truth though you must, the Devil sees us all.

About those sins of mine, I shall offer no further delays. My light is fading even now. Though it would be a grand jest to leave you with blank pages, I am a kindly devil who would reward your hospitality.

My innocence fled shrieking while I was but a boy. Fair of face, I nurtured malignity. Awful fantasies bound my mind. Insects writhed beneath pins and blades. I pinched my siblings and lied about our slaves. To witness torture was my greatest joy. Though I seldom raised my voice in anger, I dreamt of carnage, agony, and war.

What bred this taste for brimstone? Was I, perhaps, born on some tempestuous night? No. Had I been carried from the skies by a great horned owl? birthed with a caul wrapped 'round my face? Not at all. My birth, I have been told, was quite ordinary. My mother survived it to raise five more children, most of exceeding piety. I must have been the goat in the manger. Silent demons may have come to play with me at night, but if they did so, I cannot recall.

I do recall the kitten, though.

It belonged to a wash-maid in my father's service. He, being a kindly master, permitted such luxuries among his slaves. The girl was sweet-faced and supple with the softness of youth. I'd often seen her glance in my direction, but with the wisdom of the servant-born, she knew that to regard me with anything but distant awe was to court disaster and disgrace. Unlike my feeble fellow lords, who sported with their family wenches until the wretched things had to be carved out in the barn or else sent away with bastard-swollen bellies, I watched this shy doe from afar. Upon occasion, I gifted her with a word or touch that bestowed some slight haze of affection, as if I were a fine but distant friend. I even feigned affection for her kitten, a raddled mass of brindled fur that bristled and spat whenever I came near. Yes, my pious brethren, the animals know us for what we are. They see the spark of hell-flame kindled in our breasts. This tiny thing knew my destiny far better than I did myself at the time. And so, one bitter windswept night, I doused the beast with icy water as it hunted rats in the courtyard below.

By the time it reached its mistress' side, my first victim had fairly frozen stiff. It died soon thereafter. When the girl attended her chores the next day, her eyes were red and vacant. A few soft words of empty kindness brought her to my bed. My false gentleness soon turned to force. From the wetness of her cunt and the blood that flowed from it, I learned why wolves smile in the night. This world, you see, is filled with claws and bellies. With those who hold the blade, and those who turn their throats to its edge.

Until that night, I had felt alone, cold as a fortress but with a furnace within. That furnace leapt into a blaze when I embraced the blade of cruelty. And oh, my brothers, such wonders I beheld! Such powers as would make gods tremble on their thrones! Compared to the gifts of malice I could seize, the plays of men are naught but shadows. In the darkness of my room, I licked the soiled virgin's blood from her mound. It tasted honey-sweet.

To catalog my sins from that night forward would demand more parchment and light than I have at my disposal. Shall I delight you with accounts of how I stripped a beggar bit by bit of his softer parts, starting with the tongue and eyelids and then working my passage slowly inward until his bones gleamed white and his blood fouled my favorite pair of boots? Would you, my brave brethren, contest with me in the finer points of wringing agony from our fellow men? Would you count your own secret conquests against my tally of maids and wives defiled? I assure you, such contests I would win. No mad Caesar of darkest Rome could rival my indulgence. By the time I attained my first book of demonism — the *Kitāb al-Bhät*, which you found amongst my possessions — my soul was blackened as a baker's oven. No sea of *vitae sanctus* could have washed me clean by then, nor would I have wished it to. The icy corridors of my old life glowed with a fiend's intensity. My sinning made me whole.

Before your kind ministrations dethroned my vanity, I was quite handsome and well-bred. My words could grease a virgin's cunt or the tumblers of a miser's vault. After the wash-maid's violation, those faculties placed a ladder from my father's court to Hell's bedchamber. The night that nameless slave crawled into my bed for comfort, I grasped that ladder and began my ascent. The climb was long, but I enjoyed every rung of it. Even now, flensed of title, coin, and comeliness, I remain a wealthy man.

It has been argued that my wife Ysentrud, frail and sickly thing she was, had been minister in my obscenities. The accusers you favored in your quest to add her bones to your fires have claimed she was too headstrong and book-schooled to be a good Christian woman — that she was, in fact, a witch snatched back to her upon her death. But no. I cannot credit that charred broomstick with the treasures I alone procured. She was by no means a student of esoteric arts, though I must confess she was, at first, a most willing guide to the pleasures of the flesh. In her father's own bedchamber, we connived to meet, unwitnessed in our carnal splendors, may times before we were betrothed. At other times, we rutted in his barn like beasts, marking hours by the scratch of hay and the spasms of lust fulfilled again and again and again. But while my beloved

Ysentrud led me like a succubus to the heart of Lilith's garden of delights, she shrank from such discourse once it became her duty, not her pleasure. After she produced our sons, Ysentrud's lusts, like shriveled flowers, dried and fell away. If then I sought pleasures amongst ale-maids and courtesans, can I truly be blamed for such? And if I milked those cattle with increasing cruelty, would *any* husband name me unjust? If I then kindled in my heart such hatred for the dry temptress who now occupied my bed, and could it not be said that she laid new seeds for my debauchery in her own barren sex?

It *has*, as we both know, been said.

But no, it is not true.

I will admit no such guidance to my fate. You see, my most excruciating hosts, it was *my* decisions which led me to the Devil's banquet. Mine alone. In my quest to partake of all that banquet had in store, I threw aside all helpmates, apprentices, and laws. I became *my own man*. And for that, I offer no apologies. I cringe at neither the lash nor the stake. My torments, I claim by right. When I opened that final door to my damnation, *I did so as a free and independent soul*. For that distinction, I would endure ten thousand bonfires kindled just for me.

Soon, campaigns against the heretics and Mohammedans gave me cause to vent my cruelty with great acclaim. I hacked limbs, gouged eyes, and fed howling infidels to the flames in the name of your blessed Lord. And you, my brothers in Christ, adored me for it. The greater my thirst for rape and torture, the grander my imagination when devising spectacles of slow obliteration, the higher I climbed in your esteem. Your own Church, I may remind you, appended to me titles of God's favor. Though purged now by my undoing, those sacred designations won me fame and wealth beyond what humble virtues could exact. I drowned whole towns in blood. Hoisted screaming innocents on pikes to drag themselves to death beneath the sun. Generations of flies and crows fatted themselves on the harvest of my righteousness. Recall well when you watch me burn just how glorious I seemed when I brought Hell to those whom you despise. I was Satan's creature even then. Still, you honored me.

When the shine of mortal sins had dulled, I availed myself to greater wisdoms. Our plunders carried books to me — forbidden works through which I could parlay with the Lords of Deep Misrule. Coin and blade procured me knowledge with which to gain those keys to Hell. Mohammedian scribbles joined my Church Latin and a rough understanding of Hebrew signs. I grew lettered in Gothic script, High German, the eloquence of Italian princes, and the bastard scrawl of the hated French. Such knowledge pried the secrets from my books. Those secrets cracked the gates of ignorance. Beyond them, I found the truth.

My hosts, you have it all so *very* wrong.

You presume there is some grand morality in play. I assure you, there is none. Life is cruelty and everlasting pain. The elements themselves weep with anguish. Stars howl in the void. There is *no* Heaven. Earth is lies. We exist at the threshold of damnation that no amount of holy blood can quench. Your church is a fiasco. Your scriptures are ashes, and your righteousness is rags. The sentence you enact on me will be bestowed on you in turn. Your flesh will hang in ribbons from the beaks of crows.

Eternity is voracious. We are its food.

The fly's nightmare is the spider's feast. To walk his web is to know that truth.

You shall know it soon enough yourselves.

Such a pity. It appears I am running low on ink.

It would be rude of me to drain my inkwell on imprecations, so let us continue while my quill still leaves its mark behind.

Are you enjoying my library? Copious in knowledge, is it not? It will take time, I assure you, for you to catalog its contents. Presuming you do not simply consign them all to flames, I expect you and your superiors will decide those works hold greater worth for you than ash. Perhaps you believe that studying those volumes will provide you with a keener edge with which to fight my kind. Ah, but are you so certain in your faith, my brothers, that you would dare hoard such precious tomes? Or do you fear that if you *did* burn my books, the ashes would return to me in Hell?

You are right to be afraid.

Das Daemonium des Herrn Flachs? Handsome, is it not? I bound that volume in my first son's skin as my initiation into the Greater Enigmas my patron supplied. Fastening his hands and feet with manacles, I cut out my boy's tongue and stuffed his mouth with it so no screams would betray my work. It was, as my patron promised, a long and bloody task. My arms ached long before the work was through. My hands twitched as I pulled the skin free. I started with his face, so that I might half-forget that the source of this luminous parchment once sprang from my own loins. Later, when I repeated the task with Ysentrud, I saved her face for last.

My wife's skin bound *The Lesser Talon*, by DuBray. A fitting legacy, you may agree. I know you had been disappointed that I took her life before she could provide you with amusements. She was, I assure you, a lovey subject for the torture. You may, at least, enjoy the textures of her skin. DuBray's fondness for the carnal arts rekindled such memories within me as I worked that I sobbed for the youth we had together lost. Killing her was an act of love. Despite my cruelties, I am more ever merciful than thou.

I took *la Gioia del Diavolo* from a rival's corpse. Or, more truthfully, from his library, as there was not enough left of his corpse to bind that book. That binding, I am told, came from some nameless slave bought with poisoned gold. Its dark tone suits the subject well.

The Forbidden Samhita of the Lost Sons of Manu provides translations from Sanskrit sources now deemed lost. Sutras dictated by the lawgiver's fifty warring sons, these scriptures upend the dim philosophies of Greece and the pious miseries of Egypt. Their revelation of this world's trembling delusions suits the explorations I have endured with my patron's aid. Their dedication to what they call "the fearless path" inspired many degradations of my own.

The true gem in my collection, though, is not among those you secured. *The Hundred Gates of Bhät* preserves the wisdom of Babylonian deviltry. Its sigils and rites call upon Lilith's children, those fell beings born beneath the waves. Where has it gone? Oh, my brothers, I leave *that* to your imagination. Suffice to say you will see its powers when the time is right.

Those books procured through cruelty afforded me new paths toward my desires. In their strange geometries and garbled-tongued chants, I found passage through which patrons and servants greater than any king might welcome me. Through wit, threat, and barbarism, I learned the profane rituals through which I might attain their favor. You have seen the chambers where I made such alliances. Are you curious, though, to know the faces I beheld in those rifts between our false world and that greater one? Might you even, despite forbiddance, seek to open such paths yourselves?

I suspect you will. Why else, after all, does your precious Vatican preserve copies of such works for the eyes of your Pope alone? Think you such a man is holy enough to behold fell truths and remain unsullied in the face of your Lord? I know for certain it is not so.

It has been said that your Lord bestowed unto Solomon the Keys to Hell, Heaven, and all their servitors. This is a sanitized claim at best. Those gates and Keys were ancient long before his time. Though of course I mastered the Solomonic Crafts, I sought at length more venerable Arts than his.

And at such length, I found them.

Ah, but by the thinning scratches of ink upon this page, I see I must condense long decades towards a suitable conclusion! Dawn birds call beyond my cell, and your stake awaits my eager flesh.

Through the most forbidden crafts, I summoned fell advisers to our realm. Brimstone harlots and subtle imps served my purposes and filled my vaults. I treated with instructors in highest deviltry. Locks and legs opened with equal ease beneath my touch. At length, I gained the favor of a patron demon lord. Human letters would render his name as Hta'baas Du'unkaath, Keeper of the Threshold, Vigil of the Gleaming

Waste. Do not seek him in your catalogs of lesser fiends and forgeries. You'll not find him referenced there. Only the truly wise may know him, and his favor is neither cheaply nor easily gained.

On the night of our first parlay, the moon hid herself in fear. According to the Laws of Solomon, I set out the First and Fourth Pentacles of Saturn. In place of ritual purification, I stained myself with blood and dung. In place of angelic hosts, I invoked the Lords of Deep Misrule. In place of contemplation, I indulged my lusts with a legion of drunken whores. Thus defiled, I offered up the lives of those unfortunates, draining their lives into a trough. Their innards, I arrayed fanciful designs. As I burned their hearts, I bellowed prayers of blasphemy.

The Keeper of the Threshold heard, and he came to me in storm.

His voice was the cry of the fifty-score serpents who claimed Eden after the Fall. His vast wings beat the night. His dozen eyes glittered like a bishop's crest of gold. His breath was charnel flowers. His form flowed like fouled wax.

In my protective circle, I bared myself like Odysseus at the mast. *My* ears, though, were open, and I welcomed the sweet song. My patron filled them with obscenities. As cold winds lashed my dead companions into rags, I stood upon the Void of Heaven's verge. I leapt down the Throat of Hell.

The Vigil of the Gleaming Waste drew me from my mortal form and hurtled me through the cracks of this world toward the one that waits for us Beyond. We plunged together through the long eternal scream. Through shells of bygone worlds we sped, their fragments embedded in my skin. Moments stretched to eons in the ecstasies of time.

At last, the Keeper drew me homeward once again. My bones shivered from the kiss of the Beyond. Skinned and gutted in reverse, my mortal form rebuilt itself. Each shrieking nerve and organ sang. Finally, that timeless agony withdrew. As the Keeper's storm subsided, I fell into deep abyssal sleep.

When I woke, the room was nearly bare. The tempest had swept all things away. The bodies, the trough, my implements — all gone. The only light within the chamber came from five black candles guttering in fatty pools. From within my protective circle, I banished whatever spirits might still linger there. As I did so, I must confess I shivered. One does not evoke such Powers without some strain of heart.

Only then, as the last vestiges of my ritual ebbed, did I see the gift left for me as sign of favor.

A kitten. The very image of the wash-maid's cat.

Her soft mew greeted me as I stepped warily from my circle. She padded forward and nuzzled my bare leg.

I laughed so hard I feared the roof might crack.

As I took this familiar in my arms, she whipped her claws across my skin and then lapped, purring, at the welling blood.

The pact was sealed. With her aid, and my patron's, my mastery of Dark Arts began.

How *did* you apprehend me, then? If my mastery and alliances with that World Beyond are so profound, how might such clumsy agents of your Lord secure me? You believe the blessings from On High allow you to disperse my Arts?

On that score, you are once again deceived.

Have you heard them yet, I wonder? The scuttles? The whistling? Have the shadows of my cell taken on the look of fiends?

I assure you, they soon will.

The candle sputters. I must be quick.

Darkness comes.

And there she is.

My kitten.

Her footfalls greet emerging dawn.

And thus, at last, I take my leave of thee.

Come morning, brothers, you will find me gone.

As dark descends and ink runs dry, I hear the flutter of approaching wings.

Do you hear them yet? You shall.

I am far from done with you.

My flesh is not for burning yet.

But we are all tinder to the flames of Hell.

THE LORD'S GREATEST JEST

Every lord must have his cruelties, and my Lord was no exception. The horses strained against their ropes as if in horror of their forthcoming chore. Being but poor brutes, they had no true comprehension of the depth of our king's humor. Still, God's creatures are imbued with some measure of His grace... save, perhaps, we poor fallen specimens, made in our Lord's image and yet born, it would seem, to defile it.

The men cowered in their chains, some begging for mercy, a few soiling themselves. The men-at-arms grumbled at the turn of their task, yet none dared to offend the king's honor by questioning his commands. The stink of terror and vile waste offended my nostrils and compounded the dank atmosphere of the day. Clouds piled up in solemn sky-veils, as if to shield Almighty God's view from the pending deed.

Would that such mercies had been allowed to us.

It is our state to live in fear
Our poor knees to mercies bent
And fair to tremble at the threat
Of some well-pointed argument.

My liege lord availed himself to wine — fine red stuff purged from Tuscan vineyards and carried by main force through the hills. I am familiar with such techniques, as I myself was procured through such adventures. In the carpeted pavilion where my lord took his shade, noble men and women gossiped, distracting their attentions from the activities underway. He gestured to me, and I attended. It was by his grace alone that I was not within that queue, or else long gone to the crypts or shattered like some discarded plaything somehow flawed by its maker's hands.

"Hop-Frog," he said, his fingers twitching with excitement, "It is a marvelous jest, don't you agree?"

"It is," I avowed, nodding my capacious, if marginally overlarge, head, "the very toll of Irony's bell."

The king was fond of jests, which is why he sought my company. He regarded himself as quite the humorist, and if in truth his humours favored a brutish, scatological bent, none within his court would dare make tell of such. His ministers and courtiers roared at the king's japes like cruel boys with some rocks and a frog pond. It fell to me to instill some measure of refinement in that court, however poor my efforts may have been.

"The day is hot, my hopping prophet — *drink!*" My master pressed the wine cup to my hands. I took its measure, then downed it without protest. I fear, however, that I am not much fond of spirits. They skew my wits, and my lord knew this. My sardonic wit had amused him from the day I'd first set foot within his presence. Though I must confess I found his manner quite appalling, I could not argue with the favor of his office. I was one of many celestial pranks gathered into our king's court as entertainers for the noble kind. Yet it was *my* wit (if not my humor) that most pleased our gracious lord. And so, here I was, a partner in his latest jest.

The first team of horses found themselves hitched to the first man drawn from the line. He howled as if the pain had already begun. Like a kitten dangled over fire, he shrieked and clawed and struggled but to no purchase or relief. The men-at-arms hitched his legs to the team — one-half of the team to the right leg, one-half to the left.

Our good king gave the gesture, and the horses were loosed.

Arms pinioned to his sides, the man was drawn to the stake in awful mockery of the carnal act as was practiced in the halls of Sodom, damned yet sacred in appeal. For truly, what *else* could rouse such divine reproach but that which is, by some man's measure, sacred?

God cares not for petty things
To gain His favor, man's deeds must be
Keen of edge and iron-rich
Splendid in depravity.

And so, the deeds of my king were, for his appetites were as capacious as his humours... which is to say (like his belly), vast.

Delicacy forbids me to describe in detail the king's foul spectacle. Let us simply say it was an excessive jest. By evening-fall, three-score men were writhing in dances of excruciation, dancing a pine-jig of dim theatricality.

"Let it be known," said our king for the third or fourth time that day, "that such is the punishment in my realm for buggery."

And this too, may I say, dear reader, was *also* the very toll of Irony's bell.

For in all the kingdom, I knew of no more prolific a buggerer than our good king himself.

# # #

Given my close (might I say pointed?) acquaintance with our king's true predilections, I remained wary as we watched that spectacle. Not a one of those so terribly speared had *not* been a member of the King's inner secret circle — those men most tenderly taken in our lord's awful favor. Given the normal instinct for self-preserving acts, you would be forgiven for thinking that such men might avoid our lord's attentions. But just as birds often dash themselves against inviting windowpanes, so we men find ourselves drawn (if I may say so) to morbid fascinations in the hopes that some catharsis might be found. We are creatures of pity and terror by inclination, and our tastes seem sharpened by the risk of some fell thing.

In this case, that fell thing was the king himself — a magnificent hallmark of God's handiwork, I must confess, yet tinged with a Saturnian glare. His opulence — grand foods, grand drinks, clothing fit for Papal lords — was well-known, even if his bedchamber-pursuits were not. The finest musicians, acrobats, and courtesans were summoned to his palace every fortnight, to entertain men and women elevated to grand opulence by God.

And *I?*

I had the fortune to be master of his revels (both public and discreet), my chambers as capacious as my skull. I was well-barbered by a host of concubines purchased at fine price for the purpose of gilding one of God's mistakes. For just as our good king was charming and well-formed by the Craftsman's hand, so I had been tumbled off the lathe at some imperfect juncture, my wits full-formed and my body, sadly, not.

This, too, I take and gather
As sure sign of my King's wit:
To employ a half-formed Hop-Frog
In service of his etiquette.

Nor was I alone among my countrymen in being granted such an office. One other — a sweet-faced boy named by our liege *Triptolemus* — had been taken from my distant village. We forged a kinship, he and I, in shared captivity. For be assured, dear friend, royal captives is what we were — well-favored slaves, most certainly, but beaten or worse when the king's humours darkened toward night-black.

Triptolemus and I had good reason to fear our king's attentions. For by some gracious blessing of celestial wit, this young man and I shared a common secret with the king. Had truth prevailed in that forest of lies, all three of us would have been hoist upon the buggerer's spikes. But while the king's appetites were as gentle as his cruelties, Triptolemus and I held common comfort in the touch of a secret angel's wings.

I cannot in good conscience claim he loved me. How could *any* man desire in his heart an accident of flesh such as I? It speaks of strange devotions that so beautiful a young Adonis could cradle my misshapen head, stroke a perfect finger down my cheek, suffer slights and rantings from our king when tendering on my behalf. Triptolemus kneaded my bent shoulders, rubbed balm on my frequent whip-burns. He held me at night when the torments took me, whispering that he would never leave my side. What inspired such dedication, I cannot say. He never told me then, and he cannot tell me now.

Unlike the coarse blunderers who peopled our king's court, Triptolemus moved like air across a flame. So delicate that he could cross a rope across a gorge, yet strong enough to lift me without drawing a hard breath, Triptolemus shared my acrobatic skills. For though my legs force me to a perpetual half-hop along the ground (hence my name — all hail my master's wit!), my arms are strong as cables on a carpenter's high scaffold. With such ropes and scaffolds, we entertained our king, swinging like apes through torch-lit halls in defiance of death and common sense. I may have been the stronger man (or *half*-man, if you will), but Triptolemus was our Orpheus, so delicate in art that he could look Hell in the face and return to the living world unscathed.

Perhaps our bond grew from that kinship to our distant home, or from the brutal method of conveyance we shared between that home and the good king's court. The trust of wrists and well-timed leaps may well have united us. But perhaps it was our *stature* that struck such affection from our souls. For, like me, they judged Triptolemus as half a man — well-formed as any artist's statute, but far shorter than even a common girl.

What jesting Maker shapes such men? What heavenly laughter shook the clouds on the nights when we were born?

When His wits are up
And His humours sing
The Lord of Hosts
Is cruel as a king.

As our good king laughed at Triptolemus and myself, so the King of Kings must have laughed at us all.

And yet, Triptolemus showed no defect. His small height could be judged his only deformity. Diminutive in stature, he may have been; but in form? Generosity? Intellect? Grace? He was as perfect as any man I have ever seen... and far more so than our noble lord.

I miss him. Curse me for a fool, I miss him still.

Our king, of course, shared no such sentiments. We were prize foals in fools' motley beneath his royal gaze. And as we sat together, my king and I and his seven man-sized crows, drinking ourselves toward happy oblivion, the stench from our lord's jest filled the air.

I confess I was not in good humour then, myself.

# # #

Drink is my Golgotha. If someone could have taken my cup from me, I would gladly have wished it so. But my lord bid me drink, and so I did, my head growing heavier than usual with the mixture of thick wine and thicker smells. The men on stakes (still living, and what cruel jest was *that?*) writhed and spilled their entrails most pitifully. I stared down at my boots, uneasily aware that they had not escaped the legacy of humours spread out around us. I wished for Triptolemus' arms about me then, his soft words soothing my pulsating skull, but was glad to see him spared this spectacle. Back at the palace, our king had decreed a feast to be held in honor of his wit. Triptolemus had remained behind to oversee the preparations, while I followed the king's train to witness his glorious jest first-hand.

"Dance for us," my king commanded. "Raise that heavy head of yours and amuse our company."

My stomach roiled with revulsion and wine. "I fear, my lord, that I've had far too much to drink."

"Nonsense," replied Bartholomew, the most demanding of my lord's advisors. His sour moustache twitched with disapproval. "Our *king* bids you dance, Hop-Frog. Do so."

I glared at him with all the venom a slave dares display. Behind him, a man I'd known as Antony shrieked for mercy. I could not look up without seeing the forest of violated limbs and trees. Squinting, I could render them into shadows, but nothing stopped that *smell*, that *sound*. "What sort of dance," I asked our king, "would you see me do, my lord?"

"A jig of spring, my toad. As graceful as you can be."

Grace was never, I fear, an attribute of mine.

Bowing, I rose to my feet. My head swirled and throbbed. I tilted as if the world itself had tugged the carpet from beneath me. The king and his advisors laughed. I spread my arms out in pale imitation of a swan.

"*No*, my fool," the king said.

My heavy skull bobbed at the end of my neck. "My lord?"

"Not here," he said, gesturing to the carpet rolled out across the mud by his servants. "You'll soil the carpets."

"Where, then, do you wish me to dance, my king?"

He pointed, not to my surprise, to the forest of budding corpses. "Out there."

The courtiers barked flatteries at my king's command. Bartholomew cackled as he took a sliver of lamb from an ill-looking servant's tray. Caught between two pointed logics — the wall of courtiers and men-at-arms before me, the wall of staked men and men-with-stakes behind me — I bowed again and took my leave of the carpet, stumbled into the reddening mud with as much dignity as I could muster. Once there, I raised my gaze to the skies. A trio of musicians began to play beneath the pavilion, and I danced.

I wish I could say that my eyes remained closed, but that would not be true. Thankfully, tears soon blurred what my will alone could not.

# # #

"It was terrible," he said.

"It was," I affirmed. It had been my intention to shield him from the truth, to dismiss the king's jest with a few words and a shrug. I could not. Triptolemus' grasp gave me a vessel for my shudders, and so I placed them there. He himself felt shaken too, as if he'd heard more about the pageant than I would have told him myself. His sweat held a sharper edge than usual, and though I could smell the drift of garlic and meat from the kitchens, I had no stomach for a feast.

"I should have been there," he said.

"I'm glad you were not."

"We should not speak of it." He was not being kind. The king learned gossip from the roaches in the walls, it seemed, and if he wanted to add two of his favorite clowns to his next spectacle, no one would raise a word against it. Best, then, to speak of nothing and pretend that nothing was amiss.

"We will not." I gave Triptolemus a brief, but firm, embrace and then stepped back away from his arms. "How go the revels' preparation?"

His mouth bent in silent dismay. "Well enough," he lied. "By an hour past dinner, all will be ready for His Majesty's pleasure."

Such was our discourse: a forest of mirrors casting false reflections. Aware that any wrong word would bring the weight of our lord's wit and humour upon us, we chose our words like grapes among a half-ruined harvest. I nodded to him. "Surely the feast will provide welcome relief for such grand hungers."

"I hope," said Triptolemus, "that it will satisfy him." We both knew, of course, that it would not. Our lord's blood ran hot for amusement, and when it was up, no simple foods could appease it.

"I should sleep while I can," I told him, my head still spinning from the afternoon's wine.

"Will you be well alone?" he asked, his face searching my own.

It was my turn to lie. "I will."

My dreams ran wild with sharpened trees.

# # #

Humor has the breath of cruelty. Any jester knows this, and I more than most. By the time the servants tendered up their feast, the king's halls rang with noble laughter. Though I had no belly for food that night, I accepted the plate Triptolemus brought me. Starving jesters tender ill jests.

As I ate, I watched Triptolemus fly. His agile limbs cast him in an angel's role, too high and graceful for earthly weight to bind him. He danced in the ropes above our heads, shining with the glow of his exertions. Despite the swamp in my belly, I felt my heart fly with him.

Soar, my young blind Icarus,
Shame Heaven with your grace
Unbound by the dull chains of man
Gone to touch our Master's face...

And then I saw the courtier Bartholomew whispering in the king's ear, his face like countenance of a late-winter wolf.

The two men laughed. Our lord nodded.

Though Triptolemus still flew, I felt my stomach fall.

And when the angel descended, the devils caught him and brought him to the throne.

I hobbled over to where they stood, but Triptolemus warned me off with a glance. His expression closed tight, like men-at-arms in war formation. He nodded to our king, but I saw his shoulders shake.

Bartholomew nodded to one door, and Triptolemus bowed, then strode toward that portal. I looked to him. He closed his eyes and walked away.

"*Hop-Frog!*" The king's voice cracked through the chamber.

"My lord?" I knew better than to delay. Bowing, I felt my knees shudder. My thick skull blackened with the thoughts locked inside.

"To the ropes with you," he said. "We would see who flies best: the angel or the ape."

The courtiers laughed, of course. It was their nature to obey and their pleasure to observe.

Though I'm sure I fancied it, I would swear that Triptolemus' sweat lingered in the ropes, drifting over the smell of food, wine and candle lard.

In the arc of angels, I dreamed a demon's plans.

#

There are barbarities to which no man nor woman should accept. And yet, we bear them with silent shrugs and empty eyes. In such a state Triptolemus returned, stumbling to his cot with unaccustomed frailty. I rose to greet him, but he shook his head. Some novel iniquity had cut him in places my smile could not reach. "We will not speak of it," he said.

I nodded.

Our clowns' court was silent and cold that night.

# # #

"A masquerade?" our lord asked.

"Indeed," I nodded. "Like those of the Venetian courts." With words, I painted frescos of delight that should have shamed Great Michelangelo had he beheld my art. "All the kingdom will speak of it," I said. "Word of your cleverness will spread from the cold pagan reaches to the sand-courts of the infidels!"

"*What* cleverness would they speak of, Hop-Frog," he said. There was no question in his voice. For all my art, our king was no fool.

But I, of course, am a *great* fool. And though it took all my art, so I fooled him in turn.

We laid plans for the masquerade, Triptolemus still rigid from his secret pain. He embraced me while we felt ourselves unwatched, but his arms felt stiff as paving stones. I tried to will some back into him, but whatever had chilled Triptolemus lingered there beyond my grasp.

It took time and no little effort, but soon all things were arranged. The night of our king's masquerade arrived, dressed out in devilish finery.

The costumes I'd prepared arrived as well.

"Apes?" Our king seemed dubious. His advisors eyed the fur-suits with unnerved curiosity. I had taken pains to ensure that the costumes would radiate a grotesque potency. Great teeth gleamed white in the shaggy masks, and jewels glittered against night-black fur. I had coated that fur with sweet-smelling musk, oils ripe with seductive masculinity. Best of all were the claws — scimitar talons carved from bone. Such props appeal to predatory men. True apes, of course, have no such claws... but each artist must have his liberties.

I had taken mine. And in Triptolemus' distance, I had taken to drinking, too.

My head whirled and my tongue danced. Flatteries spilled from my lips like wine. "It will terrify them all," I said. "Imagine the ladies fainting with horror. Imagine the brave men trembling in the face of your ferocity! *All* will fear you — and then applaud when you remove the masks and reveal the handsome men beneath the image of fierce apes."

"It would be," the king remarked, "a most *poetic* jest." His face tightened to a grin. "And should any man flee the court, we'll know him for his cowardice. A fine jest, my Hop-Frog... and perhaps a useful one as well." Behind his eyes, I saw trees dancing with the bodies of men.

When all were attired, I produced the chains. The king's eyes narrowed behind his mask. Though I had made certain that the men would be refreshed with strong spirits as they dressed, my king's wits had managed to peek through the clouds. "*Chains*, my servant? Do you forget yourself?"

"Not at all, my king." My wits glistened with the spirits' taste. "It is an essential element of the masquerade. Who would believe that mere *apes* could be loose within the palace? You are to be *demon*-apes, my lords, straining against the very chains of Heaven. Look here," I added, opening the door. "I have even brought an angel to hold you all."

Triptolemus stood waiting, his face stern as Heaven's messenger. A pale wrap girded tight across his loins. His muscles gleamed with oil and candlelight.

It was no great task to get them into the chains after that.

#

It's small wonder that folk crave masquerades. Our passions chase us from God's sight, warding us from Eden by flaming swords we carry in our grasp. To admit to our hearts' desires is to fall from grace like the poor acrobats we are. And so, we bar the gates to our inner natures, dressing them in costumes that hide honesty behind façade. In masquerades, of course, one's true face is revealed beneath a stylish confection. We may excuse its presence with cobbled finery, but we all know (though few will admit as much) that only in such deceptions may we be free.

And do we not have excellent teachers in such masques: The Lord, our cruelest jester, and His clergy on this earth? The God of sacramental tortures, the men who bless the engines of our pain — they speak of gentleness, yet show none of it themselves. The silky kitten is tormentor to the mouse, and the laws that speak of justice give free rein to the cruel. We hide our truths from the face of the Lord, and yet it is that Lord who makes us what we are. Such ironies bind our earthly lives, and so I found rich irony in binding our lord with chains.

In the grand hall, vast candelabras shed smoky light across the ballroom. Bright-clad apparitions spun and glided on polished stone. Musicians kept a heavenly reverie, their art echoing through stone chambers to each corner of the hall.

Outside, darkness swelled with the rustle of bat-wings and skittering vermin beyond the candlelight. Hungry servants, huddled against the cold, shivered in their rags, or slapped cards and flesh and pitiful wagers in vain efforts to keep warm. Horses snorted gusts of foul-breathed mist. Dogs gnawed on bones cast there once the revelers inside consumed the best parts of the meat. Like a body on the verge of rot, the palace swarmed inside with pale-skinned maggots of ravenous degree. Not far off, the scraps of our king's jests still hung suspended on sharpened posts, their crow-tattered corpses rich with grubs. The masquerade continued apace, trading truth for falsehood with ever-present glee.

Our king and his man-crows clanked their chains. Through hidden corridors, Triptolemus and I led them towards the hall. "Wait here, my lords," I whispered as I handed the full rein off to my companion. "I will shout alarms to the masquerade, priming them for your infernal appearance."

"And what then?" asked Bartholomew, his glance skipping between myself, our king, and the angel holding his chains.

"I have prepared a shot of brimstone to herald your arrival — a fierce but harmless fire-burst. When you hear it, and the screams begin, crash through those doors and howl like the fiends of Hell."

By this time, the king and his retinue were (as goes the saying) drunk as lords. I had made certain that wine was close at hand, well-sweetened with concoctions to muddle one's wits. Truth be told, my king and his advisors stumbled like veritable *Hop-Frogs* in their chains, their normal grace hobbled by dizzied limbs.

I plied the king's guards with wine as well. We all laughed with liquid cheer. Only Triptolemus did not laugh. His face held implacable angelic calm. My chest hurt when I looked at him. Still, my office was to play the fool, and so I did, jigging like a frog on the end of a rough boy's noose.

"We are prepared?" I asked the company, but it was Triptolemus I looked to. He nodded. We had never, he and I, held much need for words between us.

In shadow, I loped up the stairs to a balcony where the brimstone cannon waited. I aimed it near the ceiling, then lit the fuse.

The hall shook with the thunder of its blaze.

Into the smoke-filled hall, I cried: *"My lords and ladies! Flee! The devil has burst the gates of Hell and set his minions loose! Save yourselves! Pray to God! The demons are free! Fly, my friends — FLY!"*

I took some small satisfaction in the ensuing pandemonium.

On cue, the king and his advisors charged into the room, their claws gleaming wicked in the candlelight. Bared fangs flashed in their fur-clad heads. Poor Triptolemus clung tightly to their chains, a gorgeous coachman with a furious team. The brimstone singed my throat and nose as I howled theatricalities to the room below. *"See them, my lords and ladies! See the angel wrestling with their chains! Fear the hot breath of their corruption, gentle souls!"* I made it clear that this spectacle was part of the masquerade. Soon, terror turned to hilarity.

The guests and men-at-arms joined the play. Ladies swooned with exaggerated flair. Men-at-arms brandished their weapons with obvious caution, wary of any true threat to the king. The demon-apes raged about the room, tearing dresses and scattering furniture. Servants fled their approach, their faces pale with genuine fear.

The king and his advisors were clearly having the time of their lives.

Leaping from the balcony, I caught one chandelier and swung out in an arc. My hand clutched the torch with which I'd lit the brimstone. "*My lord and ladies,*" I cried, "*let us have an end to this! Let the devils stand revealed!*"

Our wise king caught my cue. He stopped and roared with infernal majesty. Reaching up, he shook free his demonic ape-mask, pulled it off, and roared again.

The crowd roared in approving response.

I glanced down to Triptolemus. He glanced back to me.

And tossed the chain in my direction.

It was, by my design, long enough to reach the hook I had hung from the chandelier.

Never harm an acrobatic fool.

I swung the hook to catch the chain, caught it, and pulled. The arcing chandelier snapped the chain tight around the men below. With a heave that near-tore my arms from their sockets, I pulled the chain to anchor it on the chandelier.

The king and his men were yanked high in the air.

We swung back and forth as I drew the cursing men toward me. Years of bitter exercise gave me the strength of an angry god. "*Good people,*" I shouted, my lungs tight with exertion and brimstone smoke, "*Who is this I here behold?*"

"*It's the KING!*" some woman shouted.

"*Indeed?*" I yelled. "*Let me get a closer look!*"

And I shoved the torch in his face.

The musk-oiled fur flared. My noble lord screamed.

Indeed, I *had* prepared this jest — had crafted the costumes with an eye towards vanity *and* ignition. Within instants, the king, Bartholomew and the other courtiers shrieked in their prisons of burning fur.

Atop the chandelier, I cried:

The lord is my jester, I shall not want.

He maketh me to cry near still waters.

He lieth down with innocents and turns them to bawds.

I am Hop-Frog, and this is MY LAST JEST!

With that, I leapt to the balcony and ran for my life.

# # #

It has been said that Triptolemus and I fled the kingdom together that night; this much was true. Some tales even cast him as a woman... and this much was *not*. In a merciful world, I could say that we lived a blissful life from then on outward — and to some degree, we *did*. Through cleverness and luck, we secured a home near the edges of those lands, far from the wars and searches that combed the countryside. A wiser king soon rose to claim the throne, and the hunt for us ended with nothing to show but legends of my infamy.

And yet my angel had flown. His haunted eyes looked out toward some horizon that neither of us dared to speak of. Though his arms wound close about me at night, they held an ever-bitter chill. He trembled from the lash of some dire whip inside. No jests, no tears, no endearments could soothe him.

Tritolemus lived like a walking corpse. Not long afterward, he stopped walking and simply died.

If this was a kinder tale, I would have passed on with him then, going to whatever Hells or Heavens await creatures such as us. Yet the vitality that guided my hand that night has kept me strong through all these years. The seasons have fled. My life has not. Of all the souls alive that night, I may be the last one drawing breath today.

My vibrant strength has faded, though. What little grace I had is gone. Yet the heart beating in my chest pounds like a blacksmith's favorite hammer on the anvil of each night and dawn. I crave release, but cling to life.

It's justice, I suppose. To recall sweetness in such sour age. To smell the brimstone even when I sleep, its scent lightened by the sweat of love.

I thought myself clever... and so I was. Clever enough to see the humor of our Lord.

And even in my solitude, I have to laugh.

We are as frogs before our God
Tumbling through our graceless fall
Mortal men might play at jests
But time's the cruelest jest of all.

CLOWN BALLOONS

The floor at my feet is littered with clown-balloon corpses. Bright rubber screams into nightmare shapes. My ears ring. My wrists throb. This is my damnation, to twist and strangle rubber 'til my brain runs dry.

It isn't working, though. I'm running out of balloons.

# # #

I may have been eight when the clown first appeared, a looming bright Satan against a sea of children. Flies buzzed lazy in the summer heat but if the clown felt dizzy in his painted prison, it didn't show. He laughed instead, and did magic tricks, his face swollen and flat behind red-slashed masking. Marcie Meyers, the Birthday Girl, flounced about all pink and pretty, but it seemed like the clown was intent on me.

My world tilted. I recall that much. Sickness bloomed in my belly, greasy-sweet from too much cake. The birthday-hat elastic bit into my chin and throat. I wanted the bathroom. I wanted to go home. I nearly wet my pants when the clown leapt suddenly from the bushes, scattering children in a screeching herd. Laughing harder, he beckoned us back... and trusting, we returned to him. The Birthday Parents beamed and reassured us as the clown went back to work. The other children giggled and clustered beside him. I held back, though, sniffling. His laugh held tiny screams just for me.

I stood apart. Is that why we watched me?

I didn't need to see his eyes to know that he watched me. The feeling was clear enough. His eyes burned my skin like sunburn, prickled like peroxide on a scrape. When I dared a glance, our eyes met and locked. He seemed to giggle, then, but that may have been my imagination.

Then he fetched his balloons and it all grew worse.

I didn't want to be there. To be watching. To be caught. I didn't want to see him pull things from nowhere, to see sun glare on bright baggy clothes. To feel flaming eyes set on black-rimmed white, eyes that scurried over me like roaches. I tried to brush that gaze away.

"*Timmy!*" cried Birthday Mom. "Don't touch yourself there! It isn't nice!"

"Can I go inside?" I begged, or something like it. "I gotta..."

"I see," she said as she led me by the hand. But she didn't. Not really. The clown did, though. I caught him smiling at me as we went inside.

I heard balloons scream as we came back from the bathroom. I wanted to stay inside but she wouldn't let me. She said it was time to have fun, time to laugh, time to play. Marcie had wanted all her friends to be there, and I didn't want to miss the *clown*, did I?

How little we recall kid fears.

He caught my eye as I came out through the door. He'd been waiting for my return. At the middle of the yard, he tortured two balloons in his white-gloved hand, much to the children's delight. I winced as tiny screams broke me into goosebumps. My friends didn't notice, but I did. Dancing Marcie held a balloon-beast in her eager hands. Bruce and Katrina did, too. The clown gave his weeping balloons a final, vicious twist, then handed the result toward me.

It was hideous.

The clown was a master of his art. His creations were bent and broken things, agonizingly alive. The balloon-beasts quivered and mewled. Wet eyes pleaded for release. The one in Marcie's hands looked worst of all. I wanted to puke.

So I did.

It took forever 'til Mom showed up to take me home. I burned as the other kids laughed. Even the clown seemed amused. I wished he'd stop looking at me! On the ground at his feet, balloon-things writhed. The clown smirked as he squashed one beneath his oversized shoe. It squealed before it burst. Bright blood spattered the white of his pants. Why didn't anyone see this but me?

And still, he brought freakish things to life, handing them out like treats. Like sacrifice. He seemed to sneer beneath his paint as he wrenched pathetic beasts from garish rubber. That grin promised similar treatment to me.

Later.

I still felt him watch me as Mom came to take me home. Marcie never forgave me for puking blue birthday cake at her party.

The clown came to see me that night in my dreams. Red, wet, sticky dreams smelling of greasepaint.

# # #

Bruce Taylor called me "Party Puker." Katrina Watkins called me "Timmy Toilet-Face." Marcie called me things I never expected from a girl, and Gary Bright did a lunchtime impression of me that got him sent to Mr. Jordan's office. I was out-cast all that month, and it would be a long time before anyone invited me to a birthday party again.

I still can't eat cake, even now.

It wasn't over, though. There was more.

About a week or so later, I was in my backyard pitching dirt clods at my G.I. Joes when I heard the squeak of rubber behind me.

"I *know* you want a balloon, Timmy."

Nobody saw the clown with me, then. Nobody saw his hands on me. His eyes. His blazing white suit. I didn't scream or cry or run away. I could see the sweat sheen on greasepaint as he held me close. The whisker-tips beneath it. His hot clown suit smelled unwashed against the pine-needle scene of my back yard.

I recall a finch feeding worms to her children that day.

# # #

In high school, I could never come through. I graduated virginal, not quite a man. I'd go out on dates, sure, but when things got close, the smell of greasepaint turned me small and useless for the night. Word spread between the girls by my junior year. I didn't date again 'til college. My girlfriends, though, couldn't hear the squeak of rubber in my room back home. I didn't share that part of me at all.

The clown, I'd soon learned, had passed his gift of creation on to me that back-yard afternoon. Now *I* could make animals, too. I hid balloons underneath my bed, and when I returned from dates with Jae, or Alexa, or Sherri, or Mo, I'd dig out the bag and blow up balloons, and twist them until the skin pulled back beneath my nails and my head swam dizzily. Then I'd put the suffering things out of their misery with a pin, muffling their bursting bodies with my pillow before I slept.

I didn't want to do clown things.

# # #

Once, in college, feeling brave I dropped some acid. Big mistake. The room quickly filled with balloons and the laughter of clowns. Colored light crawled across the walls like blood. My feet brushed the bones of long-dead children as the clown stood, laughing, at the center of the room and blew bubbles shaped like heads. Balloon-creatures writhed, broken, at his feet. All around me, stoned girls watched my eyes and giggled when I met their gaze. My friends weren't really my friends, it seemed. I stared at the floor to avoid their eyes. Besides, there were bones on the floor to be careful about, too.

I just wanted my balloons.

"I know you *really* want to be a clown, Timmy," said the bubble-blowing trickster. I don't think he was right, but back then I wasn't sure.

"Hey, Tim," said a soft voice. Alison Richards, from my chem class. She took my hand in her own warm one. "Let's get you some air," she offered. "It's kinda close in here." I didn't disagree.

Outside, we walked hand-in-hand as dying stars fell to the wet cement. Branches shook with nighttime wind. Our clothes clung tight in drizzling rain. We brushed damp hair from one another's faces as we kissed beneath a streetlight.

The next time I recall seeing Alison, she covered her face and ran away from me. When I saw the clown again shortly afterward, he looked pleased. Although I never learned what else happened that night, I also never touched acid again.

#

I made many balloon-things on my wedding night. My new wife Helen never saw them. I went outside and popped them in an alley while she slept. If the clown was there then, I didn't see him.

I see him a lot now, though. At the edges of my sight, he waves at me. I buy plenty of balloons, and then fashion horrors to make him go away. Sometimes, I miss pieces of them when I'm cleaning up. Helen finds them and wonders where the rubber scraps come from. I haven't dreamed up a good enough lie.

"I know you really want to be a *clown*, Timmy," he insists. No matter how far away he stands, I smell rancid greasepaint, sweat, and birthday cake. My fingers ache, stained and stinking of cheap balloon rubber. Helen keeps to her side of the bed now, watching me with chilly eyes. Maybe I should have told her about greasepaint and pine needles. If I had, she might not look at me that way.

I *should* tell her, but I can't anymore. It's too late. Things have changed. The clown leers from every shadowed corner, now. He might tell the police where to find Alison. I don't know where she is myself, and I don't want to know.

Maybe I should tell Helen that I'm running out of balloons.

So, I sit in my den, surrounded by gasping shapes wrung from rubber, nightmares looking at me with glistening eyes. It's late out, too late to buy balloons. The clown's shadow falls across my shoulder. He brings the taste of sweet sugar cake and the tang of pine needles, and he's chuckling.

Only two balloons left. Two balloons between me and my young son's bedroom door.

Please help me, God.

I really don't want to do clown things.

THE LINGERING FIST

"Fuckinbitch! Get over here!"

Thudding bodies and anguished cries follow the demand. Just another night in Domestic Abuse Central, starring our upstairs neighbor Charlie and his long-suffering wife, Fuckinbitch. After several minutes of listening to the beating, I get out of bed once again, reach for the broom, and bang a few times on the ceiling to remind Charlie and his favorite punching bag that *some* people have to get up and work in the morning...

If this sounds callous, it's because the constant presence of traumatic helplessness tends to numb the initial horror into anger, then aversion, avoidance, annoyance, and eventual capitulation into gallows humor. Back when my then-wife Cat and I moved in under this domestic horrorshow, we responded by calling the cops and confronting Charlie personally. Neither response accomplished a goddamned thing. As many victims trapped in DV nightmares do, poor Fuckinbitch denied the abuse when other people intervened. Cops would arrive, raised voices would simmer down, the cops would depart, and the screaming and pounding would begin again.

Talking to Charlie was pointless. As Charlie put it, what he and Fuckinbitch did in *"MAH house"* was *"MAH business,"* not ours. Countering that argument with the fact that it *became* our business when we had to listen to it usually earned a half-hearted promise to "keep things down, then." That promise, like countless items of furniture and kitchenware, was inevitably broken.

It's not as if Charlie was the only culprit, either. Yelling voices and thudding bodies were part of the soundscape of that place and time. One night, it would be Charlie; another could be the guys downstairs, a dude next door, someone across the courtyard in the next building over, or arguments in the halls which occasionally boiled over into fights. Most of our neighbors seemed to spend their time in some level of intoxication. Few had jobs, many had tempers, and violence of some kind was not an "if" but a *when*. Cat and I eventually surrendered to that all-too-predictable pattern by keeping to ourselves as much as possible, minimizing our involvement until especially loud outbursts sent me into the halls with fists raised and adrenaline pumping for a fight. I got my share (and then some) of those fights in Domestic Abuse Central, too. By the time Cat and I, with our now-late friend Jae Peirce, managed to scrape together enough funds to ditch that madhouse, Cat had begun to batter me, and I'd come very close to hitting her myself.

Trauma is contagious. We caught it through immersion back in those days, and it damn near destroyed us all.

Today, with over thirty years of hindsight, I realize that calling a domestic violence victim by the only name we'd ever heard her abuser employ is grotesque. In those days, however, grotesque was our daily state of existence. Already scarred by our own histories of rare but memorable family violence and the awful experiences linked to Nancy Reagan's favorite "tough love" torture-cult, Cat and I adopted the time-honored coping mechanism of traumatic environment survivors: gallows humor coupled with a grim sense of resignation. It's easy to judge other people — or even ourselves — with a significant degree of distance from the circumstances that shape them. During the three years we lived in Domestic Abuse Central (its name another product of that gallows humor), Cat and I lived with those circumstances every day. Three decades later, we still do.

I'm not saying that every night involved a new vicarious beatdown. We could go days, sometimes weeks, without hearing the all-too-familiar sound of smashing furniture and cries for help. Trouble is, we never knew *when* we would hear those sounds next, or from which direction. By the time we'd left that awful place, we occupied our own place in that sonic hellscape. Screaming matches and sobbing jags became a regular thing between us. Cat had a breakdown that required hospitalization, and I'd become quietly suicidal. Although our personal dysfunctions and previous traumas played significant roles in that decline, the pervasive threat of violence exacerbated every flaw and scar we possessed. The quiet periods between nearby beatings, neighborly threats, occasional robberies (our apartment was burgled and vandalized once while we were at work, and our doors were kicked in twice more while we were at home), nighttime gunshots, and the legacies of someone else's bad night — bloodstains, ejected property, broken teeth on the pavement — held the constant promise that some new and gruesome reminder of our situation would inevitably appear.

Cat says now that she's blocked most of that period from her memory. I wish I could. I still relive those days every time I hear raised voices nearby, and shift into fighting postures whenever someone near me begins to show his ass in potentially dangerous ways. Although I've turned those scars into fictions, my escape from that situation hasn't helped me put those days behind me. After all, you're reading about them now.

It wasn't just the violence, though that was certainly bad enough. It was the ever-present roaches, who'd run from one apartment to the other whenever someone bug-bombed an apartment, then reappear by the time the fog had cleared. It was hot summers with no air conditioning because we were all too poor to afford one, and cold winters that the ancient steam radiators barely touched. It was the constant reek of Cat's cigarettes and the urine from our six unneutered cats. It was being on a first-name basis with the cops who'd come to clean up the literal bloody messes in your building, yet knowing those same cops might arrest you next (as almost happened to me during one especially absurd incident). It was working two jobs (or more) while selling blood plasma down the street and yet *still* being behind on the rent and bills. It was knowing that your neighbors were drug dealers, one of whom pitied me so much he offered me a job. It was living near violent drunks, like the local terror Wild Bill, who I never met personally but often *heard*. It was sharing space with folks who had dangerous mental illnesses, like the schizophrenic guy downstairs who tried to burn our building down because the voices from his radio told him we were demons. Worst of all was the fear that we would never get out of that situation alive. Thirty years after escaping it anyway, I still draw much of my righteous fury from the fact that we were fortunate to do so. That era lasted just three years for us. For many people, it's their lifetime.

Knowing how badly that situation scarred us, I cannot forgive the employers who pay their people so little that an environment like that is all they can afford. I won't accept banks charging overdraft fees that wipe out a poor person's bank account before that person's next paycheck clears. I don't see "the poor" as some abstract group of losers who deserve to be punished for perceived laziness; after all, I was one of them even as I worked two jobs, played in three bands, and began the writing career that eventually got me out of there. I can't forget that some of the people screaming in those nearby rooms were children, and that domestic carnage is the only reality some of them will ever know. Cat, Jae and I were adults, and those days left us all with lingering wounds; to have been a child in that hellscape, possibly even in the same room while those beatings occurred, maybe being the recipient of said beatings... that thought leaves me feeling cold and hateful about humanity as a whole.

And that's one of the tragedies of Charlie and Fuckinbitch: While this in no way excuses his behavior, Charlie himself was a victim of brutality. I wouldn't be surprised if Fuckinbitch stayed with him so long, and she endured so much abuse from him before she finally left his ass, because she saw the scarred man Charlie was behind those swinging fists and venomous words. If perhaps she'd tried to save him before saving herself became more important than rescuing a person she must have, at one time, loved.

Charlie, as he proudly told us, was an ex-Marine. Given his age at the time, he was probably a Vietnam veteran. Even if Charlie never saw combat, the training of that era brutalized recruits so badly that it created abusers by default. I broke off two friendships with college buddies who came back from Basic Training and promptly kicked the shit out of their girlfriends, and Cat and I nearly shared our apartment with a lesbian couple whose military-vet half later beat her partner into a hospital bed. My own dad came back from Vietnam with a head full of snakes, and although he never beat my mother, my sister and I were not quite so fortunate. "Good old-fashioned discipline" was still a thing in them-there days, especially among poor folks, military vets, and people like my father who joined the military to avoid the draft and poverty. I never heard Charlie's life story, but between the things he said when we weren't at odds, and the things I puzzled out from his drunken rages about "MAH house" and "MAH business," he was probably raised as a rural Southern boy whose masculinity demanded violent responses to every challenge.

Charlie never took a swing at me, nor me at him. It was a very near thing, though. Given both of our tempers, our relative ages and sizes, and the fact that both of us knew how unpredictable real violence can be, that would have been a mutual-destruction pact and we both knew it. I was younger and bigger; Charlie was older and meaner. Both of us saw No Prisoners written in each other's eyes, and so we shared a mutually disgusted form of respect for the other man's capacity for violence. Ironically, Charlie told me who'd robbed and vandalized our apartment: our downstairs neighbors, who sold our goodies for drug money and trashed our home because they were mad at us for calling the cops on one of them while he was beating his girlfriend and kids. Also ironically, we got our landlord to kick out both the downstairs neighbors and, the following year, Charlie himself. "It's them or us," we told the landlord, and both times he chose us because we had jobs and we always — late or not — paid our rent.

That's another thing I recall about those days: Our building was a haven for folks on public assistance and military pensions. Bored, poor, angry, and constantly in pain, our revolving cast of neighbors were prisoners of society's lower ebbs. That pain, resentment, and implacable hopelessness breed violence of all kinds. It's easy, from the outside, to judge the ways such people behave. When you're one of those people, though, or when you have been one of them, those behaviors seem as rational as any other aspect of your world.

Little about those days feels rational. Consistent, yes, but not rational. We were consistently poor, consistently anxious, and consistently waiting for the next round of Rock 'Em Sock 'Em Neighbors. Whether it involved domestic battery, drunk guys in the halls, or a fistfight in the street or in the alley behind the building, there always was a next round. When people are that consistently suffering, bored, and angry, shit inevitably runs downhill... and all of us — even Wild Bill, Charlie, landlords, drug dealers, and the cops — were downhill as far as that neighborhood was concerned.

(Cookie, the dealer who offered me a job, lived in a "vacant" building at the other end of our block. No heat, no electricity, no rent if I recall correctly, but they somehow managed to have running water even though it was always cold. Named for his day-job at a local food court's snack shop, Cookie was a soft touch who kept a small collection of girls and guys squatting with him. As far as I'm aware, he wasn't fucking any of them; he'd complained to me about that on several occasions. I enjoyed hanging out with Cookie and his tribe, if only because they were nice to me. Most of my college friends had moved out of Richmond by that time, I was between bands at the time, and I'd grown sick enough of Domestic Abuse Central and our own family spats that I didn't go home unless

I absolutely had to. The fact that a basement-level pot dealer squatting celibate in a house with no heat or electricity felt sorry for me tells you just how bad things were back then.)

On first appearances, Domestic Abuse Central didn't look that bad. A twelve-unit red brick building at the very edge of Richmond's Fan District, it wasn't falling apart in ways you could see. The landlord cleaned the rooms after each resident departed, and we always had heat even if it didn't do much to defang those nasty Richmond winters. Our previous apartment, where the heating oil ran out before the end of every month, was worse in terms of physical space. When we first moved in, the building seemed to us like a step up from our last two homes: a patched-together conversion with dodgy construction, and a brownstone hotbox perched near an intersection where three brawl-happy redneck bars converged. As Cat and I soon learned, however, that cleaner, more solid building occupied a block of low-rent and sometimes vacant demi-slums. Worse, our landlord had a weakness for hard-luck misfits, a taste for down-low rough trade, or (as we suspected) both. The first part seemed like a good idea at the time; during our three-year stay, our neighbors included a drag-queen couple across the hall; a trans Goth girl who moved into Charlie's place after his eviction (and who provided my introduction to the music of Diamanda Galas); the aforementioned dude with schizophrenia; a bunch of people on public assistance; and a Black medical resident who kept a low profile in that rather... shall we say, "traditional Southern neighborhood." Such people still need somewhere to live, and of the many flaws we would discover about our landlord, bigotry was not among them as far as we could tell. Although married, said landlord was so obviously queer that Cat and I actually considered his apparent sexuality a plus. Trouble is, he liked bad boys, especially ones who weren't so attached to their supposedly straight identity that they would decline an opportunity to pay their rent with something other than cash. As a result, many of our neighbors had criminal records... sometimes, as we learned the hard way, for valid reasons.

During our years in Domestic Abuse Central, around a dozen of our neighbors (Charlie included) got arrested and spent time in jail. Two of them robbed us, two others kicked in our doors, and over a dozen of them threatened us on numerous occasions. At least one was dealing crack and bragging about it around the building; that habit dropped him into the ICU after a gang broke into his place and beat him nearly to death with baseball bats. One neighbor got shot to death by his wife's brother after that impending corpse caught them trying to move her stuff out of the apartment. One, as I mentioned earlier, tried to burn the building down with all of us inside. Many neighbors eventually departed without fanfare, often leaving most of their stuff behind to fill the trash bins in the alley out back. And then there were the drunken parties, the arguments, the fights, the beatings, the screaming matches that Cat and I contributed to ourselves, any of which could erupt at any hour down the hall or on the next floor or right above or below your bed. We saved Jae from a boyfriend who tried to choke and rape her one evening — the incident that finally got all three of us to beg and borrow enough money to move the fuck out of that cesspit. Yeah, the building was in more-or-less okay repair. Its human contents were a very different tale.

Charlie, in that building, was the rule. We were the exception. And after a few months living there, Cat and I knew it. So did almost everybody else. Part of the seething violence in my personality back then was my response to earlier traumas; a growing part of it, however, came from self-protection and the protection of my wife. When surrounded by would-be predators, after all, the sanest response involves acting like you'll eat them first. After enough time and pressure, at least in my case, it stopped being an act. One of the reasons I despised Charlie so deeply, and still recall him now when most of the names I knew back then have faded, is because I began to see his outline in my mirror. As much as I pity the man he must have been, I can't forgive him for that reflection... and I won't let myself forget it, either.

I doubt Charlie's still alive. The way he looked when our paths crossed for the last time, he was probably dead before the 1990s ended. Hell, he seemed half-dead thirty-five years ago, animated more by spite and bitterness than by any affection for the sad semblance of life he led. Charlie was a relic of that particularly Southern hardscrabble existence — the kind immortalized in country songs and macho fiction, prized by people who don't have to live it or live with it when the music ends. He walked slow, and often stumbled. His limbs and back curled in obvious constant pain. His face was a crumpled road map of bad decisions. Charlie's voice, when sober, held that Southern lilt I learned to hate even though I have a bit of it myself; drunk, that voice bore the grating bitterness of lost causes and cheap shots of whiskey. He once mentioned that he "worked twelve hours a day playing pool"; if so, he was *very* bad at it. Whatever money he made went down his throat and eventually wound up in his fists. That dude led a miserable life. And as we all know, misery loves to share.

It still haunts me that my eventual response to the beatings upstairs involved exasperated searches for the broom we kept near our bed, a few bangs on the ceiling, and shared "jokes" about the victim of those beatings. When those nighttime beatdowns finally ended, and the worst things we'd hear from upstairs involved a drunken Charlie muttering to himself as he stumbled into bed, we assumed that Fuckinbitch had finally had enough, found the escape hatch, and left Charlie behind for good.

For a while, we could sleep most nights. Charlie's predilection for 3:00 a.m. punch-ups didn't extend to most of our neighbors, thank gods. His heavy-footed lurching notwithstanding, the noise upstairs became something we could live with.

And *then*...

The climax of our relationship with Charlie came one sunny afternoon. Cat and I had just returned from the Laundromat with bundles of clothes when we heard screams from upstairs.

Not "just" screams. Horror-movie stuff. The kind that hackle the hairs on the backs of your arms simply by recalling them over three decades later. The kind you never, *ever* forget. A woman shrieking like she was being murdered with a rusty hacksaw. Cat grabbed the phone as I flew up the goddamned stairs, her fingers punching 911 the way I longed to punch Charlie's face. Cat yelled at me to stay inside, but I think I yelled back that the screaming woman might not live until the cops arrived. From the sound and tenor of those shrieks, I might even have been right.

I also wanted to kill Charlie.

As in, for real wanted to kill him.

It wasn't Fuckinbitch screaming. This woman's voice sounded younger and more terrified. Where his departed wife sounded resigned to the whole situation even as she cried for help, this person howled in surprise as well as pain.

The screaming stopped when I hammered on the door.

Charlie opened the door.

He was buckling his pants. His shirt was still open, a dirty undershirt beneath it.

I'll spare you the volleys of masculine posturing on both sides. I threatened Charlie. He threatened back. We each dared each other to step over the threshold between the hallway and his apartment. Neither one of us was stupid enough to cross that line. I doubt either of us would have walked away under our own power if we had been. Somewhere in that verbal tempest, I recall him trying to convince me that "My old lady came back home, and she's just really drunk." I recall replying that his story was bullshit. We both postured. We both yelled. Spit and testosterone filled the air. I've had several close calls with mortal violence over the years, but that confrontation ranks near the top of that list. Finally, realizing that he wasn't going to step outside, knowing the cops were on their way, and not wanting to get myself arrested, I backed off. "Whatever's going on in there," I think I might have said, "It needs to *stop*."

I think he muttered "*Pussy*," as he closed the door and I headed down the stairs.

The cops arrived a few minutes later. Charlie tried the "*MAH house*," and "*MAH business*" line, but the cops were having none of it. Cat said the 911 operator heard the screaming in the background of the call. The cops beat on Charlie's door with a nightstick until he opened it. From what we heard through the ceiling, they beat on Charlie, too. Charlie got back some of what he'd been giving out that day.

By the time the cops hauled Charlie out in handcuffs, most of our neighbors had opened their doors, aware that shit had gone more serious than usual. We had ours open, too. We'd heard the stretcher and EMTs going upstairs to secure the now-weeping woman, who'd remained quiet and unseen while Charlie and I screamed at each other in his doorway. As Cat and I stood in our doorway, the EMTs brought the woman, on the stretcher, down the stairs, past our door, and down the next flight of stairs to the ambulance below. We'd never seen Fuckinbitch, but this clearly was not her. Though older than us, the no-longer-screaming woman was a hard-ridden thirty- or forty-something, not the elderly woman we'd heard upstairs before. This woman's face was bruised and puffy. I recall smears of blood, but that might be memory embellishing an already awful sight. I tried not to stare. I suspect Cat was looking more closely than I did. I could afford to look away from the damage done to that woman on the stretcher. Cat had no such luxury.

Then they hauled Charlie out in handcuffs. His face *was* bloody — I recall that vividly. The cops had done what I'd wanted to do. Say what you will about state-sanctioned violence, it's occasionally satisfying. His steps stumbled. His shirt was still open, and I think his pants were unbuckled again. Charlie seemed dazed. He didn't look at us. One cop did, though. In one of those *Oh dude, you seriously did not just fucking do that* moments, he turned to us and said, quite clearly, "Thank you for calling us."

You

Fucking

Dumbass

Cop.

Because of *course*, Charlie heard him. And of *course*, Charlie got out on bail. And of *course*, two days later, Charlie came storming back up those stairs, free to do whatever the fuck he wanted to do. This time, *he* was the one throwing himself at the door. *He* was the guy hammering on a steel fire door between the hallways and apartments. *He* was bellowing, "*That's RIGHT, motherfuckers, I'm BACK!*" and daring me to open the door so he could finish what we started. When Cat and I refused to respond to his attack, he hauled himself up the stairs, opened his own door, and began jumping up and down on the floor so hard he literally broke our ceiling. Charlie screamed threats, and stomped and jumped until he wore himself out.

By that time, we'd called the landlord and told him what Charlie had done.

"It's him or us," we repeated.

I suspect the landlord was madder about our ceiling than he was about Charlie beating that woman to a pulp in his apartment. He certainly made it clear that he was fed up with us, as well. Why couldn't we just mind our own business like the other tenants did?

He didn't say those words. We heard them anyway.

The coda to the Charlie tale arrived a month or two after his eviction. By then, the woman who later turned me on to Diamanda Galas (through our ceiling, around 4:00 a.m.; at least she understood tradition) had occupied the place Charlie used to call "*MAH house*" until he'd lost the right to live there. It was night, and dark, and Cat and I were reading or watching TV or something in the living room when we heard the familiar drunk muttering and shuffle-stumble steps of Charlie in the hall outside our door.

Cat tried to talk me out of going out there to confront him. By the time I proved I was too stubborn for our own good, he'd gone up the stairs and tried his keys in his old apartment's door.

As I crept up to the top of the stairs, wrangling with myself about what to say or do when I confronted him, drunk Charlie unbuckled his pants and took a piss in the hallway.

I was too appalled to shout.

"Oh, my fucking God," I growled, or something along those lines. "Are you *really* doing what I think you're doing?"

Charlie mumbled about not being able to open the door. "My key don't work, and I need to take a piss."

"That," I replied, my voice thick with disgust, "is because you don't fucking live here anymore. Remember? You got kicked out."

Charlie finished pissing, looked at the floor, and seemed to realize what he'd just done. He swayed, belting his pants closed, muttering excuses so low and slurred that I didn't really catch what he was saying.

"Just get *out*, you fucking gross disgrace." I stepped toward him. "Get. The fuck. *Out*."

I'd been standing between Charlie and the stairway. As he shuffled forward, so ripped he could barely walk, our nemesis grumbled something between an excuse, an apology, and probably a threat. I stepped aside to let him pass. He didn't make a move at me. I didn't make a move at him. Clutching the banister, the soused wreckage of our former upstairs neighbor hauled himself down the stairs. I descended behind him, slow and careful, ready to deck him if he took a swing, half-hoping he'd faceplant down the stairs, half-dreading the mess I'd have to deal with if he did.

I was not a nice person in those days.

That time and place had little room for kindness.

Reaching the bottom of the stairs, Charlie fumbled at the front door.

I stood on the stairwell, halfway between the ground floor and our apartment on the second floor.

He said nothing to me. I said nothing to him.

The last I saw of Charlie was the front door closing. The light reflecting off the windowpanes wiped out the sight of him lumbering toward the sidewalk. By the time I got to the second-story balcony to make certain he was gone, Charlie was a black shape under the streetlamp, moving off into the night.

His ghost lingers with me, though. He comes to visit every time I hear raised voices nearby, especially since one of our neighbors down the street has a Southern accent, a fondness for beer, and a tendency to belt out rebel yells when he's feeling ripe.

It's poetic, I guess, to witness someone who played a starring role in the worst years of my life reduced to pissing himself while locked out of the apartment from which I'd had him evicted. Seeing Charlie stumble down those stairs, though, I didn't feel triumphant or vindicated. Only sad.

Charlie scarred a lot of lives. Some of the deepest of those scars, though, were his own.

THE GREEN TUNNEL

Together we stand rooted on the edge, staring off with perfect clarity toward infinite horizons.

You can't download this. You can't watch it on YouTube or hear it on Spotify. The magic of technology can't share or capture this. The only way to experience it is to get sweaty and leave your comfort zone, strapping your life on your back and taking on the Green Tunnel in the flesh.

Hikers call it "the Green Tunnel" because that's how it feels inside: a vast corridor of trees and dirt and vegetation, snaking along the Appalachian Mountains, tucked between towns like some pocket dimension of incomprehensible age. You won't see it from your car window on the Interstate, though trailheads flicker on the edges of rural roads. In settlements along the way, gamey specters drift in and out of the Tunnel's course — matty-haired and earth-redolent, hauling weather-beaten packs buckled to their bodies with arcane arrays of straps. Hyper and I joined that vagabond horde a few years back; now, on the cusp of afternoon, we rise from misty wilderness and stare out speechless at the rolling scene.

Humps of earth and greenery slope up from cloud-wrapped eternity. Light-jewels of distant towns sparkle on the landscape. A pearly sheen glows across the contours of the sky, ringing rainbows in silent symphonies below. "Wow," breathes Hyper, shrugging stiffness from her shoulders. Silence. And then again, "Wow."

If I seem hyperbolic here, it's because no simple words do justice to the sheer magnificence of humping your way up a mountainscape in time to catch the last bits of afternoon clinging to a late-April sky. Hyper and I have been on the Trail for three weeks now, shedding what little fat we'd acquired and replacing it with lean tanned muscle. I've never been truly *out* of shape in my life, but twice-a-week gym routines won't give you *this* kind of build. As for Hyper, she's got the glow and eagerness of the track star she was in high school. Scraping the edge of our fourth decades, we could each run rings around kids half our age. Still, by the time we hit this clearing, not far from the mountain's peak, we're both ready to drop our packs and call it a day.

Not yet, though...

"I wish," she says, "that we could share this view with everyone on earth."

I nod. "Maybe if they could see it," I add, "folks would spend less time in front of TVs and computer screens, and more time doing shit that *matters*."

It's an old gripe of ours — one we've shared since we met up in REI almost ten years ago. It's one reason we've been friends. A big reason we'd split up this past year from the folks who'd tried to tie us down. Hyper and I both share a draw toward the woods, and we're impatient with people who think life comes over the counter in a box.

The night she'd called to tell me she was leaving Greg, Hyper's voice had held a spark I hadn't heard from her in years. My own voice might have held the same quality a few months later when I told her that Veronica and I had given up trying to make things work. When she showed up in her Amazing Flying Pumpkin Truck — a huge old Ford painted a grotesque shade of orange — to help me pack up my things, Hyper's grin had flashed like Arctic sunshine. "Ready to join the dating pool again?" she'd asked.

"Not really." I wasn't. Dating sucked.

"Oh, good," she'd replied. "Then we can just fuck."

"Huh?"

"Jerry," she told me, stepping close, "we both blew a really good thing by getting married to people who weren't right for us. I don't know what that means for us long-term, but right now..." She grabbed my shirt. "I want to do things to you that I've been thinking about for *years*."

And we did.

And oh, God — she was right. We really *did* have a good thing going on between us.

Hyper's the kind of friend you knock back beers with after shitty days at work. The kind who'll challenge you to a good-natured arm-wrestling contest — and the loser buys the next round. The sort of powerhouse that either drives guys wild or drives 'em away. She and I had seen each other through more failed relationships than God. When we finally hopped the Just Friends barricade, we both realized what we'd been missing all those years.

And so — once we'd both hashed out our respective divorces, set aside vacation time, and recognized that neither of us was "just fucking" when said fucking involved each other — Hyper and I dusted off our gear, replaced a few items that had gone creaky with disuse, and did something we'd talked about for almost as long as we'd been friends: We hit the Appalachian Trail with plans to thru-hike it from Georgia to Maine.

Three weeks into a five-month trip, we're having the time of our lives.

Hiking and camping can be an acid test to love and friendship. Paired with the wrong people (as both of us had been before), outdoor trips can become nightmares of resentment and complaint. Paired with the right people, though, a long hike becomes communion — a sharing of selves and memories that deepen more the further you get from what most folks call "real life." The aching muscles and primal smells and meager food and green monotony carve away the working-week façade. Even with top-shelf gear, you recall what it's like to be an animal.

Most people can't handle that. We can.

We'd gone rogue from the white-blazed Trail sometime early yesterday. Following deer-trails and renegade campsites, we'd decided to literally go off the beaten path. Crisscrossing the edges of the usual course, we'd bushwhacked our way to dead ends, rotting cabins, hunting blinds, and old moonshine stills gone rusty with age. Each night, we'd lay down camp, curl up in zipped-together sleeping bags, and roll in one another's musk. Four days out from our last decent bath, we smell like raw earth, raw sex, and all other good things in life.

"Wow," she sighs again, gazing out across the empty space. The cliff in front of us curves down and out, a steep slope riding into the fog and trees below. A faint purple spot darkens the haze near a ledge of the cliff, just before another sheer drop to the forest at its foot.

The cliff reminds me faintly of Devil's Tower, a tourist spot in North Carolina. According to local legend, Native American boys used to climb the cliff as a manhood rite. If they turned back, they weren't yet considered ready to become men; if they slipped, they didn't *survive* long enough to be men. I have no idea whether or not the story's true. But as we gaze off down the slope, I see mind's-eye phantoms of Cherokee ghosts struggling for a peak they'll never attain.

Hyper snuggles close to me, and I keep such thoughts to myself.

"Still glad we did this," she asks.

"Gladder than I've been about almost anything in my life."

"Me too," she agrees. "But I'm hungry. Let's make camp and have some chow."

As we pick out a spot and break out our gear, Hyper and I follow silent rhythms. Our first few tries at making camp — like the first few times you share sex with a new partner — soon gave way to a comfortable flow. Hardly needing words, we now select a good site (smooth, no bug-nests, relatively flat but not in a low spot that might flood) and then fall into the habitual tasks. I clear away sticks and stones. Hyper rigs a spot to hang our food. We pop the tent together and rearrange a ring of stones that had clearly once been a fire pit.

As I unpack the cooking gear, she walks up behind me, runs her fingers through my tangled hair, then ducks off to score some firewood. I hear her boots crack off through the underbrush.

"Hey, Scruffy," she calls softly, using my Trail name, a few minutes later. "Check *this* out."

By that point, the daylight's beginning to shade into nightfall. The thick tree-cover screens out most of the remaining sun, so when I rise to follow her voice I snag the small red flashlight I carry in my pack.

A faint deer-trail slopes up away from our campsite, winding upward toward the mountain peak. The official Trail runs close by, but our spot's tucked off to one side — close enough for safety, far enough for privacy.

Now, normally the Appalachian Trail hugs the tops of each mountain, sliding across the peaks like some back-snapped serpent. That's not true, though, everywhere. In some places, the blazed Trail slides away from the peak itself, hugging the summit but leaving the top alone. On this mountain, a dense crop of old-growth trees crowns the peak. Thick thorny underbrush congregates around those trees, dressed with flashes of bright purple flowers. A soft plushy scent, like fresh ground beef yet not exactly meaty, drifts nearby.

"Hey, Hyper — where'd you go?" My voice feels muffled in the cool humid air. I don't shout (that just feels *rude* in the wilderness) but my voice should carry more than it seems to do.

"Here. Over here." Her voice sounds muffled too. It's weird, the ways in which woods and atmosphere can play hell with acoustics. Stepping carefully around the briars, I follow the sound of the woman I love.

Yeah, it feels odd to say that: *The woman I love.* After V-Ron and I had split up, I figured I'd burnt out every shred of poetry in my soul. Much as I hate to admit it to myself... and, to be blunt, haven't yet admitted it to *her*... I fell in love with Hyper years ago. Back when Veronica and I were waltzing through hot ashes, I'd been kicking myself on a regular basis for choosing her over Hyper. What the *fuck*, I'd asked myself through many restless nights, had I been *thinking*? Until she'd made the first move, though, I'd locked Hyper up in a vault labeled "Friendship." Months later, it's still kind of awkward opening that door, even from the inside.

The Green Tunnel rustles with a rising wind. There's more than a hint of rain in its bite. "Hey, Hyper," I repeat, "it's starting to feel stormy. We'd better grab some wood and finish setting up."

"Yeah," she agrees, somehow suddenly next to me, her arms cradling a wealth of kindling. "Still, though — check *this* out."

She points up to a gathering of stones: smooth, configured, wound up in purple-flowered briars. The trees on either side give them room, as if — and I don't know *why* this occurs to me — frightened of what those stones might say, and yet fascinated by their possibility of speech.

They don't seem random, these stones. They look *purposeful*, as if huddled for some awful judgment.

"If I didn't know better — and I'm not sure I *do*," she whispers, "I'd swear someone *built* stuff up here."

"We're on top of a mountain in the middle of nowhere." Still, I think she might be right.

"People build weird shit on mountains all the time." Hyper's voice remains soft, her words half-lost in the deepening wind.

By now, the clack of branches sounds like dancing bones overhead. Again, I don't know why that image occurs to me. The Trail, to me, is usually a place of peace. This spot, though, creeps me out.

Hyper's freckled face slips into that grin of hers I adore. The breeze picks at the frazzled remnants of her braid, making it tic like a snake-tail running down her back. Her rich trail-scent blooms with mischief. "I think" she says, "there's graffiti on those stones."

Flicking on the flashlight beam, I slide it across one grim stone face. She's right. There's lettering. Nothing I can read, but it combines spray paint with age-weathered etchings. Old and new, shaming the stone.

"God," I mutter. "Some people are such *dicks*."

Hyper shakes her head. "Yep. Losers. I wonder what it was."

"Probably some old Native American stuff. Or a Civil War fortification." You see that kind of shit all over the Appalachians: mountain-man monuments, hunting lodges fallen to ruins. Civil War bunkers and pre-White Incursion sites, jumbled up with more recent additions by artistic hikers, hermits, and just plain weirdos. Most of it's pretty far off the Trail; every now and then, though, you'll find something closer to the beaten path. Since we're slightly off that path to start with, it's not really that unlikely.

See now, I know what you're thinking: *Get the fuck out of there*. Yeah, I've seen the movies. Don't camp near spooky stones.

Thing is, by that point, we don't have much choice. With night coming on and the wind picking up, we'd have to break down our campsite, re-pack our gear, and head off down the Trail in the dark... very probably in the rain as well. *Not* an option if we can help it. You want a horror movie? Try busting up a campsite and blundering around on a dark mountaintop as a storm blows in. Who needs Freddy Kruger when Mother Nature can kill you just as dead?

So yeah — while I admit that the place kinda creeps me out, I keep my mouth shut and nod back to the campsite. "We can check it out in the morning," I tell Hyper. "We should set up our stuff before the rain comes in."

"Good idea." She nods, stepping carefully but noisily through the brush. "Let's see if we can get some fire going before that storm."

That *meat-not-meat* scent rides on the breeze as I reach for some of the wood in her arms. Hyper grins again, handing some of her horde off to me.

"Hey Scruffy," she says softly. "Thanks."

"For what? For the wood?"

"For the You. Thanks for that."

"I'm just me."

"I like you."

"I like you, too."

I kiss Hyper's forehead and we take the wood back to the pit.

Thankfully, the rain holds off until after we've built a fire, had dinner, hung the food up away from our tent, and snuggled a bit by the fire. Heavy woodsmoke drowns the scent of those purple flowers up the hill. Which, I realize when it hits me, I'm good with.

"How ya doin', Scruff?" she asks me as I stretch out the kinks in my back. Sloshing a bit of filtered water around in our tiny cooking pot, Hyper cleans the dinner gear. Rolled sleeves flash the eagle-feather tats on her forearms. I've traced each design countless times with my fingertips. Hell, I was *with* her when she got the second one — the design she got after she'd dumped Greg. I haven't been inked myself just yet... but I'm thinking about it.

"I'm good," I tell her, "Hyper." Her birth-name's Hilary, but no one — on or off the Trail — ever calls her that. She picked up her name in high school, where she'd run circles around jock-boys who thought they were God's gift to girls. Even now, she shakes the sloshing pot around with fierce energy. Three weeks in the wilderness hasn't calmed her down. I'm not sure much *can*. "As usual," I continue, "you wore me out."

Hyper barks her trademark laugh. Something probably runs off in the woods at the sound. "You poor thing," she replies, "I hope you're not *too* worn out."

I lean over her and prove that I'm not. She tastes like smoke, and sweat, and rehydrated chicken with rice. I savor that sensation.

Two things about the mountains:

First off, when it gets dark, it gets *DARK*. Dark in *ways-city-folks-don't-understand*-level Dark. Unless you've got a decent moon that night, the only other light is star-shine... and if you're in the woods, the tree-cover blocks that light. Darkness on that level permeates your world. It surrounds you like a physical thing. You breathe it — just one more scent in a realm washed through with scents. Unless you're out in the open, it gets dark long before the sun goes down. In the Green Tunnel, you move through twilight as a matter of course. Full sunlight becomes the exception, not the rule. And as for the electric haze that fills any modern settlement, it's gone. Stand on top of a mountain as the sun goes down, watching the gleam of distant towns and cities, and you'll realize just how small we really are.

Secondly, it's *cold*. In spring, it can still fall below freezing at night. And while the days might grow sticky-hot near high noon, the thin air, raw earth and tree cover keep things moist on the East Coast and dry further out west. Without the heat-trapping properties of paved civilization, Mother Nature's curves stay cool by day and get downright cold after dark.

By the time wet drops of rain start to catch in our hair, the wind's picked up and the trees sway, drunken, in its pull. Branches clack their primal tongues as we gather up our gear, douse the fire, and stir the ashes black. Stripping off our boots and socks, we climb inside the tent, bring them in, and pull the zipper closed. Hollow patters on the roof and walls let us know that the storm has arrived.

Shivering with chill, we peel off our layers and slide against each other's skins. Pebbled flesh warms beneath our hands. Our lips brush against each other, then open, then go wide. Our own tongues catch the rhythm of the trees outside, tangle like vines, and seek each other's heat.

The sky cracks open with shattering light.

The answering thunderclap shakes the whole mountain.

"Holy *crap*," she whispers. I agree.

A wind-borne slash of rain bows the tent's fabric. I'd swear I hear the plastic poles creak.

Too damn close, something big cracks, breaks, and falls. Brittle things smash beneath its weight.

"Somebody," Hyper says, voice hushed, "is trying to remind us who's boss."

"She's made her point."

She didn't stop there.

Here's another one of those things you forget when you're in a nice safe house: Mother Nature's *BIG*. Bigger than us. Bigger than our gadgets and technology. When Mama ain't happy, ain't *nobody* happy. And while I can't know her mind when the storm hits our mountain, my guess is she's in a mood tonight.

Our tent ripples and snaps, its nylon sides billowing from the force of the wind. The poles bow with alarming strain. Rain pounds the mountaintop, stirring up a heady wild smell. Mud and ashes mulch into gray burnt smells blending, in my nose, with a wet-nylon bite.

"Wow," I mutter. "Glad we're not out *there*."

Flickers and blasts rock the sky in dazzling fractures of darkness and bright. Trees scream with enduring agony. Everything that can run has gone to ground, huddling — like us — in a state of terse amazement.

Skin to skin, Hyper and I wrap ourselves together. The sleeping bag suddenly feels too small to contain us. We shuck the bag, and cling, and burn. Muddy nails and unbrushed teeth dig past flesh and draw each other's blood.

Inside and outside, it's a storm we'll never forget.

# # #

Somehow, the tent holds.

In time, as they do, all storms pass.

"Didn't use the condoms, did we?"

"Uh..." I think about it. "Nope."

"Y'know," says Hyper, "I'm okay with that."

Despite the cold that snaps through me at her words, I think I might be, too.

Neither one of has used the L-word yet. Not seriously, with regards to Us... whatever Us is.

I suspect we've grown too wary to talk about it. Words like *love* get brittle when they've been burned. So in the dark, we roll together and slip back into the sleeping bags, ripe with the smell of Nature's kiss.

I keep kidding myself that the poetry I used to write had run off and died when V-Ron and I called it quits. I'd felt it cowering in dark corners of my head for years, like some kid beaten past the point of tears. With Hyper, though, that poor kid's been sticking his head up more and more often. He's not quite ready to sing just yet, but at least he's remembered how to speak to me.

As for Hyper, she doesn't say much along those lines to begin with. Feelings are something she *has*, not something she talks about. At times, when I back away from asking, I try to read her face and body language. Sometimes that's like reading Newsweek, and sometimes it's like reading Braille.

The dark has taken over now. Raindrops rustle down the tent, translucent vagabonds on a downward trail. *Wow — this woman's really turned me inside-out*. I hope she can't read the scares blooming in my head when I realize that.

As the realization settles in and we snuggle deeper into ourselves, I kiss her greasy hair and realize it's okay.

This time out, it'll all be okay.

I'm hungry.

A growl-gutted craving for something bare...

Naked walls paneled in dark smooth woods, a Brady Bunch lair gone bad. Silver implements sparkle across a white-clothed table, bright-spotted with red flowers of romance.

Cables drawn in sharp fixations bloom and open. Rose mouths crying for the sun. Pucker tight and then slide free. A course, of course. The road to blank fulfillment, wrapped in grease.

Light too spare to see by. Shadow-blank with lamentation. Reliquary blossoms quiver in the air.

Bright-synapse fires near the verge. Sliver-moon and meat perfume. Soft clenching between my jaws. Salt-slip of pink-white flavor red.

"He was hungry, so he ate himself."

I'm up.

Man, sometimes I hate dreams.

Listen to the rain hiss against the tight tent walls. Feel the curve of Hyper's back against my side.

In time, I fall back asleep, meat-perfume curling on the edges of my mind.

A warm breath in my ear. A whisper. "Hey."

A touch along my shoulder. A soft slide of fingertips.

A kiss on the back of my neck. Am I dreaming?

"Hey, Scruff. Get up."

Solid dark. Not even a hint of light. The sleeping bag rustles as I stir. Cold skates across bare skin, raising ripples in its wake.

"Huh?" An insight — the true gift of a witty mind. "Something outside the tent?" All I hear is her breath and the rustle of our bags.

Chilly fingers slide down to wrap around... "*Damn*, Hyper! Your hands are *cold*."

"All the better to wake you up with." Her voice glides warm and close to my ear. "C'mon, sleepyhead — get up."

"Not with *those* cold hands."

"I don't mean *that*," she replies. "At least, not yet. Let's go outside and dance."

Is this another dream? I'm not certain. Either way, she takes my hand and we crouch naked in the tiny tent. The zipper's growl seems especially loud in the all-but-silent night. Is it Hyper's fingers, or mine, that guide it open? Again, I'm not sure. Our skin prickles with the chilly rush of night. Knees popping, Hyper rise from the tent's doorway. She steps out, and so do I.

Outside our tent, the air trembles with pearlescent gloom. A faint shine illuminates the night. Chilly breeze stirs our hair, raising sheets of goosebumps across our flesh. I sense, more than see, Hyper's crazy grin. The cold mud, course with sticks and stones, slides against our feet. Wet sounds mark our progress as we leave our tent behind.

Something high above us shimmers, hazy constellations of uncanny luminescence. Looking up, I feel myself fall into the void. My feet stay rooted to the mud, but it seems as though some perverse gravity draws me upward without moving me at all. Vertigo spins through my guts, and I have to look down and away.

Hyper raises her hands to the sky, her nude skin glowing in the half-light. Eyes closed, she arcs her head back. Her ragged braid dangles to her waist, flicking restless as she starts to move. Her hips rock back and forth in slow-motion imitation of our dance beneath the storm.

I feel myself begin to move as well — not conscious but with pure instinct.

The night begins to sing.

It vibrates up through the ground, through my feet. A vast chorus, deep as valleys, deep as mines sunk underneath our world. Root-blind and shivering, it twines itself around my bones, a sound too low or high for mortal ears to hear. Hyper's head swivels in her neck, mouth open, a faint rumble swelling in her throat. Her hands reach for the hungry stars, crawling softly in time with the music.

Meat-perfume blossoms in the hazy air, sliding down my throat as I, too, begin to sway.

Our throats make no human sounds at all. But we *do* join the chorus as we dance.

As if standing outside myself, I see us bend and shimmer in the haze. Sweat blooms on once-chilly skins. Our heads hang back at incredible angles, our arms coiling like sunlight-shattered worms. The sounds bubbling from our throats seem to glisten in the air like slime, sounds given viscous and repugnant form. It's a dream again — it *must* be. We dance impossible things.

Sticky sounds draw me off from the eerie spectacle. I leave Hyper and myself behind, and slide noiseless to the edge of the cliff. Out past the edge, the sky still boils with pregnant clouds, their bellies torn by lightning wounds. Vertigo pulls me up and down at once, drawing my sensations in torturous directions. Back in school, I'd seen a picture in some old history book of a man being pulled apart by horses. Standing now at the edge of that cliff, I feel the way he must have felt.

A wordless scream boils up from nothingness inside.

Up the sides of the cliff, something shiny rolls across the sheer surface of the drop. Glistening balls of translucent slime, leaving slug-trail rivers in their wake. Each one larger than our tent, they roll *upward* on the steep stone. Away from gravity. Towards us. Shimmering ghost-boys made of tears.

Turning with immense effort from the cliff, I see Hyper and myself dancing near the tent.

At least, I *think* that tangle of limbs and mouths is us.

But there are too many limbs and too many mouths, and it seems to be eating itself.

And we have no faces, just bristling braids twined together like snakes.

And the stars draw me up into silent cold nothingness.

The red void sings to me.

# # #

"Jerry?"

Hyper's voice. Distant. Echoing. Alarmed. "*Jerry?*"

Fucking dreams...

Um...

Oh.

That's not good.

My legs aren't supposed to bend like that.

My arms are supposed to work. But they don't.

Purple flowers and meat-perfume.

Sharp rocks and my own shattered limbs.

When I wake up, this is gonna hurt like hell.

"Jerry? Holy fuck, where *are* you?" Hyper's voice holds *another* spark I've never heard from her before: brittle bright panic.

Somehow, that chills me deeper than what I see.

Soft luminescent haze gleams in morning twilight. Shimmering motes catch the early rising sun. Tangled purples flowers grow from sharp red stones.

The stones on the ledge where I landed when I fell.

I'd like to think that's plant-juice spattered on the stones. Somehow, though, I don't think it is.

I really want to wake up.

Except I *don't*. Not really.

Hyper's voice floats on a haze of empty space, high above me, too far beyond to see.

I *do* see something else, though.

It's not good.

Plants shouldn't grow out of your chest.

Vines shouldn't burrow into your arms and legs.

Purples flowers shouldn't inhale when you try to breathe.

Meat-smell perfume and the scent of unwashed man.

And blood — yeah, *lots* of blood.

Try to call out.

Instead, I sing.

Without words, without breath.

Sounds vibrate through my bones, grimly wrestling with the first dull seeds of pain.

"*JERRY! C'mon, motherfucker, where ARE you?*" Hyper's voice edges over into rage shot through with fear rushing swiftly towards terror. "Don't make me look..." She doesn't finish the sentence, but a vaguely Hyper-shaped darkness appears on the cliff's edge high overhead.

I can hear her voice but the words are too faint to understand.

Then, pleading: "*Please*, Scruffy — tell me that's not *you* down there."

Around then, the pain digs in, a galaxy of spiders biting on my bones.

The song in my mouth grows sharp and mournful.

My mind drifts between my body and the air.

The pain should overwhelm my thoughts.

I wish it *would*.

But my mind hovers with perfect detached clarity, *aware* but not *submerged* in my horrific circumstances.

"Hang on, Scruffy. I'm gonna climb down there and get you out."

Don't, I try to say. But nothing works. Nothing but that damned demented song rising from my throat.

The Hyper-shape disappears above me. The purple plants rustle on my limbs. I try to close my eyes... but, damn it all, I still *see*, as if I'm a prisoner stuck watching some shitty horror flick where I can't take my eyes from the screen.

I'm naked, of course. My skin glows bright with vivid red paint. It's *too* red, though, *too* vivid to be real. This is a dream. Another fucking dream. Oh, good.

I'm ready to wake up now.

Really.

"No fucking cell reception here." Hyper's voice again, moving through the mist. And again, I try to warn her off. There's nothing here she can do. But then she's on the edge and moving down, barefoot, dressed in a sweatshirt and cargo pants, her hands and feet grasping for holds on the steep cliffside. "Hang on, Scruffy," she repeats. "I'm coming down."

Quicksilver anguish swells in my throat.

Trails. Glistening silver trails. As if left by giant slugs rising up the face of the cliff.

Hyper hits one of them.

Fumbles.

Slips.

Hangs in the air.

For an endless instant.

Falls.

She cracks open like a piñata filled with blood.

Her limbs shatter in impossible designs.

We both try to scream. Neither can.

But the purple flowers sing their meat-perfume aria as vines dig into her skin.

We lock eyes in awful clarity.

Then, together, helpless, we also join their song.

Rooted, endless, to a ledge lined with broken bones and flowers, our bodies quiver with lost voices and green thoughts.

And above us both, the haze darkens, and the rain begins again.

SHAKARAH AND THE RED WHEEL

My ship is doomed.

I know it already. Before the sharp grapples from the blood-sailed ship hit our hull, I realize we are doomed. Shakarah — the "shark-herders" of the Western Sea. Innards dangle from their masts; bones chime among their ratlines. Rotted wood creaks beneath brown-spattered sailcloth. Fins crest the wake behind them, waves broken here and there with hungry mouths. The crewmen of our brave vessel clutch their swords and knives, but I know the fight is over. Already, my feet feel the slick suck of blood and entrails not yet spilled. My sight-beyond sees sharks glutted on corpses not yet dead. I offer up sweet smiles to the scared men all around me; inside, though, I know they're right. We're doomed. I see the ship being taken before the grapples are secured.

And so, like any wise woman, I prepare.

Pack it down, I hear my mentor Jaelamare advise. Years gone, now, but still she speaks to me. *Pack away compassion and ride the Red Wheel through*. I cannot, though, withdraw so soon away from my companions. Strange as I am, they've been fair to me. I owe what comfort I can bear. There's Jaklyn, with his pale shadow of chin-fur and the eyes that try so hard not to follow me as I walk. He's shaking now and so I offer him what he's longed for — a deep kiss and quick slide of my skin against his rope-roughened hands. He tastes of courage-ale and last night's sleep. From deep in my belly, I offer up sparks of glowing heat. He'll need them when the shakarah come. Nearby, Bes swallows hard and tries not to think of jagged steel. I light my smile with a touch of sun, and he answers with a brave grin of his own. One by one, I touch them — some with fingers, some with smiles, all with love and hunger and life.

Were there time, I would offer more. I cannot save them, but I can give them kindness before the blades fall.

The shakarah have not come for me. While I expect that some sharp-eyed watchboy has spotted me by now, this prize was sighted long ago. I'm just another bit of cargo, one more passenger with which to turn those deep waves red. Still, I'm not blind to the kind of prey they imagine me to be. A woman dressed only in silver jewelry and unbound hair? Even now, I'm sure, they are tossing dice and making wagers about the brazen wench on the deck of my ship. Which one will take me first? How long until I scream? How long *can* I scream? How many times will I lash out with nails and teeth and fists before surrendering at last to far worse savagery? On such things, men bet their gold.

On such bets, I plan my escape... and perhaps our ship's salvation, too.

I won't pretend I'm not frightened. My belly twitches, my fingers clench. The future feels hungry-red to me. But as I learned so long ago, Life is no tender mistress. She takes us, willing or not, with soft and savage thrusts alike. We must either meet her willingly, embracing both the kisses and the teeth, or we will be ravaged, shredded, and destroyed. So yes, I'm terrified. To me, though, fear is euphoria. Without it, I feel only half-alive.

Beneath my breath, I begin to chant, invoking Vasara and the Red Wheel. The syllables lead me back across the waves. Through years spent training, tasked, and traveled, I return. As shafts bolt through the air to rake our decks, I ride the currents of my chanting home...

...*vaulting high with spring freshness, the Eldwald took me as her own. I strode into her darkness willingly. She claimed me without question, her mist gliding thick around my path, her briars catching on my simple dress. Gritty mud, ripe with stones, helped me feel each step.*

Beneath each deep and labored breath, a prayer:

I the acorn, we the tree

Red seeds set the dayfolk free

Turn terror into ecstasy

Thus, I set my bound soul free.

Five days, it'd been like this. Alone with just my words and songs. An exile searching for a dream that had been wrapped, by others, into terror-tales. Tales of savage and remorseless cults. Cults of flesh, where hunger was the only law.

I'd ached to find out if such tales were true. Maybe there, I'd feel at home.

Distant birds and the crash of life in the underbrush. Other than that, solitude.

One step after the other, one more clutch of stony ground beneath my soles. One more league, one more mountain, one more day of loneliness. Each night, clenched within a scratchy blanket, I'd plunged my fingers deep inside, trembling with lusts no cock or finger-thrust could quench. Five days, I'd walked alone.

On the fifth night, they found me.

They'd set upon me, then, like owls. I never heard them coming. One moment, I'd been praying with my fingers, knuckle-deep; the next, I felt hard hands seize my limbs. One attacker pinned my hand inside; another slapped her palm across my lips. They moved like shadows, lit suddenly with a green and eldritch light. Tattoos. They seemed to be tattooed with light.

How could I not have seen them coming? Panic-wide, my eyes danced from face to face. My blanket fell away; hands ripped my dress to join it on the ground. They jerked me up and back without a word. Six sets of eyes appraised me. Men and women both. All fierce and wild and green-light graven. Vashayadin! *The gods had heard my prayer.*

Far from my place of birth, I had finally found my home.

The captain's shouting. His words are lost. The voluptuous sounds of war begin.

Hard-eyed men leap across the gap between ships, their blades raised, their muscles ready. "Get down below!" Bes screams, shoving me aside, but his words come from a ghost. I sense his death approach, and though I will recall him kindly, he's already dead to me.

The other passengers cry below decks. Their terror rises to my nose, running like a trickle of blood in a stream. The stream itself is combat, the rush and tackle of life with teeth. Not far off, a swell of sweat, blood, and passion rises from the fight. I've drawn both my daggers, and although my soft skin aches to dare the kiss of steel, I hold back from joining in. They trained me well, my green-lit kin. For five years, they taught me how to *live*.

I intend to live through *this*.

And to help others live through it, too.

Still, my skin itches and seethes. Sunlight ripens my bare flesh. I step back out of sight. I focus to suppress the glow from my own ritual tattoos. Whispering, I close my eyes and reach magically across the distance to the fray. Enter it. Ride it. Become it.

My skin shivers from the slice of blades. My bones shudder from hard blows. Eyes closed, I feel tears trace across my cheeks. Salt-sweat and fresh smoke join the reek of blood and bowels on the deck. Each body crashing to the wood reverberates from my naked feet to the surging in my gut.

I'll be ready when they come for me.

My captors dragged me naked through the night, their musky flesh pressed tight against my own. By the light of their vashanna *— the light-tattoos engraved upon their skin — I caught glimpses of the trees. My feet trawled through thorns and stumbled over roots. Branches lashed me as we passed. My captors did not speak, but bore me silent through the endless woods.*

I felt swallowed by the forest. She pressed in upon me, hungrily. Yet despite the hopping dread inside, I felt safe. If these wild folk had wished me dead, there'd be maggots in my eyes by now. For whatever lay before me, they were taking me home. In my lusts, they'd seen a kindred spirit. And either I would learn their arts, or else I'd perish through them.

Not till then had I felt so alive.

My childhood had been a haze of hunger no meager food could fill. I'd breathed in the ripe smells of the earth we tended, enjoyed the sharp stones beneath my feet, caressed the bark of trees as I scrambled up them to fetch fresh fruit or play some children's game. No spice nor salt nor storm could satisfy my ache for more. *Now, perhaps, among these folk, I might find what I'd desired.*

My next five years or so passed by in storms of ripe sensation. Lessons and blows. Kisses and fear. I learned hidden arts of fighting, loving, healing, and magic. My flesh was torn, my mind, challenged. They stripped me of all I thought I was.

Like all supplicants to this path, I'd remained naked through those years. No cloaks nor shawls would shelter us. The lash and luxury of each sensation danced across my skin. I learned enchantments to ward off the worst effects of weather, but those spells still left me raw to the sensations of each season. If anything, I felt even more exposed. Each touch of leaf or snowflake shivered like a lover's first caress. My feet embraced stone and ice and moss with equal joy. I capered in the rain, shivering in ecstasy at each drop and trickle on my skin.

We bundled, at night, like wolf cubs, men and women wound together in warm tangles of limbs and breath. We shared kisses, bites, embraces, and blows. Our old names, like our clothing, were stripped away. We took new ones — Illea, Darshana, Mitcal, Kolu — from old languages shaped by the sounds of the wood. My favorite teacher, Jaelamare, named me Caryanna: "The Hungry One." Even among our tribe, I craved sensation more than breath.

Despite his powerful name, Kolu may have been the weakest among us. A soft and mopey boy, he'd fled a noble life with too many brothers for the promise of naked, willing girls. Among us, though, the spoiled child whined endlessly about the cold, sparse food, and often-painful lessons. Finally, one morning, I'd had enough of his complaints. We'd been shelling nuts and putting the husks into wooden bowls. Without warning, I suddenly upended one bowl over his head, raining shells across his scalp, tangling his fine hair and generally upsetting his dignity. Illea laughed at his sputtering outrage, and we both tackled him to the ground. Pummeling Kolu, we wrapped ourselves around him and rolled in the broken shells. The sharp edges sent Kolu howling; to silence him, I stuffed his jaws open with my forearm. The jolt of his teeth and the shells beneath us warmed me deep inside. Kolu shook us off, cursing, so I grabbed Illea, kissed her deep, and pulled her down for more. By then, I was used to women's mouths; Illea, though, had lightly roughened lips, and breath like dry autumn leaves. Even now, years later, I still taste her in the autumn breeze and the tang of fresh-shelled nuts.

When my mentors brought their needles at the end of those five years, I raised my hands and spread my feet in welcome. Chanting in union, the elders lashed me bloody with Thornwood roots, then chained me to the great heart-oak at the center of our grove. Silver links pinned my shackles; silver needles pierced my skin. Cold thrills lanced my nipples — first the left one, then the right. My mentors ran thin silver chains through the rings set in each piercing, and then clasped them together in the center. Like the green-glowing vashanna patterns they pricked into my skin, these piercings marked me as a member of the tribe. Now I, too, was vashayadin *— a "carnomancer" — flesh-seer and a devotee of Life.*

They've won now, the shakarah. My ship's crew has given up or died. Below decks, the passengers moan and howl. The outlaws howl back, amused. Some ram their blades through dying bodies. Others toss men overboard to join the sharks. From a distance, I feel Jaklyn die, pulled apart deep below the waves. If I'm not fortunate, the same may happen soon to me.

Shakarah, tales say, are twice-born outlaws, too savage for any other band. Beaten or tortured to the point of death, they're fed brews of hot grog, sea salt, shark gall, and their own blood. Their wounds are treated with salt water, then sealed with hot iron. Those few who survive such baptisms become rabidly cruel. Shark-spirits, it is said, devour their old souls and possess their bodies in return. Nothing human remains within.

As the last of my ship's crew falls beneath their blades, I hope those tales are wrong.

They're ugly men and women, hideous with scars and missing teeth. Their long hair hops with lice and fleas; they stink of stale drink, piss, and blood. Most have sharpened their remaining teeth in tribute to their watery pets. Still, Life is not always comely. There is beauty in both the maggot and the butterfly.

Trembling, I step out from my hiding place.

Fearsome as it is, I accept what I'm about to do.

Trembling, I accepted kisses and caresses from each member of our tribe. The soft touch of kinship made me weep. Kolu had left in disgrace long ago by then, but Illea drew me close against her skin. Even as others crowded in, she maintained her fierce, possessive hold. I felt each stroke of her heart through our skins. She released me all too soon, then took my hand and led me toward the Elder Three, who pressed me to their chests. The Three held me for a long time as I wept. Eventually, when my tears subsided, they offered me a choice.

Vashayadin — women and men alike — follow one of three oathbound paths. Some live wild in the heart of the wood, while others return to the twelve kingdoms of settled men or wander between both worlds. We move about as emissaries, healers, warders, or spies. Most are obvious, some remain hidden, and all choose the garb we are to wear. As I trembled fresh from my initiation, Jaelamare offered me three garments.

The first was a rich brocade gown. Deep green, it glistened with finery. A thick cloak of fox fur and leather offered comfort, while jewelry and a pair of soft black boots completed the attire. This choice represented wealth and honor: rakalsa, *the sacred* courtier path. I would attend the twelve kingdoms in splendor, a prized courtesan and priestess. To the skills I already knew, I would add intrigue and etiquette. I'd have attendants, servants, rank, and funds. For my peers at court, I could offer guidance and sensual delights; for the vashayadin, I'd be their eyes and ears among the "stone folk," as we called them. If I chose the gown, I'd travel back and be set into a court of my choosing, prepared for a life of luxury.

The second choice featured a traveler's cloak, thick breeches, a warm tunic, and a pack. I could choose boots or go barefoot; in either case, my choice involved wandering. I would travel the kingdoms as tolobarda, a poor yet sacred vagabond healer. If I preferred, I could set up an herb-cottage, or journey along with traveling players. Either way, I would tend the simple folk — farmers, tradesmen, fishers, and crafters. My lot would be humble and not always welcome. Still, it would be an honest life, close to the wild and free as a leaf.

The third garment was a belt of silver links. From it hung a small pouch and two dagger sheaths. These would be my only accoutrements — I would go naked otherwise. Exposed to eyes and elements, I would become carhataya, a devotee of love and lust. My favors and lessons I could give to anyone, or to no one, as I chose. I'd pit skin and courage against wild elements and human scorn. In some ways, this was the greatest honor; in others, the harshest test. To folk who revere the oldest and most primordial ways, my silver chains and light tattoos marked my devotion to the living world; to others, I'd seem like some simple, naked fool. I would live like an animal, taking food, drink and comfort wherever I could find them.

Three garments. Three oaths. Three destinies.

Guess which one I chose.

I chose this, I remind myself as the first shakarah strides toward me. His fellows approach as well, amazed by my bravado. I'm fortunate: None of them seem to recognize a vashayadin for what she is. If one *did* realize who and what I am, he might have guessed what I'm about to do.

From their lustful chatter, I assume they think I'm just our captain's whore.

That's exactly what I want them to think.

The man before me is foul beyond reckoning. I've seen cleaner pigs feast in charnel pits. His shaggy beard crawls with vermin. His few teeth shine with brownish spit. He's bleeding from a deep cut across one arm but doesn't seem to care. He gibbers obscenities at me. I ignore him. Nothing this dead man says matters to me at all.

It's their captain I want to find.

Without him, I might wind up feeding the sharks. That might happen anyway — I'm taking a desperate chance. With the captain, though, I can gamble on the sadism such a man might have. And so, as the bold swine reaches toward me, I scan the mob for someone far more powerful.

There. There he is, toward the back of the pack. A gaunt viper of a man whose ears dangle beneath weighty bone-carved ornaments. His sun-fired face betrays some noble blood — a bastard, I assume, who chose piracy over poverty. He watches me, amused, as his man grabs my arm. He must assume I'm too frightened to use the knives in my hands.

I'm not.

A sudden slash. A sudden shock. The bold man screams.

His cock-sack splatters on the deck.

But it wasn't my intent to kill.

By now, my senses blaze. I feel the hammering of every heart on deck. Blood-perfume swirls through sea salt, sweat, and tar. Each grain of wood beneath my feet sings of trees and forests felled. I feel the wash of waves, the gnash of teeth, the struggles of those eaten alive below. Phantom tears course down my cheeks. Phantom wounds sear my unmarked flesh. I taste lust and battle in my mouth. Time freezes as I leap.

They're too slow to stop me and too dull to know how.

Before a hand can reach me, I drop one knife and slap the captain hard across his cheek.

In his mind, I place an image: Me, naked, tied drowning to an anchor. Surrounded by sharks and clutching claws. Desperate, squirming, screaming out my air at the bottom of the sea...

If he's half the man I think he is, he'll want to make that sight come true.

Hands reach out, as I knew they would.

My daggers sing of open wounds.

More blood, fresher blood, joins the red wash on the deck.

It's an impossible fight, of course.

But one meant to do impossible things.

Dodging blades, ducking clubs, I weave death between their killing strikes.

"Don't *cut* her, you bloody fools," the captain bellows. "*STOP.*"

They obey.

I do not.

With blades, taunts, skin, and blood, I draw shark-herders away from their prey. They try to grab me. I dance aside. Blood thunders in my heart, my ears, my limbs. Shouts, blows, feints, and leaps become a blur where their bodies and my own entwine. The mortal illusion of our separate selves withdraws.

I the acorn, we the tree
Red seeds set the dayfolk free
Turn terror into ecstasy...

A hand catches me at last.

A foot lashes me behind one knee.

I slam to the deck.

They fall on me.

Bloody fingers, dirty nails, slash in and bear me down. Reaching out, I pull them toward me. Fill them with an even *greater* lust. Gods yes, I'm terrified. But gods, I'm hungry, too.

I swell with their lust, and with my own.

I've been a hungry girl since birth. While my family worshipped Calacia the Brave, I favored Vasara, Queen of Life. My excesses soon drove me from our village, but I refused to feel disgraced. Vasara, then and now, remains my goddess, and in Her there is no shame, only Love, Lust, and Life.

But Vasara is a bitch. Her rites are as sensual as an open wound. As vashayadin, I passed through celebrations that would shock a courtesan. For Vasara's sake, I've fucked rose-stems, canes, and stones. She schooled me to look beyond a comely face and find beauty in foul places. Most vitally, however, I've learned to channel khal'asai — *"life-surge" the passion force within all things. To read* khal'asai, *to shape it and direct it as need be, is the core of the vashayadin arts. Khal'asai is vitality, the blood of Vasara and the pulse of Life. With it, I feel fulfilled. And through it, I am strong.*

With each blow, each grasp, each torrent of abuse, I take them in. Draw their life-force to myself. Pain becomes a whirlwind of desire, emptiness shattered by bolts of pleasure.

Beneath my sweaty, battered skin, my muscles swell with strength. My heart pounds with stolen potency.

Inside me, the Red Wheel begins to spin.

What they seek to take from me, I take from them instead.

In its place, I leave them *fear*. And *guilt*. And *pain*. Waves of pain even shark-herders would fear.

Finally, I slam, shivering, against the deck. Gasping, my captors back away. I've taken their strength, their passion, their breath. And the Red Wheel picks up speed.

The captain glowers. The crew stumbles. They all hover in a daze. Deep inside, these monsters *question* what they've done. Guilt floods them like the tide. Some glance around at the carnage on the decks. Tears glisten at the corners of their eyes. Some shake their heads; some whisper prayers. The captain roars commands. His crew responds, but sluggish. Remorse thickens in their hearts. The Red Wheel does its work.

Gasping, I recover. Their stolen strength heals my wounds. Beneath my skin, cracked bones and ruptured flesh begin to knit anew. It hurts — oh *GODS*, it hurts. But it's exhilarating beyond all words.

Beneath my skin, I'm a firestorm. I want to bite, to tear, to rend. Instead, I lay there, panting. Give the Red Wheel time to grind them down.

I scan the faces of the crew. Are they finished? Might they leave us now?

Hesitation marks them. *Hesitation*, yes, but not yet surrender.

Life and death are not so simply planned. These *are* shakarah, after all. Mercy's not their way.

Neither, then, will it be mine.

It was snowing that cold night, my first winter among the tribe. I couldn't stop shivering. My feet burned. My skin howled. "Focus," purred Jaelamare. "Focus." Naked, I whined. Not even a cloak, a blanket, a fire? "No," she insisted. "Take the cold inside you. Warm it with your own heat. Bridge the place where your skin and your surroundings meet. The borders between them are illusion. Your spirit knows the truth. If you can master the riddle of the wind, you'll survive.

"And if not..." she waved her hand at the frozen landscape... "the world slumbers, little one. Perhaps you'll slumber with it, too."

She padded off nude into the snow. Cold flakes melted on her skin. Jaelamare, then, seemed ageless as a stone. Though I could read her many mortal years across her face, she seemed as youthful, in her way, as a happy springing cat. Her feet left graceful traces in the snow. I hurt just watching her.

I huddled back against the tree, quaking to the core of my bones. The wind spoke to me like a whip. It promised a comforting pain.

For longer than I can guess, I shivered there alone. My feet and hands went numb. My teeth rattled in my skull like a gambler's dice. My black hair shimmered with tiny jewels. In the dark, the wind cut through me, merciless. Potent but invisible.

Breath. It was the breath of Life. Fleeting yet essential. Wrapped through all things yet beholden to none.

I breathed. Deeply. Held it in. Released it. Another breath drawn down and held. Warmed inside me. Set free. I watched each puff of breath as it escaped me, rose, and joined the night. Through me, the wind was warmed. Through the wind, I lived.

The wind and I are one, *I thought.* Between us, we are Life.

I began to hum. To chant. To sing. As I did so, I felt the cold recede. Felt ice and snowflakes slicken on my *skin, too. Warmth bloomed, thawing me from inside out. The numbness left me. I stepped into the snow. My footprints caught the moonlight, shimmering. I laughed deeply and began to dance. My feet sank, happy, in the burning snow.*

I've no idea how long I danced. My throat grew raw from breath and laughter. My skin glistened with sweat and snowmelt. I thrummed like a fresh-snapped bowstring. My breath mingled with the wind. I could see and feel myself both within my body and yet and from without it as well.

I challenged myself, then. I rolled through the snow. Lashed myself with icy branches. My breath smoked the air like a greenwood fire. I never wanted to stop. I left the cold behind. Only the ache in my limbs, far later, forced me to stretch out in a drift, embrace the chill, and smile as I sank into a warm and restful sleep.

Rough hands shock me back to wakefulness. The bloody deck sticks to my skin. Reavers yank me to my feet, exhausted yet enraged. Around me, they press in. They seem hungry again, like the sharks around our ships. If they simply toss me overboard, I'm dead.

Try not to smile when I see the ropes. They want me drowned, not eaten. Which means I have a chance.

As two men haul a heavy chest toward me, I breathe deep. With stolen strength, I fill my lungs. Empty them. Fill them again. Flex my limbs as much as my captors will allow. A few of them laugh. Assume I'm struggling to escape. Let them. I *will* escape, but not the way they expect.

Mumbling prayers, I reach beyond myself. To the shakarah. To the timbers of our ships. To the innocents below and the sharks beyond. To the sea that surrounds us all. *Fill me*, I pray, *with the power to live.* To dare. To defy the crushing, airless depths. I draw in strength, air, and courage. I'll need them, to survive.

My captors drag me to the chest. I resist enough to give them a good show. Nearby, some pirates begin to argue. They regret their atrocities, but it's too late for such feelings now. A handful of them want to leave. One or two look longingly toward the sea... or to the sharks below. The captain shushes them to silence. His words drown beneath the roaring in my ears.

Relieved, I see that no one has gone to savage the innocents below deck. I've captured the full attention of the crew. The vision I placed within the captain's mind whips his cruelty past madness. My ship's passengers remain safe so long as the shark-herders focus their hunger and hate on me. My suffering is this ship's security.

As one shark-herder holds my arm out for the ropes, I sweep their eyes with my gaze. *Do this*, I say silently. *Do this to me so you save the others and damn yourselves.*

A few shakarah look away as their crewmates bind me to the chest.

Beneath my breath, I whisper: *So shall it be.*

The Red Wheel's motion cannot be stopped.

"We're all entwined," Jaelamare said. *"Division is illusion. Each tree, each stone, each beast or person is united. You are one*

with the flickering flame. The dust you breathe, the dirt you walk upon — it's all part of you and you are part of it all. When you understand this deeply, you can step beyond illusions. What appears to be yours becomes another's, and what appears to be theirs becomes yours."

I was puzzled. "How?"

My mentor shrugged. Her soft white hair fell across piercing green eyes. "Because you recognize that the distance between you is false. There is no distance. There is no separation! You, me, that tree, that flame — we all exist in the same space, the same moment, the same essence. The illusion of distance is potent, but when you see it for what it is, it disappears."

She reached out and scooped up a handful of flame from our bonfire. It danced in her naked palm. She brought it to her face, blew upon it. The fire spread across her hand. Jaelamare smiled as I drew back, amazed. "You see?"

I tried to think of something to say.

With a sharp breath, she inhaled the flame. Closed her mouth. Opened it to reveal a fire on her tongue. She closed her mouth again, swallowed it. Smiled. "This is not an easy trick, little one. It's no trick at all, in fact, but reality. The fire, the air and I are one. I accept it. They accept it. It's the illusion of division that would do us harm."

"I... I..." I gaped like an imbecile.

She reached out to me. Touched my skin. Touched past my skin. I shuddered with delight and fear as that touch tingled to my core.

"The greatest act of love or magic," she said, "is unity." She snapped her fingers. I screamed. "And the greatest punishment is unity, too."

The pain shattered me like hammer-struck glass. My bones shuddered. My heart skipped. My lungs emptied in a single scream. I couldn't move. I couldn't breathe. For a moment, excruciation was my world.

Then fingers touched me. Cooled me. Stilled the echoes of that pain. I fell, gasping, to the dirt. Soft hands caressed my hair.

"We call it The Red Wheel," she said. Her voice sounded very far away. "It spins across the distance between what seems to be, and it unites one thing or person with another. If one of them hurts, the other suffers too. If there is shame, both parties share it. If one has violated the other, that trespasser feels the agony he has caused. No other punishment brings greater justice."

She helped me up, holding me close as I wept. Her skin smelled of musk and woodsmoke. We sat together, melding into one. Her heart beat with mine; my lungs breathed her air. "Why?" I finally sobbed. "Why did you hurt me?"

Jaelamare sighed. "Life is not always just, little one. Pain is not always earned — it simply is. *To understand that, you must feel it even when there seems to be no reason to suffer. For somewhere, there is always suffering. Some beast or tree or person feels pain they did not deserve to feel. By accepting that into yourself, you share unity with that pain.*

"Besides," she added in a lighter tone. "If I hadn't *hurt you, would you have so deeply respected what I said?"*

As usual, I had no reply.

Oh, Jaelamare, I certainly feel pain now. The broken bones and torn flesh barely healed still aches. Deep inside, a part of me's still screaming. There's nothing "sacred" about what's been done to me. As I draw strength from my captors, I feel sick. My belly heaves. I vomit, hard. The sharp taste burns my throat.

One or two shakarah puke as well. One hangs over the side while his fellows laugh. For a moment, as rough hemp binds my wrists, he stares at the seething sea below. Then, with a sob, he flings himself over the side.

The Red Wheel has begun to turn.

I lack my mentor's power. If I could do to these reavers what Jaelamare did to me, none of the rest would have been necessary. But I'm still young, and skin's illusions bind me. I can share touches or feelings, though, and sometimes that's enough.

I've made the shark-herders feel what they've done to us.

A few men look nauseous. Nearly all the women do. One or two shakarah stare at their fellow pirates in disgust. Still, the captain and my captors cinch their knots and pull the ropes upon me taut.

Oh gods, I'd hoped to avoid this!

They bend me back across the chest. One man reaches for the chain between my nipples, yanks it, ties a dagger to the chain, and lets it fall. I grunt at the blast of pain. He laughs, says something about "giving me a chance." His little joke, then, like those prisoners left on barren islands with a dull blade and a mouthful of water.

Some souls deserve damnation.

Practiced hands bind my wrists and ankles to the chest. I tense my muscles to give the rope some slack. All I can see is legs, feet, and the deck. My head hangs upside-down; my belly arches toward the sky. My head spins from disorientation and the rush of blood. Someone slaps the breath from my belly. I close my eyes to blot out the pain.

I hope they all die screaming.

New screams rise. Not the passengers. The reavers. Splashes and thrashing in the water. Other pirates now leap overboard. "*A WITCH!*" someone yells. "*She's cursed us.*"

Yes, I have. More deeply than you know.

I await the kiss of steel.

Instead, they lift me with the chest.

With all the strength I have, I snatch a final desperate breath. Focus stolen power and stolen strength.

Despite myself, I open my eyes.

The ship tilts. Faces and hands appear. My perspective's all wrong. My head's pounding. There's yelling. Crying. Cursing. A multitude of hands. A rush of sounds.

Release.

I watch the sky fall away.

Impact.

Shock.

Pain.

Head underwater, I gasp.

And then my world is a red storm of teeth.

The sharks.

I'm floating.

Belly up, head down.

The chest didn't sink!

And then, mercifully, it does.

Drawing me into the dark...

Darkness has always been my friend. As a child, I rarely slept through the night. Instead, I'd wait up until my family was asleep, then creep out past their snoring forms. It became a test of skill, especially as fresh siblings were born. Later, when First Blooding turned to First Lust, I used those skills to meet my lovers — always under the cover of the dark.

I think of those lovers as I sink. Around me, the sharks bolt and snap. Their teeth graze the chest, the ropes, and my skin. They've eaten too well, though, to bother with difficult prey. As the sun recedes, they swim back upwards to fetch new and easy meals.

The heavy chest drags me down as I pull against my bonds. My throat and belly strain. My spine shudders. Salt like fire in my eyes. High above, a spray of bubbles rises in my wake. Some stream from my burning nostrils and the corners of my mouth.

I can't last long like this.

Struggle with the ropes. Try to wriggle free, and fail. *What's wrong? I should be free by now.* My stolen strength, I'd hoped, would be enough to break the ropes.

And then it hits me: My mistake.

Sailors are very good with knots.

And savage as they are, shakarah are still sailors.

This is very, *very* bad.

We've been at sea two days now. The last time I saw land was yesterday. There's no telling how deep the ocean is here. Even with my stolen strength and life, I may drown before I free myself... if I *can* free myself at all. That life-force might sustain me, but for how long? How far down would I sink before I hit bottom? And what if I land badly, with the chest on top of me...?

Best to act *now*, not to think of *then*.

My wrists and ankles are bound together, tied to handles on each side. Moving one won't shift the other. My wrists are wrapped behind my head, bracing my neck with my fists. Perhaps if I can reach the handles...

The chest tumbles, end over end, into dark.

The thickening sea grows black and cold. Light fades. Crushing depths push in. My eardrums thump and pulse. My muscles scream. My belly writhes. *Whatever you do, don't breathe.*

My mouth gasps, panicked. Another gulp of air escapes.

My blood thunders like a mare in heat...

I grew up on a farm, no stranger to the mysteries of sex. As a child, I watched the couplings and thrashings of our beasts. Even then, I felt their ecstasies, and ached to feel such things myself.

One evening, during a thunderstorm, I watched a young colt mount a mare. As the rain slashed down and thunder shook the hillsides, I watched the horses writhe. With bared teeth and flying mares, the mare and colt dashed themselves against one another. Their frenzied mating matched the storm.

As the stud reared and buried himself in her, the mare screamed with joy. Bright lightning lit the hillsides. The lovers didn't care. My eyes blazed in the aftershock. My ears rang. My shoulders trembled. The mare danced beneath her colt, and I felt their passion through my feet.

That night, in dreams, I fucked a storm. In the form of our mare, I ran through naked hills. I lifted my tail and arched my back and cried out for the frenzied sky. With each bolt, I shuddered and wept with joy.

My sisters thought I was possessed.

Perhaps, in a way, I was...

The chest hits something with a jolt.

The dagger jerks the chains as it descends. The rings pull tight. My flesh holds firm. I cry out, losing precious air.

It's all dark and freezing here.

How far down am I?

I can't tell.

The chest seems lodged on a rocky shelf. The dagger hangs, held only by my skin. My head throbs, seemingly face-down. Below, I sense an endless void.

We're caught on a reef, the chest and I. Below us waits more sea and empty dark.

Shuddering, I strain against the bonds. The knots still hold. Each movement yanks the chain I wear. My honor has become my death.

Wait. The chain. The dagger. My fingertips. Perhaps...

I can't hold out. My throat burns. My belly cramps. My core pulsates with red heat.

If I can only reach that dagger...

Snarl deep. I *will* get free. I *will* breathe surface air again.

That's it.

That's what I'm missing.

Unity.

Remember this, I tell myself: *The sea and I are one.*

I think back to the fire in Jaelamare's mouth. To our dance, and the snow in which I slept. It's the illusion of division that dooms us. And my fear, if I'm not careful, will be what kills me. Not the sea.

Fish brush across my skin as I look inward. Focus. Relax. Reach out to the reef, the fish, the chest, the sea. Even the ropes — the ropes most of all. Eyes shut, I think of their fibers and strands. The hemp and tar that made them. The hands that shaped them. The shark-herders who bound me with their knots. The shape of those knots. The way they interweave.

What can be woven can be unwoven.

Focusing, I ride beyond my body, into the ropes. Glide across them; follow their paths. Then, soft and slow, guide my fingers to release them. Follow their strands with keen fingertips.

The dagger pulls against my breasts. My hunger twitches in response. I buck and ride the fire deep inside.

I use pain to reach beyond myself.

The dark sea glows green as my tattoos blaze.

The ropes slacken, finally. And my hands win free.

Life-pulse sustains me where lungs alone could not. Still, my belly clenches from the lack of air.

All at once, the chest shifts, tilts, pulls free.

But the ropes part as the chest sinks.

I yank my ankles free as the chest's weight slides away.

Now all I need to do is swim.

Up.

A very, *very* long way up.

But in the dark, which way *is* up?

The dagger remains tied to the chain in my breasts. I fumble with the knot, then stop. If the dagger pulls *down*, then I should swim *up*. Without that weight to guide me, I'll be lost forever in the depths.

That cruel bastard *did* give me a chance to survive.

I still hope he died screaming.

I release the dagger. Use its weight to guide me. To rise, I'll swim against that weight.

The pain gives me the boost I need...

The last time I saw Jaelamare, she was burning. This time, though, the fires swallowed her. *As all things do, my mentor had passed on. And so, we burned her, as is customary, and I watched her through my tears.*

I danced that night at the edge of the fire. Drums and flutes and voices kept the tune. My bare feet swept through embers, tingling; my lungs, searing, breathed sweet ash. I howled like a birthing beast, but my voice was lost in the night. I dared my skin with fire, and that fire kissed me red.

Within my chest, my heart blazed. Wood-scented tears stung my eyes. I stomped on hot splinters and sucked in hot air. No flames could match the heat inside. I was tempted, so tempted, to fling myself, full-length, across her bier. To surrender myself to the burning too, and join her "unity" in a single, precious pain.

But I didn't.

I wanted to survive.

Instead, I grabbed a burning branch. I *the acorn, we the tree,* I *whispered. Closing my fingers on the flame, I reached* beyond *that flame and felt my skin ignite. The flesh and fire mingled, danced, merged into one.*

I held the fire and the fire held me.

Together, we wept for what was passing.

And then I blew the fire out.

My hand was clean where the fire had been. The skin remained unscarred. My palm tingled where I'd held the flame, but it hurt no more than a good, hard slap.

I laughed, then. My mentor hadn't lied.

It's the illusion that kills us, not the truth. And in dying, she had transcended them both.

I still wanted to live, though. Even if it meant a few illusions.

And so, I stepped out of the fire, unburnt. My skin smelled heavily of smoke.

To defy the elements, I thought, *I must be one with them.*

The memory of fire warms me as I swim.

Soon, the sea above me glows with light. The strength I stole has left me, though. Desperate bubbles escape my lips and rise toward the surface. I see them drift yet lack the energy to join them. I'm cold beyond cold, weary beyond words. My heart surges to reach the light. My limbs cry out to stop.

I the acorn, we the tree. I use the chant to keep moving. As I did in the woods long ago, I repeat it without speaking, pacing myself to the rhythm of the words. Each phrase is a stroke. Each stroke brings me closer. Searing hands clench my lungs and belly. Like lighting, I fuck the pain. Ride the spasms into *one. More. Stroke.*

Deep in my throat, I'm moaning. *It's not fair! It's too far!*

And then I see the sharks.

High above, the water drifts with darkness. A ship's hull blocks the light. Around them, a thick stain seethes with shapes. The sharks and their refreshments. My moans deepen with despair. How can I possibly get through *that*?

Sunlight casts a red glow through the carnage. Sharks, body parts, and blood.

And then, a single killer spots me. He angles down and dives.

The knife!

With numb fingers, I reach the knot. Fumble with it. The shark draws closer. The knife stays tied. Lazy tail-sweeps bring the shark closer.

Lazy.

That's it.

He's *full*.

Curious, but satiated.

I hope...

I release the knife and spread my hands.

I the acorn, we the tree.

I stop swimming, stop moving. Reach out through the sea. The shark draws closer.

Close my eyes. Reach out and commune...

A hard jolt. Scraping. I gasp. Taste blood.

He's simply nosing me.

Open my eyes. Panic blooms. *So close! Too close!* Deep in my throat, I squeak. But there's no pain. No frenzy. Just dead-black eyes and glistening skin.

I reach out to touch his raspy hide. Touch his skin. Touch *through* it.

He slides past me gracefully.

I grasp a fin. Hold on. He draws me down.

No — not *down!*

Close my eyes. Focus. Commune with him. Beyond words, I send sensations. Light. Waves lapping. Currents. The splash of rising...

We ascend.

Hug my naked body to him. Feel the scrape of his sharp scales. Against my skin, I hold him close. We rise, and we are one.

We break surface to the cry of gulls.

My throat unlocks. My lungs expand. I gasp and gulp sea water and salt air. Choking, I cling to my shark. His jagged hide feels good against my skin.

There's a banquet floating in the sea. Dead men and women, both. I hope the passengers escaped the horror. Blood. So much blood. The Red Wheel has spun its course.

Gasping hard, I hug my companion tight. Around us, shark fins swirl. The frenzy, though, is over now. Even sharks get full. Some floating bits of meat I recognize: a head, an arm, a severed foot. Many look familiar — one especially, half-eaten: the captain, his aristocratic features naked with despair.

The shakarah have fed their sharks for the last time.

This is what *I* wagered on: A fit of group remorse. Bound to their crimes by the Red Wheel's spell, the shakarah would rather die quickly than live with all that pain. I gambled, and I won. By the look of these red waters, most — if not all — of them jumped overboard to be devoured. It's rough justice, true. But then, Life's often cruel.

Pain comes with life.

What we *do* with that pain — how we use it, how we ride it — *that* determines how we survive.

To endure Life's pain, we must love. Love each other, maybe. Love our gods, perhaps. Love ourselves? If we can. Love Life? Most of all.

Hate devours hate in time.

The shark-herders live on hate.

I live off something more.

When I can breathe enough to speak aloud, I whisper thanks to Vasara and Jaelamare. To the life-pulse and our vashayadin. To storms and mares and green tattoos. To my shark and the voraciousness of Life.

And then, I look up.

And laugh.

The sharp sound shocks the gulls.

My ship is gone — far-off and at full sail. The shakarah ship is burning, its timbers rich with flame.

I'm alone and naked in the sea, with a shark against my skin and a dagger chained to my breasts.

I laugh until I can't breathe anymore.

Life's absurdities are the richest kind of joke.

The shark feels strong. His muscles flow beneath rough hide. With salty lips, I kiss his head. "Well, my friend, it looks like you're taking me to shore."

He turns, then, as if he understands.

Chuckling, I wrap myself against the shark.

It's a long swim, but I'll survive. I have plenty of passion, plenty of life.

Drawing a deep breath, I close my eyes and dream of trees...

P.S.

"Oops, said God
As the world ended.
"My bad."

About the
Author

Satyros Phil Brucato (he/they) — aka Satyr, Phil, and Cedar Blake — has been publishing professionally in various media since 1989. One of the original creators of the World of Darkness series, Satyr's known best for his work on *Mage*, *Werewolf*, *Changeling*, *Wraith* and *Vampire*, as well as the *Street Fighter* RPG.

Outside the White Wolf pack, he's authored the novel *Red Shoes*, the webcomic *Arpeggio*, and the collections *Valhalla with a Twist of Lethe*, *Tritone: Tales of Musical Weirdness*, *Wyldheart: Tales of Primal Fantasy*, and now *Breaking the*

Devil's Bread, as well as the RPGs *Deliria: Faerie Tales for a New Millennium*, *Powerchords: Music, Magic & Urban Fantasy*, *Creatures of the Dark*, and a variety of other games for various publishers and his own Quiet Thunder and Silver Satyr imprints. Beyond that, Satyr co-created the urban fantasy film series *Strowlers*, and has written fiction and nonfiction for Weird Tales, Realms of Fantasy, Steampunk Tales, Witches & Pagans, newWitch Magazine, a variety of RPG publishers, and a host of anthologies, websites, newspapers, and blogs.

Under the name Cedar Blake, they've also released erotica, paranormal romance, RPG material, and metaphysical nonfiction.

Based in Seattle, WA, Satyr shares home and business with his spouse, partner and longtime collaborator Sandra Damiana Swan.

You can find out more at:

https://satyrosphilbrucato.wordpress.com/

https://www.patreon.com/philbrucato

https://bsky.app/profile/satyrosphilbrucato.bsky.social

https://www.facebook.com/groups/126494504028229/

https://www.drivethrurpg.com/en/publisher/11262/quiet-thunder-productions

ALSO AVAILABLE FROM NIGHTMARE PRESS

THE HURDY GURDY MAN

David Turnbull

Set in London in the summer of 1969, *The Hurdy Gurdy Man* follows Kath Dunn, who has left her home near the seaside town Berwick on Tweed, and finds herself homeless on the streets of Piccadilly. Here she encounters the eccentric Gordon Urquhart-Scott, who persuades Kath to accompany him to his large crumbling home on the edge of Hampstead Heath, where he claims to run a hostel for homeless women.

Kath finds herself inducted as one of twelve formerly homeless women who reside free of charge in the house in exchange for obeying the Hurdy Gurdy Man's strange rules, including nightly musical performances on the hand-cranked hurdy-gurdy from which his nickname derives.

Kath befriends Ruth. Together they secretly unravel terrible truths linked to the British Class system, the establishment, and the gruesome Scottish borders legends of the Redcaps. After witnessing how deep the horror within the decaying home truly runs, the two women decide to confront the evil at its source. Enlisting the help of other women, they engineer a terrifying conflict they hope will send the evil back to whatever foul region of darkness from whence it came.

BELINDA'S KEYBOARDS
PART ONE: DED'S LINE
Dedham Pond

Dedham Pond is a journalist in his fifties rediscovering how to do his job responsibly in an era that appreciates bias over truth and influencers over experts. While investigating the death of an old friend's son, Ded discovers Belinda Blessing, who is part of a conspiracy of people who enjoy injecting discord and chaos into the culture wherever they can. Now Ded must find a way to stop the destruction caused by Belinda's keyboards and bring her to justice.

SARAH CORBIN'S BLOODY REVENGE
Coyote Wallace

When Sarah Corbin and her family are killed in a midnight robbery gone wrong, she makes a deal for her mortal soul - in exchange for the chance to hunt down the men who burned her world to ash.

Violent, unflinching, and tinged with supernatural overtones, *Sarah Corbin's Bloody Revenge* takes readers into the dark heart of Texas, where the air is heavy with gun smoke and the streets run red.

On the other end of Sarah's revenge is Lono Talbot, a murderous cutthroat who has parlayed stolen gold into a position of power in the small town of Gehenna. His network of gunslingers and outlaws, reinforced with his ill-gotten gains, has made him one of the most powerful men in the Texas underground. Too well protected for lawmen, Lono continues to grow his influence and power....

....until the mistakes of his past come calling.

MURKY SHADOWS
Belinda Brady

Welcome to *Murky Shadows*, a deliciously dark world where ghosts, ghouls, monsters and all-too-horrifying realities collide, and vampires, ghosts and things that go bump in the night rule. From a vengeful fairy, to a bloodthirsty roommate, to the ghosts of a serial killer plotting their revenge, no supernatural stone is left unturned in this captivating collection of spooky tales.

Murky Shadows, by Belinda Brady, is a treasure of short stories that will take you to places you never dreamed possible, and introduce you to characters you would only meet in your worst nightmares. So sit back, relax, perhaps put a light on, and delve into this chilling mixed bag of dark stories, one that not only brings the supernatural to life, but also taps into the darkest corners of the human psyche.

Which story will be your favorite?

NO ONE CAN SAVE US
Kendall Phillips

Adam always keeps his powers in check. As the world's only superhero, he must know his limits. Defeat the master criminal, repel an army, stop a natural disaster, but never let himself go too far.

Until Syangnom.

The world has grown accustomed to the feats of its only superhuman. Adam's wife, Sara, a celebrated journalist and periodic hostage, regularly reports his exploits, and the agents of Extra-Judicial Affairs handle all the legal issues.

But when Adam becomes enraged in the reclusive regime of Syangnom, he leaves 14 million people dead and the world recoiling from the destruction he has wrought.

Now Adam's wife Sara and EJA Agent Kia Mercado must track down the conspiracy behind Adam's breakdown and discover the otherworldly source of his powers. Their search will bring them face to face with supervillains, eldritch gods, and the mysterious figure who defends Chicago from the shadows, the armored hero known only as No One.

A SOUL A DAY
Todd Sullivan

What lengths would you go to save a soul?

In the shadows of South Korea, Min Jae rebels against the Gwanlyo, an organization of vampires that tempts mortals with power, money, sex, and the promise of immortality. The catch? An eternity in Hell.

Min Jae will stop at nothing to prevent another human from becoming a vampire. He embarks on a holy quest to save those marked for damnation. Next on his list— Desmond, an expat in Seoul who lives an ordinary life of work and friends.

To stave off the Gwanlyo hellbent on acquiring Desmond, Min Jae enlists the services of Hyeri, a serial killer turned vampire who hates the organization for her own insane reasons. Will the unlikely pair be able to rescue Desmond before he becomes a vampire? Will the undead organization keep the duo from disrupting their plans?

Find out in A SOUL A DAY, a tale of violence, madness, and redemption.

SCROLLS OF RAMOSE, SCRIBE OF EGYPT

James Arthur Anderson

According to the Book of Exodus, God cast ten deadly plagues against Egypt and the Pharaoh for his enslavement of the Israelites. One wonders what it must have been like to be an ordinary Egyptian, innocent of Ramesses II's transgressions, yet still suffering the wrath of the Almighty.

Scrolls of Ramose, Scribe of Egypt retells the story from the point of view of the chief scribe of Ramesses the Great, and relives the suffering the people of the Two Lands endured during the plagues of the bloody Nile: the infestations of frogs, insects, and boils; the terror of fiery hail and darkness; and finally, the death of the eldest sons.

You have heard the stories, now see them through the eyes of the innocent merely trying to survive the deadly hand of an angry God.

STITCHES AND OTHER STORIES

J.M. Heluk

Nothing in *Stitches and Other Stories* is what it seems, leaving the reader to speculate on the origin of its horror—to root out those subtle connections and, ultimately, stitch each tale together on their own.

Stitches and Other Stories was designed to make the reader an active participant. In the end, you decide the genesis of the horror.

From a family stranded by an unnatural force on their Montana farm in "Two Miles as the Crow Flies," to "Stitches," the story of a young boy terrorized by his dead grandmother. Meet a temperamental little girl from a New York City slum who possesses a deadly talent in "The Wishman and the Worm." In "The Ovid," something has come home to roost in a less-than-quaint seaside town.

Sit back and let *Stitches and Other Stories* guide you through a frightful landscape while you read deep into the night.

JENNY'S SPOOKY LITTLE TALES: VOL. 2

The Frightening Floyds have been researching and writing about the paranormal and all things strange and unusual for ten years. To celebrate, Jenny recently compiled ten of her favorite stories from the many books she has written with her husband Jacob, which became *Jenny's Spooky Little Tales: Vol. 1*. Now, she has compiled ten more for *Jenny's Spooky Little Tales: Vol. 2*.

In this collection, you'll find ghosts, a meat shower, a haunted Disney World attraction, spirits of Hollywood stars and starlets, the Bermuda Triangle, and even spooky tales from Louisville's famed Churchill Downs. We hope you enjoy *Jenny's Spooky Little Tales: Vol. 2*.

BEALZ: PRINCE OF THE SOUTHSIDE

G.E. Moore

Hailing from Chicago's hardscrabble Southside streets, Bealz must contend daily with violence, danger, and rejection, all while having little to no contact with his mother, who aged out of the very same foster home he finds himself trapped in, and only able to wonder about an absent father, imprisoned before he was even born.

Soon enough though, he finds his parents harbor secrets that will forever change his life. Secrets big enough to rip his world apart as they introduce him to a brand new reality. A wondrous existence where legends live and breathe and monsters fight daily to destroy everything and everyone he's ever loved.

Bealz will discover he is a child of that other world, descended of royal blood, that his father hails from the Great House Askai, rulers of the Long Plains Kingdom of the Incata, and that his mother, a child of Earth, wields the powers of a goddess.

As these secrets are revealed, Bealz embarks upon a journey across two worlds, battling Saints and the demon Shitani along the way in a race to restore balance before it's all too late.

READ MORE NIGHTMARE PRESS!!!

Visit our website at <u>nightmarepress5.wordpress.com</u>

Also, follow us on:

Facebook: https://www.facebook.com/nightmarepress1

Instagram: https://www.instagram.com/nightmarepress1